DYING TO KNOW

DYING TO KNOW

A Lance Elliot Mystery

Keith McCarthy, 1960 -

This first world edition published 2010
in Great Britain and in the USA by
SEVERN HOUSE PUBLISHERS LTD of
9–15 High Street, Sutton, Surrey, England, SM1 1DF.
Trade paperback edition published
in Great Britain and the USA 2010 by
SEVERN HOUSE PUBLISHERS LTD

British Library Cataloguing in Publication Data

McCarthy, Keith, 1960–
   Dying to Know.
   1. Physicians – Fiction. 2. Antique dealers – Crimes
   against – Fiction. 3. Police – England – London – Fiction.
   4. London (England) – Social conditions – 20th century –
   Fiction. 5. Detective and mystery stories.
   I. Title
   823.9'2-dc22

ISBN-13: 978-0-7278-6897-8   (cased)
ISBN-13: 978-1-84751-244-4   (trade paper)

All Severn House titles are printed on acid-free paper.

Severn House Publishers support The Forest Stewardship Council [FSC],
the leading international forest certification organisation. All our titles that
are printed on Greenpeace-approved FSC-certified paper carry the FSC logo.

Mixed Sources
Product group from well-managed
forests and other controlled sources
www.fsc.org Cert no. SA-COC-1565
© 1996 Forest Stewardship Council
FSC

Typeset by Palimpsest Book Production Ltd.,
Grangemouth, Stirlingshire, Scotland.
Printed and bound in Great Britain by
MPG Books Ltd., Bodmin, Cornwall.

For Judy

PROLOGUE

Wintertime on the allotments – on any allotments, it must be said – is not a joyous time. It is not the kind of place to go if you're looking for companionship, or happiness, or even much in the way of life. Few things grow in winter, after all, and of those that do, few are colourful. There is much brown, a load of grey and abundant cold. Those hardy souls who venture there at such times are necessarily the keenest of gardeners – there is only so much gardening to be done at this time of year – and they are men and women of a particular stripe; they are dedicated allotmenteers, whose lives revolve around the place, who attend the committee meetings, who enter every category in the biannual flower and produce show, who know each other but rarely converse. They spend as many hours on their strip of land as they can, sitting and sipping tea from a flask, watching the seasons turn, the aircraft make their stratospheric trails overhead as they fly into Gatwick Airport, the birds as they search for scant food.

My father, Launceston Elliot, Senior, is one such. Retired GP, man of mysterious ways, urban sage and more irritating than itching powder around the scrotum, he spends more time than I think is good for him sitting outside his shed. He drinks tea laced with whisky and he has the ability that is so rare nowadays to be able to sit and do nothing; doing nothing is more than an art, it is a skill, and it is a skill that few can now be bothered to acquire.

For this I admire him.

And he is dangerous, too. Dangerous to himself and to those who love him, as he demonstrated one evening in later October, 1975.

It was my afternoon off from the surgery and I did not wish to be there, but he had asked me to come and there had been something in his voice – a familiar something – that rang a bell in my head; unfortunately, it was the bell that they usually sound when someone has passed over. The weather was cold and it was growing dark and there might have been rain in the air, it might have been damp fog; it made no difference, it was still uncomfortable.

Dad didn't notice, though, because he had found something, and he wanted to show it to me.

'It's quite incredible!' he said.

I was starting to shiver. I had a thick anorak on, but such a thing can only hold the heat so long. 'What is?'

'That I should find this. I've had this plot for eight years; I thought I'd dug every inch of it, but you can still be surprised.'

'Surprised by what?'

An old woman with an upright gait and protuberant bosom passed by in front of us and exchanged nods with my father before he continued. 'I was digging the bean trench. It's a lot earlier than most people do it, I know, but I like to open it as soon as I've got the space and then keep throwing compost into it for as long as possible.' I made little effort to stifle the yawn; I was yawning with cold, not tiredness. 'Anyway, I've never sited the trench in that particular place, so I suppose that's why I'd never found it before. Got to dig the trench deep, you see; at least four feet and preferably six . . .'

I could no longer pretend that it was a damp fog closing in; I was definitely being rained upon. I asked somewhat irritably, 'What is the point of this piffle?'

He glanced at me and in that glance there was a lifetime's love, affection and exasperation. He didn't say anything, though. Instead, he reached under his chair – a tubular frame, folding sun chair that was probably thinking that it had died and gone to hell – and pulled out a tin that had once held Crawford's Teatime Assorted Biscuits that he then handed to me.

It no longer held biscuits, though.

Now, it held a grenade.

'Bloody hell!' I nearly dropped the tin.

'Good, isn't it?' He was smiling fondly, as if it were a puppy he'd just been given.

'Is it real?'

He was genuinely appalled at my ignorance. 'Of course it is. A World War Two Mills bomb. I've thrown a fair few of those, I can tell you. There's many a Jerry who was sorry he ever encountered me when I had one of those in my hand.' He spoke nostalgically of his memories, much as he might had he been recalling a family picnic.

'And could it go off?'

He frowned. 'I'm fairly sure it's primed; I think that the detonator's been inserted.'

He didn't seem to think that this was anything more than a detail. 'Dad . . .' I began nervously, but he was off being my father again. 'The secret's in the timing, of course.'

'Is it?'

'Oh, yes. It's not the pin coming out that matters; that only releases the lever. You've got either four or seven seconds then before it explodes, so you don't want to throw it too early. There were cases when the sods kicked it back and blew one of us up.'

How unsporting, I thought. 'Didn't you know how long you had?'

He looked uncertain for just a moment, then just breezed on. 'Of course we did.'

'And this one?'

He shrugged. 'God only knows.'

Well, I thought, it's never going to matter. I asked, 'How on earth did it get here?'

'Ah, yes, I've been wondering about that. I think it must have been Fred Giles. He was an old soldier – a corporal in the Marines, I think – and he had a great collection of memorabilia from his time in the military. He had this plot before I did.' He paused, then added sadly, 'Passed away not too long ago.'

I looked at it again; rather nervously, it must be admitted. It was fairly heavily caked in clay. 'Is it safe as long as we don't do anything stupid?'

'Oh, yes,' he said confidently, and almost immediately undermined the effect that this had on me by saying, 'Well, I should think it is . . .'

I put the lid back on and handed the tin back to him, very slowly and very carefully. He looked a little hurt, as if I had rejected a Christmas present. I said, 'Get rid of it. Call the police and get it disposed of properly.'

'Why? It's a souvenir, that is.'

'It's also illegal to be in possession of souvenirs like this.'

He looked vague, a sure sign that I had said something he didn't like. 'Is it? Well, I'll tell someone . . . when I get round to it . . .'

'Dad.'

He hastened to reassure me with an insincere smile. 'Don't worry, Lance. I'm not going to do anything stupid.'

The rain began to lash down.

ONE

It was the morning of November 5th that I first heard the name Ricky Baines. My informant was Jessie Trout, who was tormented by haemorrhoids. I do not exaggerate when I use the word 'tormented'. These were not vague swellings, these were not a cause of slight discomfort; in short, these were not a joke, neither to Jessie, who had to sit on them, nor to me, who had to look at them with depressing regularity. They had attitude, these piles; they dared Jessie to rest her legs and squash them and they dared me to do anything to interfere with them.

For perhaps the tenth time that year and the hundredth time since I had come to practise medicine in Thornton Heath, Surrey, I straightened up and pulled a disposable glove off my hand. 'Right you are, Mrs Trout.'

'Well?' she asked as she pulled up her lacy underwear and was helped back into a sitting position by Jane, our nurse. Jane was quiet and empathetic and the perfect person to work with; she never seemed to get phased, neither by the antics of the patients, nor those of the medical staff.

'I think they're getting worse, Mrs Trout.'

'They certainly feel as if they are.'

I had washed my hands and was sitting back behind my desk. Mrs Trout was a very short forty-nine-year-old woman with a painfully tight perm and nervous air that led to a very slight but quite noticeable tic affecting her left eye. She wasn't unduly heavy but her lack of height made her look otherwise. Having helped Mrs Trout into a more socially acceptable position, Jane raised her eyebrows at me – *Do you need me anymore?* – and left at the slight shake of my head and my smile of gratitude.

'You really should think about an operation.'

'Oh, no!' Mrs Trout was genuinely terrified by the prospect.

'Surgical techniques have advanced . . .'

'I won't hear of it. My poor old mum went through agonies

after she had hers done. I can still remember the screams coming from the toilet.'

'That was in the forties. Things are a lot better now.'

'No.'

I knew that tone well and gave up the argument. 'Are you still bunged up?'

'Something chronic.'

'The linctus didn't work?'

She shook her head. She had a broad South London accent smeared over with pretension. 'Hardly any movement at all.'

'Oh, dear.' I had to think what to do next. Man's ingenuity, it seemed, had met its match in Jessie Trout; I was running out of laxatives; but then, I reasoned, there probably wasn't a lot of research done on improving bowel movements.

'And it got worse with all the kerfuffle.'

'Did it?' I asked this not really listening to what either of us was saying. I had picked up my copy of the *British National Formulary* – the prescriber's bible – and was once more going through the section on substances designed to shift recalcitrant bowels; it was distressingly well thumbed.

'Fancy! Two people shot two doors away from me!'

I looked up at her. 'Shot?' Jessie lived in Greyhound Lane which wasn't quite the height of sophisticated living, but it wasn't Dodge City either.

'Yes. Didn't you hear about it?' She was incredulous that I was in ignorance. I shook my head which was her cue to take the podium and proclaim; I had cheered her up no end and for the moment her constipation and her haemorrhoids were forgotten.

'It happened at Mr Baines' house. Of course, he said he was a taxi driver, but I always thought that there was something a bit shady about him . . .'

'And he got shot?'

'Yes. In the middle of the night! It woke me up and I poked Norman in the side and asked him if he'd heard it.'

'Had he?'

'No, of course not. He wears ear plugs and a blindfold, so he won't even hear the crack of doom when it opens up.'

Mr Trout struck me as perhaps a wise man. 'Who else was shot?'

'Apparently it was Mr Baines' partner! Eddie Perry.'

This was in the innocent, halcyon days of the middle 1970s when a male partner of a man automatically meant business partner and nothing else.

'Who did it?'

She made a face because I was being stupid. 'They did it to each other!' She paused. 'At least, that's what the police say.'

'Why?'

'Well, apparently they'd been in prison for armed robbery! They only got out a few weeks ago, which was when Mr Baines moved in. To think!'

Feeling somewhat battered by the constant stream of exclamation marks coming in my direction, I began to see that I had been labouring under a misapprehension regarding the relationship of the two victims. 'But why did they shoot each other?'

'It was all over jewellery, they say. Apparently they robbed a jeweller's in London. Terrible it was, because someone got killed, but then they got caught and put in prison; no one ever found the jewellery, though. It's said that only Mr Baines knew where it was, but when it came to time to split the loot, they had a falling out. Presumably Mr Baines didn't want to part with it.'

Split the loot. I wondered if Mickey Spillane featured prominently on her bookshelves.

'What's happened to the jewellery?'

She became excited and, accordingly, out came a fresh stock of punctuation marks. 'Nobody knows! The police are baffled!'

She could have got a job writing headlines.

'And you think that this has exacerbated your constipation?'

She was slightly nonplussed, I think, by my terminology, but she nodded anyway. I turned back to the BNF and discovered a new preparation that combined Ex-lax and castor oil. If that didn't shift her, then I was going to have to resort either to witchcraft or to mechanical means.

TWO

I t was cold and foggy, the dampness soaking deep into my bones, despite the heavy parka that I wore. I had wisely put on wellington boots, but even with thick socks I had serious concerns that frostbite might claim my toes for good. One of my patients – a cheerful colonel with a thin, greying moustache and eyes that were faded by decades of bright foreign sun – had lost three toes and two fingers to frostbite following a botched parachute drop in Norway during World War Two, and he had repeatedly told me in great and unnecessary detail how much it had hurt and for how long. I didn't fancy that, not for a few fireworks, a burnt sausage in a soggy roll and a liquid that might have been coffee, but might easily have been the water used to wash out the percolator.

Max, though, was enjoying it.

I loved Max madly. She was brilliantly, enthusiastically, *alive*, and contagious too. She seemed to lighten the mood wherever she went, in whomever she met. Now, staring up into the darkness, she was carrying around a smile wide enough to threaten her ears, and that ought to have made her look something like an imbecile, but it didn't. It made her strangely, impossibly beautiful; I think that this was because she was not only physically attractive, but spiritually, too. She was small in a nice way, somehow built with perfect economy, and with just the right number of imperfections to make her human: her eyes were slightly too widely spaced, her mouth ever-so-slightly lopsided; individual components that somehow summed to a whole that made me want to be with her. She was intelligent, too – a vet having recently joined a practice in Norbury, had graduated top of her year from Bristol and already had a not unimpressive list of research papers to her name. Yet the evening's trip to the fireworks display had left her excited beyond words, filled with childlike glee that made me dissolve inside.

And she was, incredibly, besotted with me.

We were in Lloyd Park in South Croydon, watching the municipal fireworks display, a huge bonfire casting not only a flickering glow but also a distinct heat to the right side of my face; it only made the chill in my feet seem more intense. Max wore pink woolly gloves and bobble hat with matching scarf over a chocolate-brown overcoat; her cheeks were cerise, her eyes bright. The smell of autumn – decaying leaves, smoke and fog – was in my nose and throat, the murmur of the crowd around us. It was difficult to judge how many people were there, but I would have said at least five hundred, perhaps a thousand. I had already spotted three of my patients, and Max had been accosted once by a little woman with tiny screwed-up eyes and strange jerky movements – she kept reaching out and touching Max's coat as she talked. Max explained later that her dog had just had a tumour removed from its spine. Not that Max had been the vet that had done it or even that the two of them knew each other; it was just that they had got talking. That was something else about Max; she attracted odd people, seeming to radiate something that allowed them to home in on her.

The final fusillade of rockets boomed across the park, causing Max to scream again, her gloved hands clamped over her ears, her face suffused with a delight that was lit by the silvers, golds, pinks, blues and greens of the starbursts above our heads. The echoes had not completely died away as the conversation of the crowd began to pick up as it dispersed slowly by breaking up into small groups that turned to make their way to their cars or the bus stops.

'Is it over?'

Max still had her hands to her ears, so I nodded as I said as loudly as social convention would allow, 'For this year.'

Her hands dropped, but her attitude suggested that she did not really believe me, that I might be tricking her into exposing her delicate tympanic membranes to unaccustomed violence, thus causing deafness or even worse. Having reassured herself of my truthfulness, she relaxed, then sighed. 'That was so much fun.'

'Wonderful,' I agreed as enthusiastically as the agony in my pedal extremities would allow.

She reached across to me and grabbed my arm, snuggling

up to me in a most delightful manner, as she asked, 'What are we going to do now?'

We were already nearly alone, the fire now burning low, the ground around us trampled and muddy. It suddenly seemed a desolate, even dangerous, place; certainly one to escape from. 'How about a Wimpy?'

'Let's!'

Another of Max's endearing traits was that she loved Wimpy hamburgers. We began to trudge back towards the civilization that was Coombe Road where I had parked my car, each step bringing yet more pain to my feet. We held hands and she looked about her with an expression of contentment. 'I'd like to move here.' At present she lived quite close to me, on the northern side of Thornton Heath.

'It's quite expensive.'

She looked at me archly. 'Too expensive for me?'

'I didn't say that.' Her father was a consultant surgeon, her mother a psychiatrist; I hadn't met them yet and was terrified that when I did I would be thoroughly dissected, both body and soul.

'I may be only a junior partner in the practice, but my prospects are good.'

I smiled. 'Today caged rodents and small dogs, tomorrow farm animals? Perhaps in time you'll get the zoo gig.'

'You swine,' she said fiercely, tightening her grip on my hand, but laughing nonetheless.

We had reached my car and I opened her door for her, then got in my side. The engine was cold and, as usual, the damp did not help; it took me several moments to coax the engine into action and even then I would have diagnosed it as suffering bronchiectasis. We moved off towards Croydon town centre somewhat jerkily as I said, 'Anyway, what's wrong with Thornton Heath?'

She laughed. 'What's right with it?'

I was hurt; I, for one, quite liked the place. 'It's better than Croydon.'

Not that, on the face of it, there was much difference. Once Thornton Heath had been a small village in its own right; now it was merely a vague increase in the density of houses, shops and offices on the road from London to the south coast. I liked to think, though, that under the surface, the village atmosphere remained. There was still a definable community and people still had an allegiance to the place; you couldn't say that about Croydon. When I voiced this opinion, Max seemed to think that I was gibbering.

'"Community"? "Village atmosphere"?' she enquired in what I could only describe as a tone bordering on incredulity. 'I work there, don't forget. You're not talking to someone who's just flown in from the other side of the world.'

'What's so special about Croydon, then?'

'Well, the centre's got a bit of life, for a start,' she said as we turned right on to the Wellesley Road and the glories of downtown Croydon were spread out before us. 'At least there's been a bit of development here in the past twenty years. It's not the land that time forgot.'

I said, 'It's dead, soulless.'

'Only this bit. A few streets away, and there are some really nice places.'

'There are some really nice places around Thornton Heath.'

She thought about this. 'I'm not sure that Twinkle would like it here.' Twinkle was her pet rabbit. A vicious man-eating thing that I suspected was in the early stages of rabies.

I swung around the large roundabout over the pass over, then took the third exit. The Wimpy was just on our left and I managed to park not too far away. We walked back and went in to find, not altogether to my surprise, that it was not bursting at the seams with clientele. I had been going in there for years and never once had I seen more than two or three tables occupied; moreover, there always seemed to be the same people in there. Inevitably there would be a group of four of five teenagers of varying ethnic backgrounds and genders, and an unkempt man of indeterminate age who had the look of madness in his rheumy eye. All of these would stare at me through clouds of cigarette smoke from the moment I entered the burger bar until the moment I left it; indeed, the unkempt man would keep staring at me through the glass of the shop front, presumably just in case I fooled him and doubled back in when he was least expecting it.

And behind the counter . . .

I had been in many burger bars, but none was quite like

this. The concept of a welcoming atmosphere did not enter the manager's retail philosophy and, I suspect, would have sat uneasily with the majority of their clientele.

We ordered two cheeseburgers and fries, standing at the counter, trying to look as if we were used to our place in the limelight and didn't mind in the least that the place had fallen silent as soon as we entered; Max stayed up-close and personal, which I didn't mind in the least. The burgers were prepared before our very eyes, with not a word from either the chef or the pinch-faced woman who served us. This was presumably company policy, because I had only ever heard her utter two things – 'Yes' when you went in and the price when the repast was presented and she wanted payment.

As soon as we were on the pavement, we both burst into a fit of giggles, clutching our supper, despite the fact that the unkempt man sustained his remorseless vigilance through the slightly steamed window.

'Where shall we go to eat it?' asked Max.

I hesitated a fraction of a second before saying, 'We could just sit in the car, I suppose . . .'

'We could . . .'

'Or we could nip home and eat it in comfort . . .'

'We could, indeed . . .'

We looked at one another, our faces bearing serious expressions that did not reach our eyes before we burst again into giggles. Without any further conversation, we hurried to the car, got in and I drove us home.

I don't know what Max was thinking, but my own thoughts were distinctly libidinous and not for family viewing.

Max was my first serious attachment since the business with the murder on the allotments back in the summer. She was a complete contrast to Charlie, my previous girlfriend, and this was a constant source of wonder to me; how could I have felt so attracted to two so different people? Yet I was.

I still had love for Charlie, you see, and would not now be with Max had it not been for Tristan.

Tristan was my brother-in-law and he blamed me for the suicide of his sister, my wife. He was a pull-the-legs-off-spiders kind of guy; one who didn't mind experiencing a bit of pain in order to cause a lot of it. He had decided that I shouldn't be happy with Charlie, that I shouldn't be happy with *anyone*. I had made the decision that for her safety, I should end the relationship. I had even strongly considered whether I should enter into any further relationships, and become a secular monk, a man alone in a crowded world.

But Max had come along and beguiled me, and I was lost.

Lost and afraid that Tristan might come back and not like the way things were going. I had not told Max about Tristan and there was within me a constant turmoil as to whether I should.

When Burns opined on the best laid plans of mice and men, he was close but not spot on; he failed to mention that other category of doomed individuals – sons of eccentrics. Perhaps his father was entirely rational and behaved normally or perhaps Burns Senior was so bonkers he was entombed in some sort of asylum, I don't know. Whatever the case, I'll bet he was never subjected to the torments that I have to endure.

We had been home no more than ten minutes and had only just sat down on the sofa, food in front of us on our laps, a nice bottle of Chianti open and begging to be drunk, when the phone rang. I ought to have had a premonition that it was trouble, and that the trouble answered to the name of 'Dad', but I couldn't believe that fate was that unkind; I think that I vaguely wondered if it might be a patient – I wasn't on call but a few with long-term or terminal illnesses had my home number and might call if they had particular problems – and consequently, although I groaned inwardly, I went out into the hall to answer it.

'Lance?'

As you've probably guessed, it was my father. 'Dad?'

'Sorry to bother you so late. You weren't doing anything, were you?'

'I was just going to eat something.'

'Were you? Well, never mind . . .'

'Max is here.'

'Is she?' This question was posed in a dismissive tone; it was not the first time that I had the feeling that he did not entirely approve of Max. 'Something's come up . . .'

The last time he had rung me late in the evening with an urgent problem, it had been because he had become convinced that his new neighbour, Oliver Lightoller, had murdered his wife, Doris. He hadn't, of course, but that didn't stop Dad involving the police, thereby causing much chaos.

'Look, Dad. Can't it wait til morning?'

The interruption made him pause and think. 'I suppose it could,' he said thoughtfully.

'Good.' I would have gone on to wish him a good night's sleep and then put the phone down, except that he hadn't finished either. In the same pensive voice, he said, 'The accommodation's quite good.'

'What do you mean?'

'It's warm, and they've offered me a bite to eat.'

'Who have?'

He seemed surprised by my ignorance. 'The police.'

I knew then that my carnal desires were not going to be satisfied that night. 'You're at the police station?'

'At Norbury, yes.'

I thought, Deep breathing, that's the key in these situations.

'What's happened?'

I had never known Dad to do anything quickly, but at times such as this, he seemed to slow to sub-glacial pace. I had time to run through at least twenty possible reasons for his presence *Chez Plod* before he spoke again. 'I've been arrested.'

'Why?' I tried for serenity but the panic I was feeling added a distinctly shrill undertone.

Another long pause, then: 'Arson.'

THREE

My father had worked as a general practitioner in Thornton Heath for all of his professional life and for over half of it he had been a police surgeon. A consequence of this was that he knew quite a few police officers, especially the older ones. The trouble was, they knew him, too . . .

Sergeant Percy Bailey was sympathetic but could do nothing for us. Dad was being interviewed by the CID and we would have to wait until they had finished with him.

'He said that he was accused of arson,' I told him. 'Is that true?'

Bailey was a large man, and fittingly portly, large lips, a nose that was slightly crooked and hair that had not exactly receded, merely faded away. His nod was part sadness, part sympathy as he replied, 'So it would appear.'

'What did he burn down?'

'His neighbour's shed.'

'Neighbour? You mean Lightoller?'

'That is the owner's name, yes.'

I closed my eyes. Beside me Max asked, 'Why would he do a thing like that?'

She was an innocent in the ways of my father; she did not appreciate that he needed no reasons; that often reasons – and reason – were not involved at all. Sergeant Bailey turned his penetrating, if ponderous gaze upon her. 'That is what we are trying to ascertain,' he informed in impeccable Constablese.

I asked without hope, 'Can we see him?'

'Not yet I'm afraid.' This delivered with the kind of implacability and finality normally associated with steamrollers. 'The inspector's talking with him.'

A feeling of despair settled upon me. 'Inspector Masson?'

He looked at me with understanding and some commiseration as he nodded and said, 'Yes.' As if the news wasn't already bad enough, he compounded it by adding, 'When he discovered it was your father, he actually smiled.'

Masson and my father were old friends, in a manner of speaking.

We retreated to the far end of the room while I regretted not calling a solicitor. I hadn't done so because Dad had insisted that it was unnecessary, that he was an innocent man and the appearance of a lawyer would only cast doubt on him.

Max asked in a loud whisper, 'Just who is Mr Lightoller?'

'His neighbour.'

She digested this. 'Don't they get on?'

'Oliver and Doris Lightoller moved in about six months ago, during the course of which their removal van blocked Dad's driveway for most of the day, and their removal men managed to damage his garden wall. Dad complained and it set the tone for their relationship ever since. It wasn't improved when Dad became convinced that Lightoller had pinched his watch.'

'His watch? How is he supposed to have managed that?'

'Dad was painting his garage doors one day. He got started, then realized that he was still wearing his watch, so took it off and rested it on the low wall that divides the two gardens. According to Dad, Lightoller came home while he was working and just about then the watch vanished.'

'Why on earth would Mr Lightoller want to steal a watch?'

I shrugged. 'Dad's always claimed that it's valuable, although I wouldn't know. It belonged to my grandfather.'

'Your father's such a nice man; Mr Lightoller must be very unpleasant if he can't get on with him.'

'He's not the most likeable of men, but then I'm not particularly objective, I suppose. And Lightoller's turned the screw a bit himself. He's instructed a solicitor claiming that Dad's boundary fence is incorrectly positioned and should be moved six inches back.'

She considered this. 'Do you think your father would do it? I mean, set fire to Mr Lightoller's house, or whatever it was?'

I wished I could reassure both her and myself that it was out of the question, but with Dad there was some doubt.

I had met Oliver and Doris Lightoller on only a couple of occasions. He was a short man, rather fat and toad-like with fleshy lips and a surfeit of hair, unfortunately most of which was not on his head. Doris was of a similar height and even more obese; she wore too much make-up and too much pungent perfume, a sure sign of an underlying odour problem. They had struck me as polite but distant, although that might have been because of who I was. The same could not be said of their son, Tom, whom I had met one evening when he was leaving his parents' house and I was just arriving for a meal with Dad. He was fairly small and delicate-looking, but he was nonetheless somehow intimidating, perhaps because of a quite startling degree of intensity with which he stared at me, while his parents whispered in his ear, presumably giving him a good dose of anti-Elliot propaganda. He was perhaps only five feet eight, with ash-blond hair and blue eyes, and a dark suit with a rose in the lapel. I remember thinking that he looked like an undertaker, which it turned out that he was.

Max and I sat in the waiting room while Percy did what desk sergeants do and, every so often, glanced up at us as we sat on the bright-red and viciously uncomfortable plastic seats. By way of light relief we watched as he had to deal with an intermittent stream of members of the public, some accompanied by police officers, others finding their way under their own steam. There were several drunk men, two drunk women, a man who wanted to report that he had lost his umbrella on the bus, another who had exposed himself to a vicar, and an ancient woman with a Zimmer frame who had assaulted a constable by thrusting her hatpin into his crotch, thus causing him to seek medical aid in the Mayday Hospital casualty department.

After two hours of this colourful pageant of human depravity and lunacy, Sergeant Bailey said, rather belatedly, 'I'd go home, if I were you. It could be hours yet.'

But we stayed and our patience was rewarded after a further ninety minutes when the familiar figure of Inspector Masson came into the room behind Percy Bailey looking just as I remembered him. He was short and grey and gloomy then and, if he was still comparably short and grey, he appeared decidedly gloomier now. He had the darkest, most impressive bags beneath his eyes, while his jowls would not have disgraced a beagle. When he caught sight of us, he stopped what he was doing and came to the counter beside Sergeant Bailey.

'Dr Elliot.'

'Inspector.'

'You're here because of your father.'

I was tired and I was worried and I thought I was being witty – and, who knows, perhaps I was – as I said, 'I see your detective skills haven't deserted you.'

And then I remembered that Masson doubtless had many admirable qualities, but a sense of humour was not amongst them. While I tried not to wilt, he stared at me for several long seconds with an intensity I knew well. Eventually he said with deadly dullness, 'He's been accused of committing a serious offence, Dr Elliot. Arsonists are dealt with very harshly by the law, and quite rightly too.'

'What, exactly, did he do?'

'He launched a rocket into his neighbour's shed.'

I confess now that I was struck dumb by this piece of news. Beside me, Max perked up. 'Gosh, did he?' This was in a wondering, almost awestruck tone, and I'm not sure it helped the situation.

'He did. It ignited some petrol and now, despite the best efforts of the fire brigade, the shed and all its contents are completely destroyed. Luckily, there was no loss of life.'

'By "rocket", you mean firework?' I asked.

He nodded.

'What the hell was he doing playing with fireworks at his time of life?'

'His story is that he bought a few to entertain a lady friend of his. A Mrs Ada Clarke.'

Dad had mentioned Ada Clarke to me before; he'd had his eye on her for some months, had even taken up bell-ringing to get close to her as she was a dedicated campanologist at St Jude's Church in Thornton Heath.

Masson continued, 'He claims that he put the rocket in a milk bottle on the garden path, lit it and retreated. He says that the bottle must have been a little unstable and when the rocket ignited, it tipped over and went at a very low altitude just over the fence and into the shed.'

At which Max giggled and I closed imaginary eyes and Masson did a bit more staring, only this time in her direction. I said quickly, 'This is Miss Christy.'

'Is it,' responded Masson; it wasn't a question, more a judgement.

'Are you going to charge my father?'

He reverted to me. 'I haven't decided yet. He claims that it was completely accidental; his neighbour, though, insists that your father has been waging a war against him and, I have to say, there is some evidence for that allegation. Your father himself tells me that he believes Mr Lightoller to have stolen a watch from him.'

'Not the watch again,' I groaned.

'So you see, it is clear that your father has taken against his neighbour.'

'They don't get on, inspector. I wouldn't describe it as warfare.'

Masson, of course, had to argue. 'I've known murder committed when two elderly people "don't get on".'

'All the same . . .'

But Masson did not want to argue. He said abruptly, 'I'm going to let him go for now on bail, but that doesn't mean it's the end of the matter. I want to make some more enquiries and then we'll see if he has a case to answer.'

He turned and I'm sure would have left us completely in the dark about details had I not called after him, 'When can we see him, then?'

He seemed surprised that I was still there and hesitated before glancing over his shoulder with a frown. 'It'll be about fifteen minutes before the formalities are over.'

With which he continued on his way. Percy Bailey smiled faintly as we returned to our seats to await my father. Max whispered, 'Gosh! He must be terrifying when he doesn't like you.'

I sighed. 'Oh, he is, Max. Believe me, he is.'

FOUR

I n fact, it was only ten minutes before my father appeared in the small waiting room, escorted by a young, ginger-haired constable in his early twenties with acne and watery blue eyes who obviously regarded my father to be a clear and present danger to life, limb and the liberty of the individual. He also had the most impressive black eye, one of those ones that you can't help staring at, that pleads with you to ask how it was acquired. Worse, it was several days old, so that it was doing the wonderful metachromatic thing, irregularly fading into greens, yellows and oranges. It was a thing of beauty.

Dad, of course, was taking everything with supernatural calmness. It was by now two thirty in the morning but his greeting to us was exactly the same as if it had been that same hour of the clock in the afternoon.

'Lance! How are you?'

'Hi, Dad.'

'Hello, Dr Elliot,' Max said and, as always, she was charm incarnate.

He turned to her. 'Hello, Miss Christy.'

He smiled politely but insisted on using excessive formality when addressing Max which, in its way, was a very loud and very clear message delivered in the most subtle of ways. True, this was only the third occasion they had met, and the previous times had been somewhat fleeting, but normally by now Dad would have been showing my female companions his shrapnel scars and telling them how I could never get the hang of wiping my bottom when I was a toddler. With Max, though, there was a distance that I found irritating.

She enquired, 'How have they treated you?'

My father considered this. He looked to me to be remarkably chipper, with no rubber truncheon marks showing anywhere, but he could be incredibly resilient and so appearances were not always reliable. 'They've got it into their heads that I did it all on purpose.'

'Which, of course, you didn't,' I suggested.

'It was just an accident,' he insisted. He glanced over at Percy Bailey as he said this and suddenly I was wondering if this was a prudent place to be discussing the affair.

'Come on, let's get you home. Max and I have to work in the morning, unlike others.'

Max said at once, 'Don't be horrible, Lance. Your poor father has been through a terrible ordeal. I think a bit more sympathy would be more appropriate.'

I noticed that Dad seemed suddenly to find something to approve of in Max as he nodded and made the sad face of a disillusioned father who has just discovered that his only son is a bit of a swine.

I asked her, 'What do you suggest?'

'Perhaps you should take your father home with you tonight, rather than leaving him alone.'

My father watched me, his face expressionless apart from the eyes that were filled with something I suspected was amusement, as I mentally waved goodbye to sharing my bed with Max for the rest of the night. This would have been a small consolation for the ruin of the evening, but it seemed that even that was not to be mine. I took a deep breath. 'Very well, then. Would you like to come home with me?'

He made a play of deep thought during which Max put in, 'You could drop me off on the way there.' Max had a house in Green Lane on the east side of Norbury Park.

Thanks, Max.

Dad eventually decided. He announced in a voice that implied he was being supremely magnanimous, 'Very well, then. I will.'

When we had dropped Max off and I was driving home, I asked, 'Why don't you like Max?'

'Who said I didn't?'

'You did.' He opened his mouth to protest but I carried on: 'Not with words, but then you don't need such mundane things.'

He had turned to me, but now looked away. 'She's not right for you, Lance.'

'Why not?'

'She's too young, for a start.'

'Age isn't everything.'

He said at once, 'Yes, it is. Believe me, I know.'

'She's only thirteen years younger than me.' Even as I was hearing these words I was thinking that they didn't help my cause. Dad said nothing, but then he didn't need to and I was left to fill in. 'She's incredibly bright. Gold medal in veterinary school, excellent academic career, then straight into a job . . .'

All he said was, 'I can see that.'

'She's kind, attentive . . . look how she was worried about you.'

'Oh, absolutely,' he agreed and somehow managed to leave me with a feeling of dissatisfaction.

'Well, then . . .'

Whenever I drove him anywhere, he was normally a bad passenger. He liked to tell me how he had been driving for fifty years and had only ever had one accident (which, of course, was not his fault). I had a slightly different perspective, though. In my opinion he drove erratically, with scant regard for other road users, even less for pedestrians; he never used his rear-view mirror, never stopped at pedestrian crossings, never let other cars in ahead of him, and never thanked those who let *him* in. It seemed to me that he paid more attention to the road and what was going on around him when he sat in my passenger seat than he ever did when he was in nominal control of the car.

Tonight, though, he was uncharacteristically subdued; I assumed that the events of the night had taken more out of him than he cared to admit. For a few moments there was only the sound of the engine and the tyres on the road, when he said, 'I can see that she's a very attractive, very bright, very kind girl, Lance. It's just that I don't think you and she are right together.'

I wanted to argue, to point out all the holes in his view, that he was being unreasonable and frankly *old*, but I didn't. I wasn't sure why, but perhaps it was because I knew he was tired, perhaps because I was tired, perhaps – conceivably – it was because I was afraid he was right.

In an effort to escape thinking too much more about all this, I asked, 'So, you were entertaining Ada Clarke, then.'

'I was. And it was going very well, too. I'd cooked her a nice bit of braised steak with mushrooms, and we'd had a drop of wine, and I thought that, in view of the occasion, I'd finish the evening off with some fireworks. Ada likes fireworks. Who knows what might have happened if things had turned out differently?'

I broke all the rules of road safety and closed my eyes, partly in horror at what he was implying, partly in exasperation as I thought about what might have happened for *me* if things had turned out differently. I had to grit my teeth as I said tightly, 'Don't you think you're a bit old to be playing with fire?'

He was indignant. 'I wasn't playing. I was entertaining a lady, nothing more.'

'It was bloody irresponsible to stick a rocket in a milk bottle without burying it; of course it might have toppled over at the wrong moment.'

He did not reply for a long while and it was not until we were almost at my house that he murmured, 'It didn't happen *exactly* like that . . .'

A sense of horror that I knew well began to creep up on me. 'What does that mean?'

His head bobbed from side to side as he stared straight ahead while he admitted the awful truth. 'It was completely accidental that I burned down his shed . . .'

There was a 'but' at the end of that sentence, and it was a bloody big one. His voice dropped quite noticeably as he supplied it. 'But that's because I was aiming at his conservatory.'

'What?' My eyes came off the road and he reacted at once because the car veered dangerously close to the parked vehicles on his side. I jerked the steering wheel and we just avoided a collision. He had to comment, of course.

'Be careful, Lance. How many times do I have to tell you to keep your eyes on the road at all times?'

'You really were trying to fire rockets at Lightoller?'

'It was just a bit of fun. Ada thought it was most amusing. She doesn't like them either. They were most rude about the bell-ringing. Said it was an awful din that should be banned.'

'Dad . . .'

'Don't worry. She won't say anything. They can't prove a thing.'

He didn't seem to have grasped the point and I hastened to put him right. 'You set fire to his shed! Supposing you had done the same to his house? You might have killed both of them.'

'Oh, don't be melodramatic, Lance. That's always been your trouble – over-egging the recipe. Your mother was the same; she always saw disaster when it wasn't there. I remember once—'

'Dad, it was the height of irresponsibility.'

'Oh, tosh. Anyway, Masson confirmed my suspicions about the Lightollers.'

'What suspicions?'

'That there's something shady about them.'

It didn't sound like the kind of thing that the Inspector Masson I loved and adored would say. 'In what way shady?'

'Well, he didn't say, exactly . . .'

'So what *did* he say? Exactly, I mean.'

But Dad, as he so often did, retreated into vagaries. 'He intimated that Lightoller isn't quite the upstanding citizen he makes himself out to be.'

In other words, Dad had heard what he wanted to hear and seen what he wanted to see.

We had reached my house and I turned right off the road and on to the hardstanding in front of the attached garage. As I turned the engine off, I said, 'Dad, whether Oliver Lightoller is an archbishop or the greatest criminal mastermind since Fu Man Chu is irrelevant. Trying to hit his house with a firework rocket is reckless and potentially disastrous.'

He had opened the door and was climbing out, so he delivered his response – his considered response – across the partly melted frost on the car roof. 'That's what Masson said. It's poppycock, of course, as I told him. The chances that a small firework rocket will result in a conflagration are minuscule. Having strenuously reassured him that I had never had any intention of hitting the shed, I pointed out that it was only because the fool had left the door open and kept large bottles of white spirit and turps on the shelves – where they could have fallen off and smashed at any time – that a fire had started. Otherwise, I am convinced, there would have been little damage.'

He slammed his door shut to emphasize his certainty, apparently under the impression that all my neighbours were deaf.

As so often before, I had the distinct impression that normality was a pathetically fragile thing, easily broken by the lunacy of my ancient progenitor. I needed to get to bed and to sleep quickly, before the gates of insanity opened never to close again. As I let him in, I said tersely, 'I only hope that Ada supports your story.'

'Don't worry. She will.'

FIVE

The next day's morning surgery dragged like a Wagner opera played andante. General Practice is about helping people as much as treating them, which means that you spend a lot of time just listening to people's problems, their disappointments and their successes, even though they may walk through the door complaining of a cold, backache, pain in their belly or mouth ulcers. I can probably only effectively treat half of the medical conditions they bring to me, but I like to think that the psychological support I give them is just as valuable and this gives me great comfort. That morning, though, I was just too tired; by the time Samuel James Metcalfe Hocking hove into view, I was ready to surrender, the white flag unfurled and waving in the breeze.

It wasn't his fault. To be fair to him, he wasn't a particularly regular customer – unlike some of my patients who seem to regard the surgery as a day centre – and when he did present, it was usually for a good reason. Unfortunately, on this day, it was with backache. Now, modern medicine has made fantastic advances in almost all areas, save one: this one. Moreover, it hasn't progressed one whit. Why? Because to you the back is just a bit of your body you can't see, the place where the limbs meet and that keeps your head well above your bottom. To a doctor, the back is an incredibly complicated musculo-skeleto-neural structure that we don't really understand. Patients are completely incapable of appreciating why, when all they've got is a simple problem, I rarely seem to have a simple answer.

I knew at once what he was going to say, could see it written in his stiff posture, the tightness of his face. 'I can barely get out of bed in the morning.'

It took him a good sixty seconds to lower himself into the chair, all the while his face an eloquent testament to the pain he was in. He had a broad face with light-blue eyes and laugh lines around his mouth.

'When did it start?'

'About two days ago.'

'What were you doing when it started?'

He shrugged. 'Work, I suppose.'

'Does that involve a lot of lifting?'

He frowned. 'Of course.' This was said as if I should have known. When I looked through his notes, I saw that he was a baker.

'A *master* baker,' he corrected me when I confirmed it with him; clearly, in his eyes, there was quite a social chasm between mere bakers and the masters of the art.

'And that involves lifting what?'

'Dough, and lots of it.'

Obvious, really.

'Have you ever had back trouble before?'

'The odd twinge.'

And so on through all the usual questions about pain down the legs, performance of the waterworks and bowels, numbness and tingling, until it came to time to examine him. As he stripped off his shirt (slowly), then stood up with his back to me, I was able to appreciate that he was a muscular man.

It was a painful examination both for him and, indeed, for me when he overbalanced and trod heavily on my corns. At its end, I didn't really have much idea what was wrong with him, although I thought it unlikely to be a slipped disc. In my best voice I pronounced, 'I think you may have strained your sacroiliac joints.'

He looked alarmed. 'Is that bad?'

I smiled reassuringly; how to smile reassuringly is the first and most useful thing they teach you at medical school. 'Not at all. I'll arrange for you to have some physiotherapy at Mayday. In the meantime, some painkillers will help.'

'I've tried paracetamol. That didn't touch it.'

Lesson number two was the ever-so-slightly condescending tone. 'I think you'll find these a little bit stronger,' I said as I wrote his prescription and handed it to him. 'And you need to rest it. Ideally, you should be sleeping on a firm mattress and taking time off work.'

He shook his head firmly. 'No. I've got to keep working,

I'm self-employed. The bills don't pay themselves, you know.'

Words of wisdom from my father came back to me. *Never argue with the buggers. You won't win and, if you do, they'll never forgive you.*

I shrugged. 'It's up to you, Mr Hocking.'

SIX

At last, my torment ended and I could escape to the restroom for some coffee and a biscuit. I felt as if I had been awake solidly for thirty-six hours.

Jack, of course, spotted it immediately. Jack Thorpe was a good doctor but that didn't necessarily mean he was a kind man; expose your neck to Jack and it was odds on you'd find teeth marks in it the next time you looked in the mirror.

'Good God, man. You look worse than me, and I was the one on call last night.'

'I probably feel worse than you, too.'

'Couldn't you sleep?' This question was immediately followed by the abrupt appearance of a leer on his round, rather bulging features. 'Oh, I get it. You and that bit of totty of yours. What's her name? Chris? Tina?'

'Max. And, no—'

'That's it. Max. Had a good night, did you?' He shot a glance over at Brian, the third partner in the practice, to see if he were enjoying the sport, but Brian wasn't listening; I think that Brian had long ago decided that since listening was a part of the job, he wasn't about to start doing it in his spare time. He was biting into a bourbon biscuit, crumbs falling on a slightly stained dark-green tie.

I said, 'It wasn't that . . .'

Which, of course, only made matters worse.

'Oh! Turn you down, did she? Been lying alone in bed with an ache in the groin and a feeling of inferiority?'

Jane, our nurse, came in and I turned to her. 'Help me, Jane.'

Jane was tall and self-possessed and beautiful, just as a nurse should be. If you're going to have to bend over with your trousers at half-mast while a nurse sticks a hypodermic needle in your rear end, it's important that she looks like Jane.

'What is it?' she asked.

In a fit of sex equality to keep in with the prevailing social trends, we had agreed that she might be allowed to share our coffee breaks; we were quite enlightened for those dim, distant days. She poured some coffee and sat down, eschewing the plate of biscuits that Brian offered her.

'Jack's being unpleasant.'

Having sipped the coffee, made a face and put the cup and saucer down, she said, 'Really? I can't believe that.'

Jack countered with: 'Dr Elliot's feeling sorry for himself. Couldn't get his end away last night.'

'It's true that I didn't have a very good night, but that was because my father got into a little bit of trouble.'

As I would have expected her to, Jane said at once, 'Not serious, I hope.'

I sighed. 'I hope so, too.'

'What's he been up to now?' asked Jack. Dad's foibles were well known, especially amongst the medical community.

I didn't want to give details – not, at least, to Jack – and said vaguely, 'Oh, just a small dispute with a neighbour.'

Brian made a contribution while masticating the last of his bourbon, thus slightly muffling his elocution. 'I wouldn't minimize the importance of arguments between neighbours. They can get quite nasty.'

'This one is nothing,' I said firmly.

Over breakfast that morning, I had confronted Dad over the matter, trying to find out exactly what were the problems between him and the Lightollers.

'They're such a peculiar couple,' had been his first reason and one, moreover, that caused me to suppress the obvious rejoinder.

'In what way?'

'Secretive.'

'So?'

'And mean. Do you know, they were positively abusive last week when I called on them to collect for Remembrance Day. They said they were pacifists and didn't agree with the whole notion.'

I could see that this would upset Dad. 'Perhaps they really are pacifists,' I said gently.

'In my book, whether they're pacifists or just mean, they're still a bad sort.'

'In future, then, don't call on them when you collect,' I suggested.

'Don't worry, I won't. And I've made sure that they're on the blacklist at the British Legion.' He made this sound as if the Legion were equalled in vindictiveness and unpleasantness only by the Cosa Nostra. 'It's more than that, though. I could swear that they're up to something. Something illegal.'

'What?'

To which his answer was a shrug and I reflected that as a standard of proof, it lacked a certain something. I asked, 'What does Lightoller do?'

'He *says* he's an antiques dealer.' He emphasized the second word to tell me that he believed not a word of it. 'He's got some sort of junk shop on the London Road opposite the site where Sainsbury's used to be.'

'One man's junk is another man's desirable.'

'Complete and utter tripe. Most junk is junk, no matter how you describe it, and that's what's in his shop. I've had a nose around. I know.'

'If it's junk, how does he manage to sell it?'

Continuing to smear butter while looking up at me, he said, 'That's a very good point. How does he?' To which, since I had not the answer, I could make no reply, thus allowing my dear papa to launch himself into his theory. 'I think he's a fence.'

'A fence? For stolen property?'

'Of course for stolen property. Apart from things made of chain-link or wood, what other kind is there?'

Conversations with my father could leave me more short of wind than a ten-mile run. After a moment or two of speechlessness, I asked, 'What proof do you have of this slander?'

'It's as plain as a boil on the end of a nose. He sells rubbish and, anyway, he hardly has any customers in that shop. I know; I've stood and watched.'

I didn't know which was more disturbing, the fact that he spent his time hanging around street corners keeping tabs on innocent citizens, or the fact that he thought it was normal behaviour. For a moment, the vision that he conjured before me held my attention, then I shook my head. Firmness was what was required here; give Dad any room and he'd be off after wild geese with a loud cry of pleasure, and have me following behind. 'Don't, Dad.'

'Don't what?'

'Don't fantasize. Lightoller's just an ordinary shopkeeper trying to make an honest profit.'

He stopped buttering his toast so great was his incredulity. 'What an oaf you are, Lance.'

'Am I?'

The buttering resumed with twice as much energy before he put the knife down and reached for the marmalade. 'Where's the spoon?'

'Use your knife.'

This produced a sad shake of the head. 'An oaf and a slob,' he commented as he stood up to fetch a spoon from the cutlery drawer.

'Thanks.'

He sat back down and showed me how a refined and civilized man behaved when faced with transferring marmalade from jar to toast. 'He's taken against me, Lance. I can't help that. They started it, but I'm damned if I'm going to lie down and take it.'

'You did accuse him of killing his wife.'

He dismissed this as only my father could. 'A perfectly understandable mistake. They'd had some sort of argument and then, suddenly, she's not there any more. No explanation, no nothing.' It occurred to me that there was no reason why Dad should have been given an explanation, but I said nothing for he continued, 'It was a real humdinger of a row, too. I had to bang repeatedly on the wall to get them to shut up.'

Gently, I said, 'I'm sure that your motives were beyond reproach, but can't you see that in the aftermath of the accusation there is going to be a tincy-wincy bit of resentment on his part?'

'An innocent man has nothing to fear,' he proclaimed pompously.

'Fear and feeling pissed off that your neighbour's accused you of murder are two different things.'

He ignored this. 'He was the one who notched things up by taking out that claim that my fence was on his property. He should have left things as they were.'

I asked with considerable trepidation, 'Out of interest, *is* the fence on his property?'

He had got up to fetch some more toast from the toaster so his back was to me as he replied, but I could see even from this disadvantageous view that he was wishing I hadn't asked. 'It's very complicated,' was his only response.

For a while, he chewed toast and I drank tea and there was no more said on the subject, but I couldn't let it lie.

'You ought to make an effort to repair the relationship. No good will come of the affair if you don't.'

He was outraged. 'Me?' he demanded, or rather squeaked.

'Yes. You. You're the professional, the pillar of the community.'

He sat back in the chair, staring at me, knife in hand and fleck of marmalade in his beard; I wondered how many other flecks of marmalade had gone into that hairy wilderness over the years, never to be seen again; a jarful, perhaps? He pointed out, 'I didn't start it.'

'No, but you can be the one to finish it. At least talk to him, Dad. I'm not suggesting that you should take the blame—'

'You'd bloody well better not! The man's a poltroon and a blackguard. I'll be damned if I abase myself in front of such a milquetoast.'

'But you can at least suggest that you and he should put the past to one side and start again.'

He relaxed, leaned forward and began ingesting more toast, his beard acting as a sort of safety net for wayward crumbs. Through the crumbs that had not escaped their fate and were being masticated in a most enthusiastic manner, he said, 'He wouldn't be interested, Lance. He's only happy when he's making trouble and having arguments.'

My mug was emptied of tea and I stood up to put it in the sink. 'All the same, I think you should try.'

He grunted, but whether it was with acquiescence or defi-
ance I couldn't tell. I had to leave at that point, no nearer a
solution to the problem of my father and the Lightollers.

And so, I repeated to Jane, 'Absolutely nothing.'
    I saw more reassurance on her face than I felt in my heart.
As it turned out, I was right to remain uncertain.

SEVEN

My midday calls weren't too arduous, thank goodness, so that I managed to stumble through them without too much mayhem and without, as far as I was able to judge, doing anything that might cause the General Medical Council to come knocking. My last call was in Strathyre Avenue, quite close to where Dad had said Lightoller's shop was, and so, when I drove back down the London Road, I looked for it. I didn't spot it, though, so turned left on to Warwick Road, parked the car a little way down and walked back.

That stretch of the London Road is not particularly prepossessing. To the north lie the leafier glades of Norbury, to the south the interesting example of suburban culture that is The Pond, a large roundabout in Thornton Heath surrounded by pubs, shops, a bingo hall and a small exhibition hall where the Horticultural Society show off its produce twice a year.

On foot, I found the shop easily. It was snuggling between a baker's and a grocery shop, but looking rather like their poor cousin. The sign above the grocer's read Parrish's Family Shop and, even more interestingly, the sign above the bakery read S.J.M. Hocking, Master Baker. Not for the first time I wondered what a master baker did that an ordinary one could not.

Despite the fact that it was early afternoon, there was a 'closed' sign hanging in the door of the Lightollers' shop, which I thought was rather odd. I peered in and, at first sight, it appeared to be quite tidy but this impression – which was gained from the relatively uncluttered display in the front window – did not survive inspection of the inner recesses. These were difficult to make out because it was intensely gloomy, but the more I looked, the more I realized how disorganized, almost chaotic, things were. There were piles of books on the floor, heaps of papers on chairs, boxes and crates half-emptied everywhere. Ornaments lay scattered on

the tops and shelves of items of furniture, mannequins were
dotted around, and there was even a suit of armour. I
remember thinking that Dad was right, that this was little
more than a junk shop.

More detailed perusal, though, showed that there were a
few jewels amongst the pebbles. In the double front of the
shop, framed by peeling, in places rotting, painted wood,
were various items of dirty brass, a staggering array of pottery
and porcelain, a military standard, a pair of duelling pistols
in the tatty box, services of cutlery, a backgammon set, a
pack of ornate Tarot cards, a teddy bear (both eyes but no
nose), a china doll (no eyes but a nose) and a stained hobby-
horse (neither eyes nor nose). Further back, I could make
out in the dim fluorescent lighting, that this was only a small
collection of the delights on offer, and that there were innu-
merable items of furniture, carpets, musical instruments and
three brass telescopes of varying size.

At this point a woman, dressed in a sort of housecoat of
fine, light-blue check over which was a cream-coloured apron,
came out of the grocer's and stood looking around, presumably for customers. I thought at the time that she was quite
attractive in an exhausted sort of a way, that with time and
care and a bit of money she could make something of herself.
She was blonde with a small nose and pale lips that supported
a lit cigarette. She caught sight of me and stared for a while,
as if affronted that I should be showing interest in Lightoller's
retail establishment and not hers. I glanced across at her and
smiled, but received nothing similar by way of response and
looked away, back through the shop window. I would have
left then, but for the fact that I then caught sight of the
brooch.

It was near the front but to the extreme left, displayed on
a felt board with other items of jewellery. It had a central
emerald cluster with two surrounding rows of diamonds, all
in an ornate silver setting and, although it was difficult to
see from a distance of about eight feet, it looked old.

It also looked like one that had belonged to my mother.

One that had been stolen from my house six months before.

I think Lightoller's a fence. Dad's words came back to
mock me. Could he be right?

I wondered what to do. Presumably the premises were empty and Lightoller was back in his house, in which case I might have been best served by going to the police. Except that I wasn't completely sure if I was correct, if that really was my mother's brooch. If I waited, though, it might go, never to be seen again.

Perhaps Lightoller was in . . .

I knocked on the glass of the door, peering in, looking for a response.

Nothing. I knocked again, peered in some more, still saw nothing; so, before leaving, I tried the door handle.

Which turned and opened the door.

Surprised, for a moment I just stood there. Perhaps he had left the premises and forgotten to lock up behind him. Perhaps, though, he was asleep in the back room, spread out upon an ancient ottoman, handkerchief covering his face, as dust-covered as his wares. I called out, listened, then stepped inside.

A musty smell smote my nostrils, as if these were more than mere antiques, these were artefacts from the other side; moreover it struck me as cold, giving the whole place a Dickensian air, with Little Nell waiting in the back to make an entrance. I nearly knocked over an ugly, cumbersome-looking vase merely by opening the door, and was almost stabbed by an African tribal spear that was lying against the back of a winged armchair.

I did not call out again, because I thought then to get a closer look at the brooch without hindrance. It was difficult to get at, as it lay behind an Ottoman and a large box of metal toy cars, but by putting one knee on the Ottoman and stretching over the box, I could look at it more closely.

It was, without doubt, my mother's brooch.

I stood up, and looked around.

'Mr Lightoller?'

When there was still no reply, I began to make my way to the back of the shop, taking great care not to knock anything over, gaining the impression that it had all been laid out as a series of booby-traps to catch the unwary. 'Mr Lightoller?'

At the back of the shop there was a door with frosted glass in its top half, and beside this there was a rather striking stuffed grizzly bear on its hind legs. There was no writing on the glass but it was obviously an office door and behind it the light was on. I knocked on it and called out his name again.

No response.

I grasped the handle, twisted and walked in.

You'll already have guessed, of course, what I found.

EIGHT

Masson ignored me for the first hour that he was present at the murder scene. He arrived about thirty minutes after my 999 call and about ten minutes after the first, uniformed officers. I had gone at once to the grocer's shop and asked the woman if I could use their phone; she had looked doubtful until I explained why; then she looked nothing less than prurient. Then I hung around outside while the grocer and his wife kept peering into Lightoller's shop, perhaps afraid that he might come back to life, or that his murderer might still be lurking, possibly in the suit of armour.

For Oliver Lightoller had been murdered and, when I say 'murdered', I mean well and truly done in. Somebody had run him through with a sword; they had done this so enthusiastically that it turned out that he was pinned to the chair. Mr Lightoller bore a surprised expression on his rather corpulent features, his eyes wide (and not clouded), his mouth open to reveal teeth distinguished by nicotine staining and a dental bridge that had become slightly dislodged in his death throes. His arms were flopped over the sides of the office chair, but I could imagine that he had perhaps had them raised just before he died.

Masson spent a long time in the office, looking around, directing men taking photographs, dusting for fingerprints, and picking up things that might be of interest to put in thick plastic bags. I sat in the shop with my back to the office door, aware of the intermittent light-bulb flashes coming through the frosted glass and accompanied by the same plain-clothes police constable whom I had seen at the station last night. It turned out that his name was Smith and he was afflicted with a seemingly permanent and indelible frown. He was quite big and muscular and, had his face not been forever creased by worry, I think that he would have been handsome.

He took my details and asked me questions and did so competently, although I had the feeling that he found the

whole process rather perfunctory. About halfway through
this, a small man, immaculately dressed in a blue three-piece
pinstripe, came into the room. He had on his face a look of
superiority mixed with distaste and was treated with due
deference by the police who were showing him the way to
the back of the shop. Constable Smith barely noticed him,
however, as he was wrestling with his next enquiry, chewing
the end of his pencil while staring at his notes that, I could
see, were rather untidy and poorly spelled.

'Who's that who just came in?' I asked.

He looked over at the retreating figure, the stern, cropped
grey hair. 'The prof,' he explained. 'Prof. Tyrell Cavendish.
The pathologist.'

I had often wondered what use a pathologist was in such
cases. They seemed to be there merely to confirm the bleeding
obvious and, in my experience, refused point blank to cede
any useful information, like precisely when the death
occurred, or who actually did it.

Smith and I continued the tedious process of taking the
statement for half an hour, at which point Professor Cavendish
emerged from the room, his manner as imperious as before,
followed this time by Masson, whose expression suggested
that I was right in my suspicions and the good professor had
not solved the case for him.

Masson stopped before us. Had he been chewing on a
hornet, he couldn't have been in a meaner mood, nor had
an uglier look on his face. 'Right,' he said nastily, ignoring
Smith and talking only at me. 'I'd like a word with you.'

I knew the answer I was going to get, but tried anyway.
'How long is this going to take, inspector? I've got evening
surgery . . .'

'And I've got a dead body, doctor, which trumps everything.'

'I don't think my patients are going to agree with you.'

He didn't warrant that with a reply. 'Come with me to the
office.' He turned away, turned back and added in a sarcastic
tone, 'I assume you're not squeamish?'

'It's just the sight of my own blood that makes me faint.'

The only differences that I could see were that Lightoller's
chair had been turned so that he now faced to his left, and

that various surfaces were covered in dark-grey powder where they had been dusted for fingerprints; indeed, two gentlemen were still hard at work looking for them. A photographer was packing his equipment away in a heavy-looking metal case.

'Another dead body,' Masson said, rather unnecessarily.

'Yes.'

'It's been hardly any time at all since we had all that malarkey on the allotments.'

My first encounter with the good inspector had been during some unpleasantness at the local Horticultural Society. 'No.'

'And do you know how much time and effort I've expended, how many sleepless nights I've had because of the deaths on Greyhound Lane?'

I didn't connect what he was talking about with what Jessie Trout had told me. 'A lot?'

He scowled. 'And now this.'

I said nothing.

'And you're in the thick of it, again.'

I definitely wasn't going to say anything to *that*. My silence seemed to make his mood worse. He worked himself up a bit and then began to bark out the questions as if practising for a role in the Spanish Inquisition. I should imagine that it was the kind of voice heard by those confined in deep dungeons while Torquemada warmed up the coals a bit in the background.

'What time did you arrive at the shop?'

I had previously gone through all this with Smith but kept my counsel on that one and confessed that I couldn't remember precisely. 'I suppose about three in the afternoon.'

'About three? Can't you be more exact?'

I tried to concentrate but I was tired and his manner was, as usual, getting to me a tad. 'I remember leaving my last patient, Mr MacNamee, at about two fifty. He lives in Strathyre Avenue, so I would say that it was just before three.'

'How much before three?' he insisted.

'I don't know. Why don't you ask at the grocer's? The woman there saw me.'

He glared at me. 'I provide the questions, you provide the answers.'

I shrugged. 'I'm telling it as exactly as I can. I think it

was just before three, but can't be certain. You'll have to corroborate it.'

He admitted sourly, 'She says she first saw you a couple of minutes before three.'

I said nothing, but I did smile faintly and for just a second. He was wearing a crumpled, tired suit of dark-grey worsted, a dark-blue tie and a light-grey shirt; the suit was misshapen, as if the pockets held all sorts of bulky items. I speculated what they might be – perhaps handcuffs, perhaps a note-book, perhaps even a firearm.

He moved on to another tack. 'Why did you stop?'

'Out of curiosity, I suppose. I just wondered what the shop looked like.'

Masson frowned. 'Curiosity? Nothing more?'

'It's a fault of mine.'

With a shake of his head, he asked, 'You expect me to believe that? You're a busy man, doctor. Do you really have time to wander around peering into antiques shops when the fancy takes?'

'It was on my way.'

His hand went to the pocket of his jacket and he pointed out, 'But you came inside.'

I hesitated. 'Yes . . .'

The hand stayed there and I could see his fingers playing with something. 'Why?'

'I wasn't planning to come in at all, the "closed" sign was up.'

I could see that he didn't believe me from his facial expressions, his sighs and his generally dissatisfied demeanour. 'In which case, why did you?'

'I saw something when I was looking through the window. Something I thought I recognized.'

At last he produced what was in his pocket; a packet of cigarettes. As he set fire to one, he asked, 'What?'

'An emerald and diamond brooch; the diamonds are fake, of course, but it looked like one that I used to own; one that was stolen from my house at the start of the year.'

The inhalation of cigarette smoke seemed to change him, make him more suspicious, more intense. 'And was it?'

'I think so. I tried the door and was surprised when it

opened. I came in and called out, but got no reply, so I thought I might as well check the brooch out. I couldn't get at it easily, but by leaning over a few things, I managed to see it up close.'

'You said the "closed" sign was up, but you still came in?'

'When I discovered that the shop wasn't locked, yes.'

He was staring at me and I could see things going on in his mind as he did so; I wondered rather uneasily what they might be. 'What did you do then?'

'I called out once or twice. When that produced no result, I made my way to the back of the shop, still calling out his name.'

'During all this time, did you see anything untoward?'

'Nothing.'

'You're sure?'

'Quite sure.'

'You never thought that someone else might be about?'

'No.'

'What then?'

It struck me as a stupid question. 'Then I came in here and found Lightoller.' This reply brought forth that stare again; it was most disconcerting. So much so, in fact, that I asked, 'What's wrong?'

Masson shook his head. 'I really can't decide if you're very bright or very stupid, or both.'

Unsurprisingly, I was a trifle affronted, but tried not to show it. 'What do you mean?'

'You really didn't see anything wrong in the shop?'

'No.'

He sighed. 'Wouldn't you say that it's rather untidy?'

I considered. 'Well, yes. I remember thinking that it could do with a bit of a clean . . .' I stopped, because I saw what he was driving at. 'It's been searched.'

While examining me intently, he muttered sarcastically, 'Bravo.'

I rushed to defend myself. 'I just thought it was always like this. Dad said that it was a bit of a junk shop, so I assumed that this was normal.'

'It isn't.'

'How do you know?'

I suppose he interpreted this as impertinent, although it wasn't meant to be. Whatever the case, his face assumed a mean look and his voice became clipped to the point of staccato. 'Not that it's any of your business, but I'm not unacquainted with Mr Lightoller, doctor. In fact I was in here only last week, and it wasn't like this. Far from it.'

I recalled what Dad had said about Masson supporting his theory that Lightoller was a bit shady, but said only, 'Oh.'

'So, when you found the body, what did you do?'

It was such an idiotic question, I took a moment to answer. 'I called for help. I went next door to ring you.'

'You're sure of that? You didn't touch anything?'

'I touched the door handle, obviously.'

'What about inside the office here?'

'No.'

He was frowning. 'You're a doctor; surely you tested for signs of life.'

'What would have been the point? He'd been skewered to the chair by a sword. That's not something they see much in the minor injuries clinic.'

'But even so . . .'

'His eyes were glazed and he was cold to the touch—'

'Ha! So you did touch something.' He was triumphant and cross at the same time, a difficult trick but he did it well.

'Only the back of his hand.'

'But you said you touched nothing.'

'I touched nothing important.' I admit to a degree of exasperation at this point.

He sucked on the cigarette and I saw its end glow bright orange while the unburnt portion shortened noticeably.

There was a knock on the door and Smith popped his head in, shiner on prominent display. 'They're here to pick up the body, sir.'

'Tell them to wait.'

'But—'

'Tell them to wait, Smith.' His voice was not raised but was distinctly more commanding. Smith's head disappeared at once, whence it had come.

Masson stared at the spot for a while, as if convinced that Smith was liable to be insubordinate and reappear anytime soon. When he didn't, he turned to me and asked rather unpleasantly, 'How do I know you didn't kill him?'

You will not be surprised to hear that I was slightly flummoxed by this question.

'Me?'

'Why not? You have means, motive and opportunity.' Almost to himself in nostalgic reverie, he added, 'In the old days, people were hanged on less evidence.'

'No I don't. I don't have any of them.' The proposition was preposterous but it had me jumping.

He suggested with grim enthusiasm, 'Let's see, shall we? I think we can assume for the time being that the sword is one of Lightoller's stock items, so it would be easy to acquire the means. As far as opportunity is concerned, I'm sure you won't argue.'

'I was only here five minutes . . .'

'Quite long enough to stick a sword in someone.'

'Why the bloody hell would I want to do that?'

He smiled. 'You're moving on to motive, I see. Well, there is the little matter of your father's feud with the deceased.'

He had moved from preposterous into silly and come out the other side, heading for ludicrous. 'You think I did away with Lightoller because he was bickering with Dad?'

'Last night, your father deliberately tried to set fire to his house. That's more than "bickering" in my book.'

'It was all an accident.'

He shook his head. 'I have a signed statement from your father's companion of last night stating categorically that your father was trying to fire rockets into Oliver Lightoller's house. The only accident about it was that he hit the shed instead.'

Dad's confidence in the fidelity of Ada seemed to have been misplaced. I had to retreat and try a new tack. 'Whatever happened last night, I don't see that it gives me a motive for murder. Why should I get involved?'

He shrugged. 'You and your father are very close.'

'Oh, yeah. We're so close, I act as his hired assassin. The milkman's next on the hit list because he overcharged Dad by ten pence last week.'

If this made Masson see the idiocy of the theory, it didn't

show on his face. 'And, of course, the means is easy. You pop inside the shop, walk to the back while picking up a sword on the way, burst into the office and pin him to his chair before he can get up.'

Even though this was now well beyond the ludicrous and entering the outskirts of insanity, I could feel slowly rising panic as I tried to find the flaws in this argument that I knew must be there. 'He's been dead for some time . . .'

'Professor Cavendish estimates death at between twelve noon and two.'

'There you are then.'

'So it would seem,' he admitted, paused and then continued maliciously, 'but a clever murderer would perhaps confuse matters a little by killing Lightoller earlier in the day, say around lunchtime, with no one to see, then popping back three hours later, this time making sure he was seen; perhaps even discovering the body.'

He rendered me speechless for a few seconds, what with the audacity and sheer imagination he was displaying. 'You're barmy! If I'd managed to kill him without being seen, why pop back and advertise my presence?'

If he saw how bizarre his theory was, he didn't show it. 'Double, maybe even triple, bluff,' he suggested. 'Put yourself in the frame and then, when we discount you, you're home and free.'

'In the name of all that's holy, why would anyone do that? If they weren't seen at lunchtime, why draw attention to themselves unnecessarily?'

I thought that was unanswerable, but I underestimated the deviousness of the police mind. 'Just in case we find a fingerprint or two. Then, you could say, for instance, "Oh, I forgot. You're quite right, I did accidentally touch the sword, or the chair."' He nodded, pleased with his thinking, and even elaborated upon it. 'Perhaps, as you were visiting your patient in Strathyre Avenue, it suddenly occurred to you that you left fingerprints on the handle of the door, and maybe one on his hand; you had to think quickly, and you decided to risk pointing suspicion at yourself by rushing back here and pretending to discover his dead body.'

There's a rule in psychiatry: never argue with a madman.

Unfortunately, I was in no position to follow that one.

I took a deep breath, partly to calm myself, partly to allow a little time to pass while these delusions settled, then drew attention to the basic flaw in his thinking. 'All of which hinges on my being here at an earlier time, and a few enquiries will quickly assure you that I couldn't possibly have been. I've been seeing patients non-stop since just after eleven and before that I was in surgery. I've given a list of the home visits I made to Constable Smith, so it'll be easy enough to check.'

I could see that he was slightly shaken by my confidence but he was too much of a copper to let it defeat him completely. 'Have you? Good. We'll start talking to them straight away.'

'Can I go now? I've still got evening surgery to get through.'

'Not quite yet. I want to see this brooch first.'

So I led him to it. He examined it closely without picking it up. 'Did you touch *this*?'

'No.'

'It doesn't look very expensive.'

'It was my mother's.'

He grunted, then straightened up. 'We'll see. Do you recognize any of the rest of this stuff?'

'No.'

His sudden shout of 'Smith!' towards the back of the shop made me jump. Smith came hurrying and was told, 'Get this into an evidence bag. Then I want you to check through Lightoller's paperwork; check to see if there's a receipt.'

While Smith was doing as commanded, Masson allowed me to leave, but not before pointing out that, whilst not formally charged, I was still under suspicion and I should make him aware if I were considering leaving my home address for any protracted period.

When I got home that evening, I was almost comatose with fatigue, feeling as if I were in a fugue, observing but not really controlling a body that was mine and yet not. Luckily, for all his faults, Dad was scrupulously neat and so I was not surprised to find that all the breakfast things had been

tidied away, the crockery and cutlery washed and dried, and
the kitchen left cleaner than it had been before. I restored a
bit of normality to the universe by making a cheese omelette
and leaving a mess in the kitchen. I made some coffee and
tried the crossword in *The Times* for half an hour. As usual,
I failed to finish it – in fact, as usual, I barely started it –
and had to throw it to one side, telling myself that I would
have more success if I were less tired. It was only nine thirty,
but I went to bed anyway.

The phone rang in the deepest depths of the night, an
intolerable din that took my brain and shook it violently. I
came to at once because such things are a part of my life,
but was already cursing because they were most definitely
not supposed to be a part of my life when I wasn't on call.

'Yes?'

'Ah, Lance. How are you?'

'Dad?' I couldn't believe it. Surely my father had more
sense than to ring me at . . . I looked at the alarm clock to
find, incredibly, that it was just after eleven.

'Yes, of course it is. Who else would it be?'

Who, indeed? I sighed. 'Actually, I was in bed.'

'Were you?' He seemed distracted, just like he had the
night before.

And a dreadful feeling of foreboding came down upon me.

With the kind of trepidation that only a condemned man
on his way to the scaffold can know, I asked, 'What's wrong,
Dad?'

'Spot of bother, again.'

A deep breath. 'Where are you?'

He paused, then announced gravely, 'The police station.'

I closed my eyes and mouthed an obscenity as I thought
of what Masson had told me about Ada grassing on Dad. 'Is
it arson? Have they charged you with arson?'

He said at once, 'Good grief, no!'

He sounded affronted and I breathed out relief. 'What's
going on, then?'

'It's murder,' he said matter-of-factly. 'They've arrested
me on suspicion of murder.'

NINE

The rest of the night followed a pattern that was familiar from the night before, except that this time I was accompanied by a solicitor. Alexander Holversum was small, with blond hair that had a distinct coiffure and nails that were neat. He was, as my father was wont to say, 'well-trousered', an expression that I suspect meant all things to all men. He was not what I would have chosen, had I had a hand in the matter, but I did not. He became mine – or rather, my father's solicitor – because his was the name on the duty roster for that night. I try to reassure myself with the thought that, if I could not attest to his legal abilities, I was certainly impressed by his teeth that seemed to me to be things of perfection. Whenever he smiled, I feared for my optic nerves.

I met him outside the police station and explained the situation. 'Ah, yes. Mr Lightoller,' he sighed.

'You knew him?'

'I had the pleasure of working for him on the odd occasion.'

'Well, first of all the police thought that I had done it, but now they seem to have got it into their tiny heads that my father is the guilty party.'

He considered this. His lips were barely elastic enough to stretch over his dentition and when they did the effect was a succulent pout. 'Why would they think your father to be a murderer?' he enquired.

So I explained about the feud and the business with the fireworks.

He didn't laugh, didn't even smirk, which I regarded as a bit of a black mark against him but, as he was the only lawyer available to me, I filed it for future reference and said nothing.

We went inside and were greeted by the familiar corpulence of Desk Sergeant Percy Bailey; a variation on the theme was that on this occasion he was considerably graver and less inclined to proffer sympathy. In fact, if truth should be told, he was what can only be described as 'icy'.

It did not start well. Mr Holversum announced himself in a manner that suggested that his name carried some weight. Percy was writing something in a big ledger; he looked up but only slowly and without great enthusiasm. He clearly knew Holversum and, I suspect, knew him well, but that did not mean he was going to fall on his knees in awe. 'Good evening, Mr Holversum,' he said, his voice the kind of voice that people use when they think they're talking to a prat.

'I believe you are holding an innocent man, sergeant.'

Percy either smiled or snarled – it could have been one, or the other; it could even have been both. 'Not that I know of.'

Mr Holversum flashed his smile and I realized what it was. It was the Swiss army knife of expressions: it signalled pleasure, it warned and it staved off misfortune. 'Now, now, sergeant. You know that I'm here about Dr Elliot.'

Percy returned to his paperwork; I saw that it was something about overtime. His voice was slightly muffled but quite clear as he said without looking up, 'He's being interviewed by Inspector Masson.'

'I wish to see him.'

Which made Percy look up again. 'When the inspector's finished, you might be able to. Until then, I'm afraid that's not possible.'

'But—'

'Mr Holversum, you know the rules.'

And, of course, Mr Holversum *did* know the rules. He turned to me. 'I'm afraid we will have to wait.'

We retreated and Mr Holversum gave me the benefit of his dental work. 'This is par for the course,' he said. 'They like to intimidate by pettiness. Do not worry. We will overcome.'

His optimism seemed to me to be out of all proportion to the evidence.

And so we waited, the whole affair seeming to follow more or less the same course as it had twenty-four hours before. The decor remained as it had, my emotions were certainly similar, and the entertainment seemed peculiarly familiar, for through that same waiting room passed a stream of people who, whilst differing in most respects to those I had seen the night before, in the most important were identical.

I began to realize just how boring Percy Bailey's job was.

From where I sat, I could see the clock on the wall behind him, and this only made the waiting worse, the time slow, the tedium swell. My bladder swelled, too, but the only toilet was on the far side of Percy and I didn't fancy my chances of a positive response if I asked to be excused.

Then Constable Smith appeared in the office, looking rather tired. I called out to him, 'Constable Smith?'

He looked up; he was still frowning, presenting the impression of a man with severe troubles on his horizon. 'Hello.'

'We're here to see my father. I understand you're questioning him about Oliver Lightoller's death.'

The frown deepened. 'Yes,' he admitted. 'We are.'

I was about to ask why but my new-found attorney decided to start earning his crust. 'May I ask, constable, on what grounds you are holding him?'

Smith looked over his shoulder, as if afraid of being overheard by Masson in conversation with the enemy. 'No grounds at all,' he said at last.

Holversum perked up, clearly sensing a victory. 'Ha! In that case—'

'He volunteered to come in and help us.'

'Oh.' Holversum turned to me sadly. 'Nothing we can do, I'm afraid. The blighters have got us on that one.'

I ignored him and asked of Smith, 'But why are you questioning him at all? Just because they didn't get on together? That's absurd. And why at the police station? Surely you could have done it all at his home?'

Smith looked at Percy, who just kept on scribbling, refusing to have anything to do with the matter, before he said, 'I really think you'll have to ask the inspector those questions . . .'

Whereupon, as if summoned, Masson opened the door at

the back of the office and, leaning on the handle and the door frame, bellowed, 'Smith!'

He looked very hot, very bothered and very impatient. Smith almost left the ground as he spun around; Percy didn't move any part of his considerable musculature. 'Just coming, inspector.'

Masson caught sight of us and, I could see by the way his face turned from light pink to lightish mauve, he could have done without the vision. Mr Holversum smiled and called out in a friendly way, 'Hello, inspector.'

Judging by Masson's expression, this proved far from helpful. He advanced into the room. He was in shirt sleeves and his tie was loose, his top two buttons undone; I had never seen him in such a condition before. He said in a dangerously steady voice, 'Dr Elliot.'

He ignored Holversum who, nonetheless, did what he was paid to do. 'Inspector, I am here to represent Dr Elliot, whom I believe you have been interrogating in regard to the death of Oliver Lightoller.'

Masson said loudly and forcefully, 'It was murder, Mr Holversum. None of your verbal tricks here, please.' The words 'Mr Holversum' were said in a coldly polite and totally disrespectful manner.

Holversum bowed his head to concede the point. 'Nonetheless—'

'Since Dr Elliot is here of his own free will and hasn't asked for legal representation, I don't really see that you have any business here.'

'So we are led to understand by your constable. However—'

I had had enough of Masson's stonewall defence and Holversum's pretty but ineffective footwork. 'Inspector, you can't possibly believe that this has anything to do with my father.'

Masson looked surprised. 'Yes, I can,' he countered, as if I were being stupid.

I stared at him. 'What?'

Masson repeated himself and, for my benefit, did so slowly. 'Yes, I can.'

'I told you. The disagreement was nothing. Two grown-ups having a silly argument, that's all.'

Masson looked less than impressed. 'You think so? You think we should forget about what's gone on between your father and Lightoller?'

'Yes, I do.'

'Tell me, doctor. Was your father in the habit of social-izing with Oliver Lightoller?'

I said carefully, 'No.' I felt like a man wandering into a forest full of gin-traps.

'They didn't ever go around to each other's houses for a spot of tea and a couple of Bourbon biscuits?'

Again, I said, 'No.'

'Never?'

'Never.' But I knew as I said this that I was being led by the ring in my nose exactly where Masson wanted me to go.

'Then perhaps you'd tell me why your father visited Lightoller in his shop at just after noon today.'

What could I say? The words had yet to be invented that would adequately describe my feelings then.

Holversum stepped in smartly. 'Whether or not Dr Elliot visited the deceased, I still do not see why you are holding him as a suspect.'

Masson turned to Holversum and if ever a human being could be described as 'smouldering', this was it. 'I will hold him for three very good reasons, Mr Holversum. Firstly, this is a murder. Secondly, Dr Elliot has refused to explain why he chose to pay a call on a man whom he seems to have cordially hated. Thirdly, as far as we can ascertain, no one called at the shop after him until his son here did. Since we've established by our enquiries this afternoon that it is highly unlikely that his son could have done it, I think he has some questions to answer.'

It was obvious that Holversum had practised law for so long that incontrovertible arguments presented him with no problems at all; had he been defending Pontius Pilate, he would have argued quite cheerfully that the one-year-olds had it coming. 'Have you any fingerprint or bloodstain evidence to implicate him?' he demanded.

Masson actually smiled. 'No.'

Holversum pounced. 'In which case, I demand—'

The smile was returned to store as Masson interjected, 'Mr Holversum, as I have already told you, Dr Elliot is here voluntarily. He is not charged with anything.'

Before Holversum could start quoting case law and invoking the Geneva Convention, I asked what I thought was a reasonable question. 'Surely by now he's explained matters. Why is he still here?'

Which was when I saw just what a hard time Masson was having. 'Because,' he said, 'he refuses to explain himself. In fact, he refuses to say anything useful at all.'

Mr Holversum used every trick that he had learned in the many years in his profession, flashed his smile at full strength, and generally talked a lot, but Masson was not to be persuaded. My father was to remain in custody overnight and, if necessary, beyond; and since he had not asked for legal representation, he was not going to get any. As Mr Holversum remarked to me sadly afterwards, 'Inspector Masson is such an obdurate fellow.' We finally left the police station at just before three in the morning, he still smiling despite this lack of success, I unable to match this positive attitude.

'Isn't there anything we can do?'

'Not really, not unless your father requests legal representation, or is formally charged.'

'Great.'

He patted me on the back. 'Never fear, Holversum is here. We will prevail.'

He seemed to find great pleasure in this maxim, so much so that he repeated it as he began to walk away, throwing it over his shoulder at me, then laughing.

TEN

'How's your father?' Jane asked the next morning.

I didn't know. I had tried ringing several times throughout the morning, but had met on every occasion the seemingly indomitable stubbornness of the constabulary. In a voice remarkably similar to Percy Bailey's, the policeman who answered the phone refused repeatedly to answer any of my questions, telling me only that my father was still being questioned. I managed to contact Mr Holversum, who assured me with a high-pitched laugh that he was moving 'even the stars in their firmament' to gain access to my father; unfortunately, since my father had apparently still not requested legal representation, there was little that he could do.

I struggled through the day, beset by exhaustion and worry, wondering what my father was going through, able to think only about the kind of interrogation techniques employed with such relish by Jack Regan and his colleagues in *The Sweeney*. It seemed to me unlikely that Constable Smith would partake in such exuberant methods of questioning, but Masson was another matter; he had always struck me as a man who was relentless in the pursuit of those he saw as criminals. I wondered what my father was playing at by neither answering Masson's questions nor asking for a lawyer, and was concerned that perhaps he had . . .

I met Max at seven thirty for a drink in the Railway Telegraph in Beulah Road; she had just had to put down a large golden retriever and was somewhat melancholy; the news about my father jerked her out of this, however. 'My gosh! Murder?'

I nodded.

'Who?' She drank whisky and coke, but I still loved her; a large proportion of the contents of the glass disappeared inside her.

'Oliver Lightoller.'

A look of epiphany lit her face; her large eyes became positively hypnotic in their size, her mouth hanging open, her delicious tongue just visible. 'Oh . . . I see,' she decided.

There was something about the way she said this. 'Do you?'

A nod, then more whisky and coke, but she said nothing. 'What do you mean?'

I knew the look of unalloyed innocence well. There was nothing nasty in Max, and that made her very dangerous to know; very dangerous indeed. She looked around, as if police spies might lurk anywhere and everywhere. 'Well, I can understand why he might have done it. I mean, this Mr Lightoller sounded as if he were a very unpleasant man—'

'He didn't do it, Max,' I interrupted a tad forcefully. 'He's innocent.'

This concept was novel to her and apparently disappointing. 'Oh.'

She swallowed the last of her drink and prevailed upon me to go to the bar and order some more. When I returned, her next question told me that she hadn't quite accepted the possibility that my father might not commit homicide at the slightest provocation. 'If he didn't do it, who did?'

'I don't know.'

The silence that followed between us was an awkward one before she suddenly said, 'We should find the real murderer.'

Which was all fine and dandy in principle, but I still had vivid memories of my last encounter with a murderer and their return came back to me with sufficient clarity to make me shudder. Before I could say anything, she continued, 'If the police aren't doing their jobs, then we'll have to do them.'

'I'm sure the police will come to their senses and realize how absurd the idea is.'

She frowned with more than a touch of incredulity. 'You really think so?'

'Of course.'

'Well, I remember when the old lady over the road from me was attacked in her own house and left for dead, and they didn't ever catch who did it. They were useless.'

'They don't fail every time—'

'And there was the time that my parents were burgled; all

the police did was turn up, wander about for twenty minutes and make some fatuous comments about the inadequacy of the locks. They never even pretended that they were serious about looking for the thieves.'

I might have argued still further, except that I knew that there was a degree of truth in what she said; Masson hadn't exactly covered himself with an air of infallibility when it came to investigating the deaths on the allotments a few months before.

'What can we do?' I asked somewhat pathetically.

'Investigate,' she said at once, as if that were a magic word that immediately bestowed on us the abilities of Sherlock Holmes and James Bond in one.

'How?' I enquired, and my tone was partly curious, partly trepidatious.

Well, if she had had anything in her mind, it went out of it at that point and her opened mouth gave forth no bounty. After a short pause, she said uncertainly, 'We'll have to think about that. It's too late now to do anything, anyway.' She finished her drink.

By the time I had returned from the bar again, I had made a decision. 'If Masson's dumb enough to charge Dad with Lightoller's murder, then we interfere. Until then, we stay out of it.'

She was on the point of arguing, so I leaned across and planted a large kiss on her open mouth, which proved effective in silencing her. I had to keep it up for quite a while, but decided on balance that it was worth it. Slightly numb of lip, we parted eventually and Max looked distinctly happy.

After which, things went quite well. In fact, they went brilliantly . . .

At about three in the morning, as Max lay sleeping peacefully and with quite astonishing pulchritude next to me, the phone rang and two thoughts entered my head instantaneously. One was that this must be news about my father, that perhaps at last Mr Holversum had worked his promised magic and managed to get my father released; the other was that in five hours' time I was on call for twenty-four hours and a night's strenuous hokey-pokey with Max was not the best preparation, especially following on from two nights in which I had barely amassed a total of seven hours of sleep.

'Yes?'

Dad's voice was bright and breezy. 'Hello, Lance. Couldn't give me a lift home, could you?'

ELEVEN

T hankfully, it was a relatively quiet call. There were two cases of influenza, three of measles and three of chest pain (at least two of which were, I'm fairly sure, indigestion), all fairly non-taxing. Which was just as well, since I had not managed to get back to sleep after picking up Dad from the police station and ferrying him home.

The conversation had been fairly one-sided, as I had spent most of the time listening while he prattled on as if I were picking him up from a coach trip to the seaside. He was cheerful, almost triumphant, constantly repeating the refrain that, 'I knew I'd win in the end'. I wondered if he had been as verbose in the police station and if that were the reason he had finally been slung out on his ear.

'They had no proof, of course,' he proclaimed for the fifth time as I pulled up outside his house. Some peculiar piece of operatic tripe came on the radio; I vaguely thought that this was odd, as it was tuned to Radio One, but thought nothing of it.

'So I gather.'

He looked out of his window. 'We are at my house,' he said, apparently surprised.

I mentally applauded his observational skills. 'We are.'

A deep frown. 'You're not taking me to your house, then?'

I thought of Max tucked up in my bed, and thought then of his reaction to such a situation. 'Not tonight, Dad. I'm due on call in less than four hours, so I'd like to get back to bed as soon as possible.'

His expression was unreadable; it contained elements of disappointment, suspicion and disapproval, but in what proportions I could not say. 'Very well,' he decided, somewhat huffily.

'I'll hang around until you're settled.'

'It's all right. Don't worry.'

He was out of the car and heading up the garden path. I hurried after him. 'Dad, I'm sorry, but—'

Fumbling for a key in the brown paper envelope that the police had returned to him when they had let him go, he mumbled, 'You go home, now. I might have been through a frightful ordeal for the past twenty-four hours, but at least it's over now.'

'Dad . . .'

'No sleep, constant harassment, intensive interrogation.'

Which was odd, because that wasn't the impression he had been giving me up until that point. He got the door open, and stepped inside. I tried to follow him but he held up his hand. 'Lance, it's time you were back in your bed. I'm very grateful for what you've done, but enough is enough. You must think of yourself.'

With which the door was shut quite firmly and with enough of a crash to loosen my fillings.

My news that I had diagnosed cases of influenza and measles the night before left my colleagues in deep gloom.

'Here we go,' predicted Jack in a voice of sepulchral doom. 'The winter's come and with it the pestilence.'

Brian said nothing but his nod was the nod of a man taking no pleasure in agreement. It was left to Jane to be positive. 'Perhaps it won't be too bad this year.'

Jack scoffed. 'Even when it's not too bad, it's bad, isn't it, Brian?'

Brian nodded again. He was due on call that night and he tended to the taciturn when faced with this prospect. Not that he was ever especially voluble.

It was Jack who changed the subject. 'What's happening with your father?'

'He's been released.'

Everyone was pleased. 'So I should bloody well think,' said Jack. 'Can't have PC Plod running around arresting doctors whenever they get the whim.'

'Absolutely,' agreed Brian.

'Not a stain on his character, I hope?'

'Well, almost . . .'

Jack detected my uncertainty. 'What does that mean?'

'He's still on police bail.'

Jack was outraged. 'On bail? You mean they still think he might have something to do with it?'

I shrugged. 'I don't know the details.'

Jane said, 'They surely can't still think your father had anything to do with it. That's absurd.'

Jack, as always, had some good advice. 'If I were you, I'd go and see them and find out what they're playing at. Tell them to get off their backsides and go and find the real killer. Tell them they're a useless bunch of good-for-nothings.'

I made out as if I were seriously considering this advice, all the while thinking that he clearly had never met Inspector Masson.

I went straight home and thence immediately to bed where I fell instantly asleep.

And was instantly awake some twenty minutes later as the phone rang.

'Yes?' I admit now that I was rather short.

'Lance?' It was Henry Lamb, one of the general surgeons at Mayday Hospital.

'Henry, it's my half-day and I'm rather tired. Can't it wait?'

'Your dad's been admitted.'

Which woke me up no end. I sat up, suddenly very, very alert. 'What's happened?'

'He's got a serious head injury. He's unconscious and the X-rays show a skull fracture.'

TWELVE

E ven in those days Mayday Hospital was a busy place, the casualty department never seeming to empty, the nurses forever dealing with people crying or screaming with pain, vomiting, shouting or staggering around, not infrequently even verbally abusing them. I had done six months of house jobs there and I knew just what the staff were going through as I went up to Martha, a large, friendly but nonetheless formidable West Indian woman who staffed the reception desk.

'Hello, Dr Elliot,' she said as I approached. She had just finished dealing with a man who had his hand wrapped in a bloodstained tea towel and who looked as if he were going to faint. Normally she would have had a huge grin on her face and her eyes would be sparkling as she tried to persuade me to marry her, but not today.

'My father . . .?'

'He's in side room number two.'

I walked in without knocking just as a short, plump nurse with bobbed brown hair was bending over Dad taking his blood pressure. She had a stethoscope in her ears and so didn't appreciate my entry, nor did she hear me express my surprise that they were not the only two people in the room.

Constable Smith was reading a tatty copy of the *Sun* as he sat in the corner beside a hand basin, one that he now peered over as he said, 'Inspector Masson said I should wait here, just in case your father became conscious.'

'Why?' It seemed a reasonable question but it got no answer, merely a forced smile.

I went over to Dad, disturbing the nurse who straightened up, initially with some annoyance. Dropping the bulb of the blood pressure cuff and taking the stethoscope out of her ears, she asked, 'Can I help you?'

'I'm his son. Dr Elliot.'

If I had hoped that my status as next of kin, and doctor

to boot, would butter a few parsnips with her, I hoped in vain. She said severely, 'You'll have to wait a moment until I've taken his blood pressure. He's on four-hourly obs.'

He looked awful. Because of his exuberant facial hair there wasn't much of his face that was visible, but what there was had a sickly hue, drained of life. He appeared to have lost weight already, as if he had been in a coma for months, not just hours. His head was tightly bandaged and in each forearm a cannula had been inserted; both were attached to a clear plastic bag that hung from a metal stand, crystal clear fluid in each.

The nurse completed her task, made a note of the result on the chart that hung from the metal frame at the end of the bed, then said, 'There you are.'

'What's his blood pressure?'

'One-forty over ninety-five.'

It was high and that was not a good sign. 'Has he shown any signs of regaining consciousness at all?'

She shook her head, then left quickly.

Which left me with Constable Smith. I couldn't work out why he was there. Was there some sort of danger to my father? I thought of what had happened when he had interfered in the deaths that had occurred on the allotments a few months ago, when he had again been brought into hospital unconscious . . .

'What happened?' I asked.

'I think you'd better to talk to the inspector about that.'

'Is he in danger? Is that it?'

The constable remained silent.

'What's going on? Why aren't you telling me anything?'

That got only a shrug. Rising frustration made me want to keep on at him, but I knew that it would be counter-productive. I asked tightly, 'Where is Masson?'

At least he felt able to answer that one. 'He's at Oliver Lightoller's house.'

It wasn't surprising and, with a terse 'Right', I left the room. I thought that I had the right to know what had happened to put my father in a coma with his skull cracked, but before I uncovered the past, I wanted to know what the future had in mind. I went back to Martha's desk and waited

for her to book in a young man with a crew cut, a lazy eye
and a dart sticking out of his head; he didn't seem to be too
bothered about this last, but was more concerned by the fact
that Martha was black. She coped as she always did, by
ignoring his hostility and remaining remorselessly cheerful.
He didn't stand a chance.

'What is it, Dr Elliot?'

'Can you contact Henry Lamb?'

She picked up the phone and contacted Henry's secretary.
Five minutes later, Henry came into Casualty. He wore a
bright-red bow tie, check braces and commiserating smile
as he came up to me, hand held out. He was slightly younger
than me, a rising star in the surgical galaxy, his expanding
private practice a testament not only to his abilities, but also
his charm. 'Lance. I'm so sorry. Have you been to see your
father?'

I nodded. 'He's stable at the moment.'

'Good, good.' He had floppy brown hair and bright-blue
eyes; the female patients fell in love with him as soon as
they came round from the anaesthetic and found him
inspecting their stitches. There was an awkward moment as
he waited for me to ask the difficult questions and I waited
for him to volunteer the answers. Into this the sound of an
approaching ambulance siren began to make itself heard and
I broke first.

'What's the prognosis, Henry?'

I looked closely at his face and body language, and listened
intently to his voice as he answered, on the lookout for the
lies that all doctors sometimes have to tell. He took a deep
breath in (not a good sign), then hesitated (another bad one),
before saying, 'Clinically, he's had quite a large bleed.'

'What about surgical intervention?'

His expression became hesitant, even reluctant and I
reflected that Dad was racking up the bad prognostic signs
with alarming rapidity, but then he said, 'I've been in contact
with the chaps at Atkinson-Morley. They say they'll take a
look at him.' Atkinson-Morley Hospital was the local neuro-
surgical centre, situated in a rather pleasant part of
Wimbledon. Henry continued, 'They've got a CT scanner
and everything.'

I'd vaguely heard of it; it was some sort of fancy X-ray machine. 'Will that help?'

'Oh, yes. It allows them to see the soft tissues in the skull. It's a great help when planning neurosurgery.'

I couldn't see how it would work, but it wasn't the time for an in-depth discussion of novel medical technology. 'When's he being transferred?'

'Any time now. I've just been arranging the ambulance.'

Which was some comfort.

'Do you have any idea how this happened?'

Perhaps it was because I was looking so closely at his body language that I spotted so easily that this seemed to cause him some discomfort. He noticeably stiffened, became almost embarrassed. 'Don't you know?' he asked, but it was more by way of dissembling than because he wanted to know the answer.

'No.'

'Oh . . . Well . . .'

'What's going on, Henry? No one wants to tell me how this happened.'

'I don't know the details,' he began and, having done so, failed to continue.

'But?'

'But apparently he was found in his neighbour's house.'

Well, of course, Dad has two neighbours, and it was entirely possible that he had been visiting Leslie and Jasmine, two middle-aged ladies who lived together in perfect and (according to Dad, anyway) lesbian happiness, but I knew at once that that wasn't the case.

'The Lightollers' house?'

'Yes.'

I could tell by the way he said this that there was more. 'What the hell was he doing there?'

Henry smiled but it wasn't the kind of smile that I wanted to see; it was a thing of sadness, of sympathy. 'Well, the police seem to think that he was murdering Mrs Lightoller.'

THIRTEEN

M y father's neighbours were well used to having their entertainment provided for free, because they could be fairly confident that, merely by looking out of their front-room windows at the right time, they would see something that would keep them talking and reminiscing for many hours. His car alone – a bright-red Hillman Avenger that sounded less like a means of road transportation and more like a Lancaster Bomber with smoker's cough – told you that here was no normal human being; when one added in the fact that he suffered from recurrent bouts of lunacy in which he indulged in various obsessions, then they need never be bored again.

It wouldn't have been so bad, had it not been Pollards Hill. Every town has a Pollards Hill; it's the place that, when you're young, your parents talk about in hushed tones, a place to aspire to when you're living in an end of terrace two-up, two-down and life's a bit of a drag. Such places are always infested with huge numbers of retired dentists, solicitors, chiropractors and military men, and these are people who can glower, tut-tut, head-shake and whisper like no others. They frequently had opportunity to do this with my father in their midst, but, that afternoon, the circus had really come to town.

They assembled in small groups and couples, some just outside their front doors, some by their front gates, and boy did they gawp. Just looking around as I walked along the road from where I had parked the car, just behind a baker's van (there were so many police cars I could barely get within a hundred yards of the house), I saw so much prurience, so much naked nosiness, so much desire for scandal, I could smell it in the air, as if the drains had overflowed.

I made my presence known to a policewoman who was standing at the garden gate next to Dad's looking bored. She wasn't about to let me in, but she signalled to a colleague who, in turn, went through the open door of the house. Masson appeared shortly afterwards to beckon me in. As I walked along the path, I waved and tried an unconvincing smile at Leslie and Jasmine who were standing, hand in hand, peering over the decrepit wooden fence that separated their property from Dad's.

In the hallway, Masson asked, 'How's your father?'

'Not good. He's being transferred to Atkinson-Morley; they may operate.'

Masson nodded and actually looked genuinely sad.

Like my father's house, the hallway we were in was large but, unlike his, this one was crowded. It was also dark and therefore not unlike Lightoller's retail establishment. Also like that, there were a lot of old things; most of these looked to me like junk, but I know nothing of antiques. We were standing just inside the door and from there I could see that over by the foot of the stairs there had been some sort of struggle, for several items of chinaware lay smashed on the carpet, amongst which were some brass ornaments and the remains of a carriage clock.

I asked, 'What's going on, inspector?'

The sadness was switched off, the tartness returned. 'Mrs Lightoller has gone the same way as her husband. She's been murdered.'

'With a sword?' It was a genuine question but perhaps Masson thought it sounded facetious; certainly he glowered a lot.

'No. With a hammer.'

I could not stop myself wincing slightly. 'I heard some ludicrous story that you thought my father might be involved.' I tried proffering this in a light tone, a sort of 'you'll agree that this is absolute tripe, I'm sure' voice. Masson was having none of this.

'I do.'

The same photographer I had seen at Lightoller's shop came heavily down the stairs. 'All done. The prof's just finishing up.'

Masson grunted by way of affirmation and then turned back to me as the photographer squeezed past us and nearly knocked a strangely hideous porcelain shepherdess to the floorboards. 'Preliminary enquiries from the neighbours have identified your father calling at this house at approximately twelve noon today; we have two independent sightings.'

It was yet more evidence that, as far as his neighbours were concerned, my father starred in a sort of real-time soap opera, that he made not a movement without at least one pair of rheumy eyes observing his every move. Masson continued, 'He banged on the door, apparently in a very agitated state. He was shouting something, although we have yet to ascertain precisely what, but received no response from the house. After a couple of minutes of this, he then made his way back to his own house.' At this point, he paused, perhaps to let me make comments as I wished, but I could think of nothing that would help Dad's case so he continued. 'What he did then, we have no direct knowledge of at present – as you will be aware, the back of these properties is not overlooked – but at twenty-five past twelve, the Lightollers' cleaner arrived. She has a key to let herself in should the house be empty. She rang the doorbell and, receiving no reply, entered.'

We were at the crux of matters. Masson was a good story-teller, instinctively building the tension at the right rate and at the back of my mind I wondered if this came through telling his story in court on many previous occasions.

'She discovered a man lying at the bottom of the stairs, unconscious; that man we now know to be your father. Not surprisingly, she became extremely emotional and started to scream. This attracted the baker who was delivering from his van just up the road. He checked to make sure that your father was still alive, then instructed the cleaner, Mrs Madigan, to phone for an ambulance while he investigated further. He made his way up the stairs where he found Mrs Lightoller.'

Professor Cavendish came down the staircase, his tread considerably lighter than the photographer's had been; he still carried with him the same air of unconquerable super-iority. 'You can have the body removed, inspector. I have completed my preliminary enquiries.'

Masson's face told me that he did not appreciate the game that the pathologist was forcing him to play as he asked, 'What have you found?'

Cavendish paused but did so in a manner that suggested he was impatient to be elsewhere, that almost anything else he could be doing would be more useful, more enjoyable and less tedious. 'Multiple blows with a heavy blunt instrument, I would say at this stage. Quite a frenzied attack, I'm afraid. I found her false teeth some distance away. Very bloody; very nasty.'

Quite a frenzied attack. The good professor pronounced this well-worn phrase with enough academic haughtiness and patrician condescension to make it sound an objective assessment rather than a tabloid headline. It angered me and I like to think I would have said something rather cutting had Masson not then asked, 'The hammer we found . . .?'

'That is most likely to be the weapon, I would say. Of course, I will know more when I have performed a detailed autopsy. That I plan to do this evening.'

Masson managed a smile, and bowed his head. 'Thanks.'

Cavendish walked off, his eyes merely raking me without interest. I could see which way this was going and didn't like it.

Masson said, 'The hammer was found by the unconscious form of your father. There is only one set of fingerprints on it.' He paused and before I could ask the obvious question, he went on, 'I don't know yet whose they are.'

'Are you insane?'

Masson looked at me coolly, 'No,' he said, although it is difficult to envisage circumstances in which that question ever receives a positive answer.

'You know my father. He's a retired GP. Slightly off-the-wall, I'll admit, but not crazy, and certainly a long way from the crazed killer type. In fact, I don't think he's capable of "crazed"; he'd do his back in if he tried to raise a hammer above his head too quickly. He's gentle, rather considerate and rather nice to everyone he meets.'

Masson observed dryly, 'Except, by his own admission, the Lightollers.'

Constable Smith came in. 'Can they pick up the body, sir?'

'Another ten minutes.' To me he said, 'Would you like to see what was done to her?'

'Not particularly.'

'It's not very nice.' he said.

'You're saying nothing to make me change my mind.'

He might just have been disappointed as he suggested, 'Come with me.'

We walked through to the back of the house. Being the mirror image of Dad's, it was familiar and yet strange, a looking-glass world, a fancy that was strengthened by the bizarre miscellany of antiques that filled every available space. In the back room where there was only a small, fold-away dining table and even more pieces of bric-a-brac, mostly still in cardboard boxes, he indicated the French windows. 'The rest of the house is secure, but these were unlocked. The same fingerprints as were on the hammer are on the handles.'

'But not necessarily my father's.'

'The house has been searched,' he said. 'There's nothing to suggest that anyone else was there. No witnesses saw anyone else enter it or approach it, and there is no physical evidence that anyone other than the deceased and your father has been here.'

'That doesn't mean anything. A clever criminal could have easily obliterated any sign that he'd been here.'

He exuded quiet and extremely distressing confidence as he said quietly, 'We'll see, shall we?'

I had to pick up a few things for Dad from his house, a task that ought to have been relatively quick and easy, but for the fact that I was trying to gather my father's belongings and not those of a rational human being. It took me twenty minutes to locate his pyjamas because he chose to store the ironing on the top shelf of the larder in the kitchen, above tins of fruit and Ambrosia custard. I had previously been somewhat surprised to discover that the airing cupboard, where I had first gone in search of said articles, was given over to the production of mushrooms on what appeared to be an industrial scale. I wondered what he did with them all, for he could surely not be eating all of his produce; to do so would surely have produced torrential and ultimately fatal looseness. Feeling fairly confident, however, that he would want to know that I had watered them, I emptied several gallons of water over the mushrooms before leaving.

And then I saw, over the low garden wall that separated Dad's house from the Lightollers', two men in dark suits carrying between them Doris Lightoller covered in a pale-red blanket on a stretcher. Behind them came her son, Tom, head bowed. In the background, I vaguely registered that there was a black Bedford van, completely unmarked, parked in the road. Tom spotted me immediately, became fixated on me, his face stony and his blue eyes suffused with emotion. I didn't know what to say, but thought that I ought to say *something*. Accordingly, I stopped and said, 'My commiserations.'

The effect was dramatic. He stopped at once, and the stretcher-bearers did likewise; for a moment there was what felt very like a face-off. He stepped towards me as the stretcher-bearers looked on closely, the one closest to him having to crane his head around. I was suddenly very glad that there was something between us, even if it was only a rather insignificant and decidedly frost-affected brick wall. He asked in a low and venomous voice, 'What did you say?'

'I offered my condolences . . .'

'Are you kidding?'

'No.' I said this because I wasn't.

The two men with the stretcher put it down slowly and with reverence, then came to stand behind him. Because I'm stupid I had not until that moment appreciated that, since Tom Lightoller was an undertaker, he would of course be taking care of the arrangements himself.

'Your old man did this.'

'No . . .'

'Yes, he did. The police said so. They also said that he might also have killed my old man.'

His companions were not handsome. One was well over sixty but clearly still muscular and wiry; he had white stubble around his chin and a nasty looking sty in his left eye. The other was younger and taller and fatter, but equally mean of face and I didn't particularly care for the way that he kept rubbing the knuckles of his left hand in the palm of his right. Either of them could probably have punched me into oblivion

and both of them together could almost certainly have
dismembered me within a couple of minutes, so the fact that
they were both making heavy breathing noises and glaring
at me caused not inconsiderable alarm in the Elliot bosom.

'That's rubbish. It's just an unfortunate coincidence of
circumstances.'

'My mother told me that he tried to burn them to death a
few days ago.'

As if they were pantomime extras in some provincial
repertory company, his companions – now completely trans-
mogrified from respectful attendants of the dead to goon
squad – reacted with expressions of surprise and outrage.

'That was a misunderstanding.'

'Oh, yeah?' He moved forward and, presumably to make
sure that they did not lose contact, so did Bill and Ben, or
whatever their names were. Tom looked down, perhaps to
judge how easy it would be step over the wall, which was
only two feet high; I looked down too and saw that it was
unlikely to keep the Barbarian hordes at bay.

'Look, Mr Lightoller . . . Tom . . .'

'Can I help you gentlemen?' Masson's voice had never
sounded so sweet to my ears. Tom Lightoller looked around,
and softened his face a little as he moved back an almost
imperceptible fraction.

'Dr Elliot was just offering his condolences.' This was
accompanied by a lot of nodding from the decidedly un-
Greek chorus.

'And you were accepting them in the spirit in which they
were offered? That's nice. Very heartening.'

Tom looked back at me and, with just a brief pause to
give me the once over, presumably by way of compensation
for not giving me a going over, said sweetly, 'Thank you so
much.'

With which the three of them turned and walked back to
the blanket-covered figure on the ground, picked up the
stretcher and continued conveying it to the van. Masson
watched them and then turned back to me. 'Everything all
right?'

'He was threatening me.'

'He was upset.'

'No. He was menacing, especially when he was backed by a couple of Neanderthals.'

He glanced back at them. They were climbing into the front seats of the van without a glance in my direction. He sighed and then said to me, 'Perhaps it wasn't the wisest thing to engage him in conversation. He has just lost both parents to a murderer.'

He didn't need to add that all the evidence suggested that the murderer was Dr Launceston Elliot, MBBch, retired.

FOURTEEN

Dad was finally transferred across to the considerably greener and more refined surroundings of Atkinson-Morley Hospital – known to all and sundry as AMH – at about six that evening. He still had a police escort, just in case he made a miraculous recovery en route and jumped out at the traffic lights, never to be seen again. By that time Max had finished work and, after I had told her what had happened, we followed the ambulance through the rush-hour traffic north-westwards to Wimbledon. It was inevitable that we would lose the ambulance and we arrived nearly half an hour after it; by that time Dad was already being assessed by the on-call senior registrar. We waited in a slightly shabby but nevertheless not squalid waiting room, talking nervously.

'I just can't believe it,' she kept saying. She was genuinely upset, almost crying, and I loved her for it.

'What I can't believe is that the police think he's capable of smacking someone repeatedly on the head.'

'I'm sure that when they've checked the fingerprints, it'll prove that he's innocent.'

She was endlessly optimistic, endlessly positive; in that regard she was like a child and it made me want to protect her. It would have been cruel not to agree with her. 'Of course.'

But what I really meant was that it wouldn't matter if he didn't get through this, and the probabilities were against him. I knew neurosurgeons, knew that they were choosy when it came to their patients and then, even if he fulfilled their stringent criteria, the odds were not those one would choose. I had not told Max this, could not have told her because I am fundamentally a rather nice person.

The registrar came in. He was Australian, tall and fair; I thought I noticed signs of interest on Max's face and found myself skewered by jealousy.

'Mr Elliot?' he asked. His accent was broad.

'*Dr* Elliot, yes.' I hated myself for saying it; hated myself even more when he grinned knowingly and said without a trace of apology, 'Sorry, Dr Elliot. My name's Ed Keeping. *Mr* Ed Keeping.'

I ignored his attitude problem. 'What's the verdict?'

Max was sitting beside me and I felt her move closer to me, which helped all round. His face became grave and my insides became cold. 'He's got a massive subdural causing severe midline shift. He's in serious danger of "coning".'

Max whimpered. 'Coning' is as lethal as the axe that severs a head. I waited, wondering if that was it, if this man who had the ability to read out a sentence of death on Dad was going to do just that. I am sure that he wasn't being deliberately sadistic when he seemed to be pausing, to be assuming an expression of supreme graveness before he said, 'We're prepping him now. I'm sure that we can relieve the pressure.'

Max squealed with delight and burst into a huge smile. 'Oh, thank goodness!' she said breathily, her eyes filled with awed reverence as she gazed upon Mr Keeping's countenance and he smiled back at her. As elated as I felt at this reprieve, and as dependent as I was upon his surgical skills, I felt like smacking him in the gob.

We managed to get one last glimpse of Dad in the anaesthetic room before he went into surgery. Smith was standing outside and tried a sympathetic smile as we went in. Dad's head was encased in an elasticated bandage under which, I guessed, someone had shaved his head; his face looked far, far paler, even closer to death and I realized with foreboding just how quickly he was marching down the road to the end of his life. Max was openly crying as I squeezed the old fool's hand and wished him good luck. Then the anaesthetist moved in and, picking up the same hand, held it by the wrist and slapped it to bring up the veins. With practised ease, he took a green butterfly cannula from an assisting nurse and inserted it into one of them; as he withdrew the needle, it filled with blood. I watched as he pressed the plunger of the syringe, forcing the blood in the tube back into the body, mixing with the anaesthetic. Although there was no visible change, Dad was now anaesthetized and paralysed. The anaesthetist quickly put a laryngoscope into his mouth and used it to guide an endotracheal breathing tube into place; this was in turn connected to a manual breathing bag which he squeezed regularly while the nurse taped the tube in place. With this done, Dad was ready to be wheeled into the theatre, and to have his head opened.

He was in theatre for six hours, a quarter of a day in which I felt as if I were in complete sensory isolation, the rest of the world without meaningful existence. Max fell asleep, contracted into a foetal curl, mouth open to just the right degree to make her, under almost all other circumstances, impossibly attractive. I tried to sleep, perhaps I even succeeded, but it was the lightest, most inconsequential brush with the arms of Morpheus, and it was without effect. When I prowled the room, I was tired enough to cry, yet when I lay back in a stiffly upright chair upholstered in bright-red PVC, my brain throbbed with awareness.

And the more that I waited to hear if my father would live through the night, the more I began to wonder just what was going on. I knew my father and I knew therefore that he would no more attack someone with a hammer than he would run naked through a nunnery, which meant that whatever he had been doing round at the Lightollers' house, it had been innocent and misinterpreted by witnesses. What followed from that, therefore, was that despite the evidence, there had been someone else in the house, the real murderer. It did not take an intellect the size of a planet to deduce from all this that whoever had bashed Mrs Lightoller over the head had also run her spouse through with an antique pattern sword.

That, though, proved to be a temporary stop upon my deductions, for it brought me back squarely and inevitably to the problem that, once again, my father was the only one who had been seen in the vicinity at the estimated time of death.

I had a horrible feeling that the next time I spoke with Masson, he would be informing me with quiet satisfaction that the only fingerprints found on the hammer and in the house generally (apart from those of the Lightollers) belonged to Dad. I wondered then what he would do. Would he consider that sufficient evidence to cease serious investigation of the two deaths? Would he wait for my father to recover and then charge him? Of course, if he didn't recover, he would not be formally charged, but he would die a murderer in the eyes of the world . . .

Thus the night passed, seeming to become slower and more turgid with every minute, threatening at any moment to stop completely, perhaps to die there and then, leaving me in stasis, condemned to oblivion.

The first sounds of a hospital waking up began to come through the door: the odd echoing call, something metal falling to the linoleum floor, the quick clipping of footstep heels past the room, an increase in the noise and volume of traffic outside the frosted glass of the window as grey light began to seep through it.

Max was just coming round when the door opened and in came our Australian neurosurgeon. He was dressed in light-green theatre ware, a silly disposable balaclava around his head, a mask hanging loosely around his neck. He looked very tired, almost morose.

I stood up, Max uncurled and sat bolt upright; both of us stared at him, waiting, wondering.

'Well,' he said with a tired drawl. 'He's made it so far.'

FIFTEEN

Everyone was very understanding when I phoned and said that I wouldn't be in. The receptionists – Sheila and Jean – were charged with contacting all my appointments that day and seeing if any could be rescheduled for a later date and between them Jack and Brian said that they would handle my calls. As it was Friday, that meant that I had three days off work to try to begin work on clearing my father's name.

I returned from the public call box to the ward where Dad now reposed to find Max sitting beside him, holding his hand. Also present was DC Smith, looking official. I said to him, 'Hello, constable.'

He nodded. 'Sir.'

Dad had shown no sign of returning to consciousness but, we had been warned, that might not happen for several days, perhaps even weeks. What had not been said, but was clearly evident between the lines, was that it might not happen at all. To Smith I said, 'I don't know why you're here. I don't think he's faking it. He's not going to do a midnight flit on the *Orient Express*, you know.'

And Smith, taking it all as seriously as ever, said, 'Just doing what I'm told, sir.'

Max asked, 'Did you get through to the surgery?'

I explained the arrangements. 'What about you?' I asked. 'What about your work? You're going to be late.'

She looked at her watch; it was just after eight. 'I'll never get there in time now and, in any case, I'm too tired to be any use. I'll have to ring them and tell them what's happened. I'm sure they'll understand.'

We agreed that there was no point in hanging around by Dad's bed and, leaving instructions with the nursing staff to call if there was any change, we left the ward and I showed Max where the phone was. I left her making the call, then went out of the main entrance, intending to wait by the car for her. Masson, though, was just coming in.

'Dr Elliot,' he said.

'Inspector.'

'I was just coming in to see how your father was doing.'

I told him the situation. He nodded and then his face twitched into what might have been a grimace, might have been a smile. 'Well, that's something, I suppose. It's not all bad news.'

I couldn't feel quite as positive as that, but said something non-committal. Max came up and joined us just as Masson, after what I could only describe as an embarrassed pause, said, 'The results of the fingerprint tests are through.'

'And?'

That twitch again, which told me the answer before he opened his mouth. 'Your father's prints are the only ones on the hammer handle and, apart from Mr and Mrs Lightoller's, they are the only ones anywhere in the house, including the French windows at the back.'

So, I had been right; somehow, I wasn't surprised. There was a pattern here, and this new piece of information fitted it exactly. I said tiredly, 'You surely can't believe that my Dad's guilty of these murders.'

When I said this, Max's mouth fell open; I hadn't told her the details of Dad's accident and, most particularly, I had not told her that all of the available evidence put him in the dock for two murders. Masson, predictably, seemed to consider my doubts to be both superfluous and incomprehensible. 'Can't I?'

'Surely it's obvious. Someone's framing him.'

Masson asked, 'Really? Who?'

To which I had no answer.

Then, frowning deeply, he asked in a falsely curious tone, 'Whilst we're about it, why? Why would anyone want to frame your father?'

I wasn't sure and he knew I wasn't sure. It was surprising for both of us when Max suddenly said, 'Maybe because he saw something at the first murder scene.'

For the first time, perhaps, Masson took her in and looked at her seriously. He appraised her for a moment, then turned back to me. 'Is there somewhere we can talk?'

We showed him into the waiting room where we had spent

the night. He looked around, grunted, then sat down; Max and I did likewise. Masson fiddled in his coat pocket, I would guess for cigarettes; I'm not even sure he was aware that he was doing it. Eventually, he said, 'All our enquiries have failed to reveal any sign of anyone coming to the shop during the time in question, except for your father.'

'You can't prove a negative.' I knew as I said this that, by resorting to scientific principle in a case of murder, I was backing a hopeless cause.

Masson did exactly what he should have done and ignored me. 'The door at the back of the shop was locked.'

Max chipped in, 'Someone could have come to the back and been let in by Lightoller. Then left the same way after killing him. Was the key in the lock?'

'No . . .'

'Have you found the key anywhere?'

'It's on the windowsill by the door.'

This rather deflated Max for a moment before she rallied with: 'Is there a window by the door?'

'There's a fanlight.'

'Was it open?'

Masson clearly objected to being the questioned rather than the questioner. 'It was ajar, on a latch.'

Max pounced. 'Then, whoever it was let themselves out, locked the door and then dropped the key on to the sill through the fanlight. Easy.'

Masson did not bother to conceal his annoyance. 'Enough of this fantasy. No one else was seen entering the shop either from the front or the back, except your father. He has now been found unconscious at the scene of a second murder, with his fingerprints on the murder weapon. No one else has been implicated in either death.'

I was tired of hearing all sorts of reasons why my father should be number one suspect, while the only reason that counted – that he was a good, decent and honourable man – was being ignored. 'And I say again, this is totally and completely ludicrous! My father is innocent!'

Masson shook his head but instead of entering into a debate on the point, he said gently, 'I haven't got anything against your father, you know.'

It was an odd thing for him to say and seemed out of character; I didn't know how to respond and it was Max who said, 'You could have fooled me.'

'Perhaps you might understand if I give you a bit of background.'

She snorted. 'I doubt that.'

Masson stared at her; he had such pale eyes that, when he stared at you, you felt as if he were doing more than merely looking, more even than assessing, as if he were looking into you and seeing things that he shouldn't be able to. Max stood up as well, staring at him in return and after a while he just grunted softly, and smiled.

'What do you know of the Lightollers?' he asked.

'Not much.'

'In which case, let me fill you in on them. Oliver Lightoller was sixty-nine, his wife, Doris, was sixty-eight. He's owned that antiques shop for thirty-seven years, starting it just after the war. He had originally worked as an apprentice for a firm of auctioneers in Bromley, where he learned the trade. He met Doris when he fell and received facial injuries whilst redecorating the shop not long after he acquired the lease; he was taken to Mayday Hospital where she was a casualty sister.

'Before moving to Pollards Hill, they lived in Colliers Wood; we've talked to their neighbours there and the rather sketchy picture we've drawn is one of a couple who kept themselves to themselves, who were courteous but not overly inviting. They had a single son, who you've met, I think.'

'There's something about that Tom Lightoller, inspector. Are you sure he's just an undertaker? Judging by the men he employs, I think he might be something in the underworld.'

'Undertaking's quite a hard, physical job,' he pointed out. 'It's no good employing someone who's too weak to act as a pall-bearer, is it?'

'One of the two I saw looked as if they could bend a lamp post with their bare hands, and the other one looked as if he'd fillet you with a knife if he got half a chance.'

'I've looked into Tom Lightoller's background. He had

behavioural problems as a child but nothing since he left school.'

'What sort of behavioural problems?' I asked this in more than just professional interest. When I had seen him he had radiated an air of cold menace that struck me as almost cruel.

'A fair amount of petty thieving and bullying, mostly. One spell inside for persistent joyriding.'

'Bullying? He doesn't look big enough.'

'He got his friends – his bigger friends – to help him out. There was a suspicion of some sort of organized extortion racket, but the school authorities couldn't prove it.'

I thought of his pall-bearers when Masson mentioned 'bigger friends'. 'There you are, then. He's the criminal type.'

Masson sighed. 'Tom Lightoller's odd, I'll own up to that, but he's become something of a philanthropist, if anything. His little sojourn in the nick had a salutary effect. He realizes how hard life can be for ex-cons and makes a point of giving them a job as a start to going straight.' I reflected that this explained the decidedly dodgy appearance of his employees. Masson went on: 'He's done well for himself. He started out as his father's apprentice in the antiques shop, then moved on about ten years ago. He got a loan from his father and has never looked back. The business is in West Croydon.'

'It's a bit of a funny transition, isn't it? Antiques to corpses.'

He shrugged. 'There's no accounting for human beings. I wanted to be an engine driver when I was young.'

The unbidden and faintly disturbing vision of Inspector Masson dressed as Casey Jones in the cab of a huge steam locomotive vied for my attention. Max asked, 'Who inherits now that both the Lightollers are dead. It's Tom, I bet.'

Masson was imperturbable. 'So would I.'

'There you are then!' She was triumphant and I own that I suspected she was a little premature in this.

There were times when Masson could treat patience like a miser treats gold sovereigns but, at other times, he doled it like sweets, as he did now. I thought it was probably because Max was a pretty girl, but I'm prejudiced. Anyway, whatever the reason, he said calmly, 'We'll check the value of the estate, of course, but I doubt that it comes to more than a hundred thousand pounds.'

'A lot of money.'

'Considering Tom Lightoller's got at least that already, and that he has no significant debts, I would discount it as a motive.'

Max opened her mouth to argue but I interrupted by saying, 'So he was a real antiques dealer?'

He replied, but only after the briefest of hesitations, 'Yes.' Then he asked, 'Why?'

'Because Dad was convinced that he was nothing more than a junk dealer, maybe even a fence for stolen goods.'

'Most antiques dealers handle a lot of junk. They have to, because by sorting through the junk, they find the treasure . . .' He trailed off, the sentence ending with a silent but very loud, 'but', which I supplied for him and he continued, 'Lightoller has been dancing on the line between legal and illegal for years, but he's by far from alone in that.'

'Does that mean he was or was not a crook?'

'I think – no, I know – that he was handling stolen goods, but nothing was ever proved. Ironically, I think we've now got the proof, but a day too late.'

'What proof was that?'

He felt in his pocket and pulled out my mother's brooch. 'This.' He handed it to me as he went on: 'It tallies with the description you gave when you reported it stolen, and we've been unable to find a receipt amongst his papers.'

So Dad had been right, for once; I only hoped that he would live to gloat about it.

I held out the brooch for Masson to take back but he said, 'Keep it. It's of no use to me as evidence. We're not going to prosecute, are we?'

Max suddenly burst out, 'That's why he was murdered!'

Masson looked across, his face neutral. 'What was?'

'Because of something he had that was stolen. The thief wanted it back, I bet.'

Masson said gravely, 'That's exactly what I thought.' It was obvious from the way he said it that he was being patronizing and Max, who was sensitive to condescension, asked at once, 'Why do you say it like that?'

'Only my theory involved a man who wasn't himself a thief, but who thought that Lightoller was.'

It took only a moment for me to get what he meant. 'The watch?' I asked incredulously. 'You think that Dad bumped him off because he wanted his watch back?'

Masson looked at me impassively. 'It strikes me as quite a good theory,' he admitted.

'What about Doris Lightoller, then?'

He said slowly, 'I suppose if he didn't find his watch in the shop, he decided the next most logical place to look would be the house.'

'That's almost as barmy as one of Dad's theories. You cannot possibly believe that my father has become a homicidal maniac because he wants his watch back. It wasn't even particularly valuable.'

'Your father told me himself that it had great sentimental value.'

'Even so . . .'

Suddenly Masson had had enough. 'Look, Dr Elliot, I've seen murder committed over a single pound note, over a cigarette and even over a football, so a couple of killings because of a watch doesn't surprise me in the least.'

'Yes, but not my father.'

It was with the air of a man who did conjuring tricks as a party piece that he produced from his jacket pocket a plastic bag that he held towards us on the flat palm of his hand.

And in that plastic bag was my father's missing watch.

I stared at it and Max stared at me, guessing, I suspect, what it was. I croaked, 'Where did you get that?'

'In Lightoller's house, at the bottom of the stairs near where your father was lying. It had rolled behind an umbrella stand.' He looked into my eyes, and I saw within him a blend of triumph and sadness. 'It's got your father's fingerprints on it. He must have dropped it as he fell down the stairs.'

I like to think I tried, for I said with lips and tongue suddenly dry, 'This doesn't prove anything . . .'

'Maybe not,' he conceded, 'but it does strengthen the suggestion that your father was actively looking for the watch and, quite obviously, he found it, apparently at Lightoller's house.'

I felt myself to be desperate. 'He wouldn't murder anyone over it, though.'

'Why not? Anyone can be a murderer; it's not an exclusive club, you know.'

I was running out of arguments, reduced to repeating forlornly, 'Yes, but not Dad.'

He didn't deign to reply to that, instead saying to the audience in general, 'So, since I can't find a single reason why Tom Lightoller should want his parents dead and, in fact, I can't find a single reason why *anyone* else should want them dead, I have to consider the possibility that your father is guilty.'

'You're wrong. Utterly, totally, disastrously wrong.'

Masson stood up. During the whole conversation he had had his hand in his pocket, grasping his cigarettes. He said, 'I might be wrong, but not disastrously so. We'll wait to see what your father has to say.'

'In the meantime, you are going to carry on investigating these deaths, aren't you? While you wait for my father to recover.' I said.

'I've made all the enquiries I need to make for now. There's not a shred of evidence to implicate anyone else. Until I find out your father's explanation for what happened yesterday, I'm concentrating on other matters.'

With which he walked off to the ward to get an update from Smith.

Max was outraged. 'What's wrong with him? Can't he see that he's completely wrong? If he doesn't get after the real murderer, he could get clean away.'

I sighed. 'The official mind doesn't think like that. Dad ticks the right boxes in Masson's list of things a murderer should have; if there's nothing to suggest in the slightest that anyone else had anything to do with it, why waste time chasing phantoms?'

'It's criminal,' she said vehemently, unaware of the irony, I think. I said nothing by way of reply, was too busy thinking, and she took this as a sign of reluctance to act. 'We've got to do something now, Lance. There's no one else who is going to look after your father's interests.'

I sighed, then said slowly, 'I really rather think you're right.'

She was so excited, she was almost jumping around in the seat. 'Come on, then!'

'What, though, Max? What do we do?'

'Ask questions, find witnesses, look into the history of the Lightollers . . .'

Good suggestions all, but I had a better one. 'No. The first thing we do is go home. We need some sleep.'

SIXTEEN

I wasn't going to get any, though; not straight away at least.

For the first part of the journey, though – as we made our way through Epsom – there were no smoke signals on the horizon and I was gulled into a feeling of relative security. The cod opera music was on the radio in the background again.

'What is that?'

Max did a bit of eye-rolling. 'Honestly, Lance. Don't you know anything?'

'Apparently not.'

'Isn't it fantastic?'

I began to suspect that she did not share my opinions regarding the piece's musical virtues. 'Well, it's different.'

'I think it's wonderful.'

'But what is it?'

'It's called "Bohemian Rhapsody".'

'Really.'

'It's by Queen.'

I'd heard of them, but they'd passed me by, like leaves blown in the wind. There was quiet between us for a while, perhaps that was a mistake for Max suddenly announced, 'If the police won't do anything, then we'll have to.'

From somewhere she had found a Bounty bar and we were each munching half. I could remember all too clearly what had happened when Dad dragged me into the affair on Thornton Heath allotments and I wasn't keen for a repeat dose of the kind of thing that had befallen me then. 'We're both tired. We're going to go home, get some sleep, and then go back to AMH. We leave the sleuthing to the police.'

'But they're not doing anything. You heard him.'

'So? We both know that Dad didn't do it. I'm sure that when he recovers he'll have a perfectly rational explanation of what he was doing in the house. He'll probably even be able to identify the true killer.'

But I remember a small doubt at the back of my mind, one that pointed out that my father's reasons for what he had done might seem to him to be rational, but there was a fair chance they would appear completely cuckoo to the police and the courts.

And there was also the possibility that he wouldn't recover at all . . .

Max said nothing more as we cut through Sutton and made our way towards the Purley Way and then on to Thornton Heath. Then she said, 'You'd better take me home.'

I was hurt. 'Don't you want to come back to my house?'

'I think I'll sleep better in my own bed.' Perhaps she realized that I was slightly hurt by this, for she then said, 'I'll ring you later this afternoon, I promise.'

So, I dropped her at her house and we parted with a kiss and I drove home. The Bounty bar had helped but I hadn't actually eaten a proper meal for twenty-four hours and so I made some breakfast of toast and Marmite and tea, then dragged my legs up to bed, confident that I would be in the land of Bedfordshire before the Sandman had even found the address on the map. I had forgotten the brooch in the pocket of my overcoat; I didn't realize then how lucky that was.

Two hours later I was still awake. The reason for this was multifactorial but mainly partly because my mind wouldn't stop going over Dad's predicament, partly because they were digging up the road about a hundred yards away and using no fewer than three pneumatic drills, and partly because I was (as I remember my mother used to put it) 'overtired'.

Accordingly, when the phone rang, it did not drag me from the deepest depths of slumber, merely from the shallows of sore-eyed frustration.

'Yes?'

'Lance?' This was a low, urgent whisper but unmistakably it was the voice of Max.

Accordingly, I enquired, 'Max?'

'Lance, I need help.' Still the whisper.

'What's going on? Where are you? Are you at home?'

'Shhh!' This vowelless syllable was issued even more urgently.

'Max?'

Nothing.

'Max?'

There was another passage of silence, then she said, 'I'm in the house.'

'Which house? Yours?'

'Lightoller's house!' Her whisper signalled frustration at my obtuseness.

I sat up straight. 'What are you doing there?'

She didn't answer directly. 'Can you come at once?'

'Max, what's going on?'

'Please, Lance. Can you come at once? I think that—'

And she stopped speaking. All that I heard was a clatter as the receiver was dropped. I shouted, 'Max? Max?' The only sound I heard came about five seconds later. It was the sound of the receiver being put back on the cradle and then there was nothing other than the soft whisper of the ether.

My first impulse was to rush around there at once, to charge into the house and come to her rescue, but reason whispered in my head and slowed me. Although part of me felt that it was possibly wasting time as I waited to be connected to the police, another part told me that I was doing the sensible thing, that they would be able to get there before me. The woman who took the call was irritatingly slow and matter-of-fact, seeming to become more so as I became in turn more and more stressed. Eventually she was satisfied and I dropped the handset on the base, then ran to my car and drove there as fast as my new BMW series 3 and traffic conditions would allow. Thankfully there were already two police cars parked outside the house and I skidded untidily to a halt behind them.

The door to Lightoller's house was open and there was the usual small cluster standing on the pavement under a lime tree, talking amongst themselves. I thought bitterly that they must have been delighted to have yet another drama so quickly enacted for their own personal entertainment. I ran past them, aware of their judgemental gaze, their desire to be shocked by what they hoped was more disaster.

There was a uniformed police constable just inside and he stopped me with an official palm but then allowed me past when, from the back of the house, Constable Smith called out, 'It's all right. Let him through.'

I hurried towards Smith who was standing in the doorway to the kitchen, just managing not to knock over a large brass table lamp as I went by. Smith looked genuinely worried as he said, 'It's all right. We've called an ambulance.'

He let me through into the kitchen. A uniformed police-woman was down on one knee behind a round pine table, bending over the body of Max. My heart went into spasm. I said urgently, 'Let me see her.'

The woman stood up and allowed me access to Max. Her face was white and there was some blood on the floor beneath her head. As I knelt down beside her I remember feeling neither anxious nor sick, just numb; completely divorced from everything. I was hovering above the world, giddy and yet perfectly focussed; holding my breath and yet hearing deep, undulant sighs in my ears.

The first two fingers of my right hand reached out to the side of her neck, felt nothing; somewhere inside my body there was a rising feeling of panic but, as I moved them slightly, the pulse came to them, strong and regular. I sighed a deep breath and with it the world became normal again; I rejoined my body, time seemed to speed back to its habitual pace, and I felt elation.

I looked into her eyes, saw contracting pupils that were equal in size, thought somewhere at the back of my mind that they were a beautiful hazel in colour, then heard her moan. Smith said, 'Is she all right?'

I was feeling around the back of her head, my fingers encountering the sticky viscosity of coagulating blood and, without altering my position, I replied, 'As far as I can tell, a single blow to the head but she'll be all right, I think.'

'The ambulance should be here presently.'

'Good.'

Max's eyes opened, looked at nothing for a moment, then found me. 'Gosh,' was her only remark.

'Are you all right?'

'I don't know.' She winced, moved her head, then winced more deeply. 'Ow.'

'Is it just the head that hurts?'

She considered this question. 'I think so.'

'Well, lie there anyway. There's an ambulance coming and I want you checked over.'

'I'm all right.' Of course, she tried to get up and, of course, she said, 'Ow,' again, even before I pushed her gently back down.

Smith leaned over me. 'Could I ask what you were doing here?'

She moved her focus to him, and frowned. 'Doing where?'

'In Oliver Lightoller's house.'

'What am I doing there?'

Smith's voice expressed some exasperation. 'That's what I want to know. This is a crime scene and it's a criminal offence to interfere with a crime scene.'

Max said, 'Crime scene?' in a bewildered voice.

I said over my shoulder to Smith, 'Post-traumatic amnesia. It's a sign of concussion. I don't think it's wise to continue this until she's had a chance to recover.'

'I'm not sure. The inspector will want to know—'

'Sod the inspector.'

Smith straightened up. 'I'll have to report matters.'

'Please do.'

He vacillated for a moment, then took me to one side. 'Look, Dr Elliot, I'm sure that the young lady has a perfectly reasonable explanation of what she was doing inside the house, but the law's the law, you know. The inspector will have to know, but I don't suppose he'll want to take it much further.'

It was, in a way, the first sign of proper humanity he had shown and it changed my opinion of him from a slightly incompetent, robotic jobsworth to a man trying to do his job and finding it all a trifle tricky.

A call from the front door told us that the ambulance had arrived. Within ten minutes Max was in the back of it and I was left with a disgruntled Smith and the policewoman. We looked at each other. 'Do you know what she was doing here?' he asked.

'Not the foggiest.'

He didn't believe me. Just in case I'd forgotten, he repeated, 'This is still a crime scene. It's an offence to interfere with a crime scene.'

I looked around and said facetiously, 'It doesn't seem to be interfered with to me.'

'That's not the point. I want to know what Miss Christy was doing here.'

'As I said, constable, when she's fully recovered, I'm sure she'll tell you. What I want to know is who attacked her and, more specifically, what *they* were doing here.'

SEVENTEEN

By normal medical criteria, and even though physical examination and an X-ray of her head revealed nothing untoward, Max should have spent the night in hospital under four-hourly neurological observations, but because I promised to keep a close eye on her, she was allowed home after just five and a half hours. Somewhat oddly, though, her amnesia remained more or less unchanged, so that Constable Smith's repeated attempts to find out what had happened to her and why she had been in the house were thwarted. She seemed unfocussed and distracted, no matter what he asked. When he complained to the senior A&E registrar about this, implying that he thought that she was faking it, he received a condescending explanation that such things occasionally happened and that, as a layman, Constable Smith had no right to question clinical diagnoses. He departed shortly afterwards and I was able to thank the registrar for his assistance. Then I returned to the cubicle to collect Max. She was sitting on the couch, swinging her legs. She had an adhesive dressing applied to the back of her head, just to the left behind her ear, but she seemed to have improved remarkably from the slightly bewildered urchin who had been lying on the couch.

She asked, 'Has he gone?'

'For now.'

'Good.' She hopped down. 'Can we go now?'

I like to think of myself as quick and so it was not long before I twigged. 'You're all right.'

'My head hurts,' she pointed out.

'But you're not concussed.'

'Of course I'm not.'

I took this in, thought about it and then, with light dawning all around me, I asked, 'Can you remember what happened?'

She made a show of deep consideration. 'I think so . . .' she said hesitantly, then spoiled things by smirking.

'You never had amnesia, did you?'

'Not exactly, no.'

'Not in any way, I think.'

She made big eyes, and looked up at me. 'I was a bit confused for a while.' She had a look of unalloyed innocence, but then, I suspect, so did Lizzie Borden shortly before she took up indoor lumberjacking.

'Why all this charade?'

She said disdainfully, 'You heard what Constable Smith said. It's a criminal offence to interfere with a crime scene. I didn't want to get into trouble.'

I sighed.

Duped again.

'Why were you in the house?'

She opened her hazel eyes wide, gave me a full view of the light-green flecks in the irises, as her rather pouting lips formed a circle that tried to portray puzzlement. We were in the car, waiting behind a queue of cars to turn right on to the London Road. She said, 'I went there to nose around.'

I sighed. 'I guessed as much.'

'It just seemed a good opportunity to see whether we could find any clues.'

Find any clues. It was a naive thing to say, a naive way of looking at things. 'I told you we were going to go home and get some sleep before we did anything.'

'You told me that *you* were going to do that. That doesn't mean I have to do likewise.'

'Yes, it does.'

'No, it doesn't.'

'Max, yes, it does.'

We were becoming slightly heated in this puerile exchange and, because we were both tired, neither of us spotted it. Her face was taking on an intransigent, angry look as she responded, 'No, it doesn't, Lance. I'm not an underling. If I want to snoop around, I will.'

'And look what happened. You could have been killed. It was a stupid, juvenile thing to do. We're not members of the Secret Seven, you know, Max.'

But I had gone too far, as I appreciated at once, because her face became suffused and set and I could see that she

wanted to cry but was damned if she was going to succumb
to the desire. I had broken the taboo and alluded to her
age, to the age difference between us, and that made neither
of us comfortable. There was silence for the time it took to
get from the Pond roundabout to the Granada Bingo Hall
where I asked in a gentle voice, 'What did you find?'

She refused to answer until I was in the act of turning
right off the main road, then mumbled, 'Nothing.'

'Oh.'

'I had only just got into the house when I was interrupted.'

'How did you get in?'

'It was absurdly easy in the end, although when I got there,
I suddenly realized that I might have a problem. I thought
about going around the back, but I couldn't get around there.
For a while I was stuck and I just sat on the wall staring at
the front of the house and the door with all that silly yellow
tape across it. I don't know why, but suddenly I got up and
ducked under the tape and just shoved against the door. To
my surprise, it opened. For some reason, they'd left it on the
latch.'

For a moment I was as surprised as she was, then I appreciated the truth of the situation. I murmured, 'I'm not sure
you can blame the police.'

She glanced across at me, for a moment uncomprehending,
then her face showed that she followed me. 'Oh, I see.'

I turned into my road, past the roadworks where symphony
for pneumatic drill and pickaxe was still being assiduously
practised. 'What did you do when you got inside?'

'I began to look around.'

When I asked, 'What were you looking for?' it was
genuinely because I did not know and when she didn't answer
I realized that neither did she. 'Anything,' she said at last,
and I contented myself with nodding knowingly.

I parked the car and we got out, went into the house. Max
volunteered to make some tea while I phoned AMH to discover
that there was no change in Dad's condition. In the kitchen
over a steaming mug, I asked, 'What happened, then?'

'I was in the back room, looking around when I heard a
noise; I think it was someone coming down the stairs. It gave
me such a fright.'

'I'm not surprised.'

'I panicked, and suddenly I felt trapped. I ran for the door and, through the banisters, I saw the bottom half of someone coming down the stairs. I turned left and crept as quietly as I could into the kitchen. I thought that he hadn't seen or heard me, so I just crouched down in the far corner of the kitchen and waited.'

'He? It was definitely "he"?'

'Oh, well, I suppose it could have been a woman . . .'

'What did he – or she – do then?'

'I heard someone moving around. It was then that I spotted the phone extension on the far side of the kitchen and went across to it to call you. Whoever it was came in while I was making the call.'

I reached out across the kitchen table to take her hands. 'Whoever it was could have killed you,' I pointed out gently.

Her eyes were large and underlined by tears as she nodded. 'I know.'

I squeezed her hands and said, 'I think you need to get some sleep, and I know I could.'

I led her upstairs, leaving the tea undrunk.

EIGHTEEN

We managed all of two hours of sleep before the doorbell rang. It was Masson's formidable face that greeted me as I answered it. He managed what he supposed was a smile and said, 'Sorry if I'm bothering you, doctor. Mind if I come in?'

Being a policeman, it didn't matter much to him what minding was going on in my head, so he stepped past me and I was left, in my dressing gown, trailing him as he made his way into my house. 'Isn't Miss Christy going to join us?' he asked.

I was awash with embarrassment and therefore on the point of arguing when Max started coming down the stairs. When she came in, dressed only in one of my shirts, Masson asked dryly, 'How's the concussion?'

'Not too bad.'

'I'm glad to hear it. Anything coming back to you about why you were there?'

She held her hands open, shrugged her shoulders. 'Sorry.'

He turned to me. 'I think I've told you before how irritating I find amateur detectives, doctor. Invariably they place themselves – and not infrequently others – in extreme danger and, almost always, they hamper the professionals. I can't afford the manpower to have a permanent guard on the house, but I am going to make sure that regular foot and motor patrols are keeping an eye it, so please don't try any more stupid stunts.'

Max burst out, 'Hamper you? How could I have done that? You're not doing anything!'

Masson contented himself with a tired smile and made himself at home by going into the front room and sitting on the edge of one of the armchairs. I pointed out to him: 'Whatever you may think about the wisdom of what Max seems to have done, at least you have to admit that it proves that Dad isn't Doris Lightoller's murderer.'

'Oh, dear,' he said with mock sadness. 'Is that what you think?'

'It stands to reason. Clearly the real murderer has been looking for something all along. He must have gone to the house, been interrupted before he got going by Mrs Lightoller, they struggled and he killed her; Dad comes along and the murderer has to scarper. He came back to finish his search but this time he was interrupted by Max.'

Masson said slowly, 'There are signs that the house has been searched . . .'

'There you are, then.'

'But . . .' he continued, 'he seems to have been a lot kinder to Miss Christy than he was to Mrs Lightoller, don't you think? He contented himself with a single, non-fatal blow to the head, as opposed to trying to smash her skull to bits.'

Max said, 'He heard me on the phone and knew that he didn't have long.'

Again Masson considered this and I could see that he knew things that we did not. I asked, 'Are you going to tell us what you think, then?'

He did one of his nasty smiles. 'I think you have no need to worry your little head about it any more, doctor. We've caught him.'

We were both impressed, and surprised, by this demonstration of constabulary efficiency. 'Who is it?' we asked together.

'Victor Robbins.'

It left us both none the wiser and so Masson elucidated. 'He's thirty-five years old and well known to me. He's a petty thief and swindler, nothing more; he's been in and out of the magistrates' court more often than the magistrates' clerk. Certainly not a murderer.'

I thought I was being clever when I quoted his own words back to him. '"Anyone can be a murderer." Isn't that what you said?'

Of course, he took that badly. The fridge lights came on and I battened down the hatches for a wintry blast. In a voice that was as frosty as Frosty the snowman he said, 'He's got a pretty unbreakable alibi for Oliver Lightoller's killing in that he was in police custody that afternoon, having been found drunk and disorderly near the Pond that morning.'

Max demanded, 'What was he doing in the house?'

'Stealing, of course. It's what he does. He saw the house, realized it would be empty, and thought it would be worth a crack. The last thing he expected was an amateur private eye barging in.'

Max lowered her eyes so that he did not see the flush on her face. I asked, 'How did you catch him?'

'We got a partial description from an old woman who lives opposite. It wasn't much, but Smith thought he recognized who it was. He did some checking through records and put a name to the face; Smith picked him up a while ago on suspicion of dealing in forged MOT certificates.'

Once again, I saw a new facet to Constable Smith's persona. 'That sounds like fairly smart work.'

Masson nodded. 'He might come across as a bit of a hesitant dimwit, but in the few weeks I've known him, I've found that he's got a little more going for him than you might think at first sight. He's actually quite bright, and he's not afraid to have a go when the occasion demands.' He then added, I know not quite why, 'He actually asked to be transferred across to Croydon. Seems he wanted to work with me.'

I honestly tried to squeeze all the astonishment out of my voice as I said, 'Really?' I'm not sure that I succeeded, though; certainly his look was suspicious as he carried on, 'We picked Victor Robbins up an hour ago. At the moment, he's denying it, but Smith tells me that he's found some old book at his house, and he reckons it's a first edition, though God only knows how he would recognize one. Anyway, if he's right, it's odds on that it came from Lightoller's house. With any luck we'll be able to identify it from Lightoller's records and pin him to the break-in.'

'He assaulted Max,' I said. 'He should be charged with that as well.'

'That's going to be a bit difficult unless her memory returns,' Masson replied sarcastically.

Max muttered, 'Yes, well, I expect it will . . .'

Partly to take the attention away from her, I asked, 'Has he got an alibi for the time that Doris Lightoller was attacked?'

Masson said unconcernedly, 'Not much of one, I'll admit; he says he was in the pub and, of course, he's got a list of cronies as long as your arm who will back him up.'

'So maybe . . .'

'Forget it, Dr Elliot. Whoever skewered Oliver Lightoller also did for his wife, and I know that Robbins didn't do the first murder. Which means, I'm afraid, that your father's still got some explaining to do. I understand that there's no change in his condition as yet.'

'No.'

He nodded and stood up. 'I'm going back to have another chat with Mr Robbins, although Alexander Holversum is doing his best, as usual, to make my life difficult.'

'Holversum's representing him?'

He scowled. 'Holversum's sole purpose for existence is to make the lives of honest policemen impossible. He spends every waking hour defending the indefensible and, more often than he should, he succeeds. If I were you I'd find another solicitor to defend your father; having Holversum on your side won't make you any friends.'

Having showed him out, Max and I sat in the kitchen and talked. The one positive that I had hoped would come out of Max's escapade was that it would show Masson that my father was probably innocent, but that hope was now destroyed. I felt very low and Max had her work cut out to cheer me up.

'I'm sure your father will be all right, Lance. They seemed quite optimistic at the hospital, didn't they?'

'I hope they're right to be so, Max. You can never be sure, not at this stage; possibly not for days.'

'They're the experts, though. If they're hopeful . . .'

But I had met enough medical 'experts' to know that infallibility was not a prerequisite for the office. I didn't say this though, contenting myself with a vague, 'Of course, of course . . .'

'And in the background are the Lightoller killings, with your father as number one suspect and I have a horrible feeling that there isn't a number two.'

'We don't know that for certain; we don't know precisely

what the police are doing. Maybe Masson will find something to clear Dad.'

'Will he, Lance? Are you really so sure? As far as Inspector
Masson is concerned, your father's got means, motive and
opportunity. He strikes me as the kind of man who doesn't
waste his time looking for unnecessary work. And what
happens, God forbid, if your father doesn't wake up? Do
you think that the inspector will have a change of heart,
because I don't. I think that the case will be closed there
and then.'

It was the most passionate speech I'd ever heard her make
and it made me feel ashamed of myself. She was right. No
one else was going to do anything to clear Dad. If we didn't
do it, the chances were that he would be found guilty, whether
or not he ever got to court. I knew that I was in for trouble
– I just didn't know in what form it would come or how
painful it would prove – as I said, 'You're almost certainly
right, of course.'

She was at once impassioned, ready to fight the cause.
'Then it's up to us to discover the truth, Lance.'

Whilst I agreed with her, I wasn't sure that I wanted her
involved. 'Max, it could be dangerous. You nearly got killed
earlier today.'

'I'll be more careful next time.'

'No. There won't be a next time.' I like to think that I was
firm. 'He's my father and it's up to me to help him. I can't
put you in harm's way.'

Her face showed surprised hurt. 'You can't mean that,
Lance. You need me to help. We make a great team, don't
we?'

'Well, yes,' I began to agree and was about go on to say
something about this not necessarily implying that we were
going to prove to be the world's greatest detective duo,
but she did what Max does, which was to jump in at once.
'There you are, then. With my brains and your brawn,
we're unbeatable.'

NINETEEN

Which was easier said than done. I admit that I was at a loss to know how to start, but Max wasn't. Far from it.

'There are two things we must do. First, we've got to keep an eye on the house,' she announced.

'Why?'

'Because someone's looking for something and they haven't found it yet; your father interrupted them. I think that they'll be back.'

'Maybe,' I said doubtfully.

'Definitely,' she assured me. 'So, if we keep an eye on the Lightollers' house, we might spot who it is.'

'How will we do that?'

'From your father's house, silly. It's perfectly positioned. Come on, get dressed.'

'But Masson's arranging for a watch to be kept on it.'

'But not a permanent one, remember. That's where we come in.'

'Max, I'm not sure that this is a good idea.'

'It won't be dangerous. Have you got a camera? We can take pictures of anyone suspicious, like they do in the films.'

I had the distinct impression that to Max this was a game, nothing more; her brush with violence seemed to have had no dampening effect whatsoever. But, on the other hand, I reasoned that she was probably right: what was wrong with staying in my father's house while he was in hospital, keeping an eye open for anything odd going on next door? Something that she had said sounded a warning bell in my head, though.

'If that's the first thing, what's the second?'

'Really, Lance. I thought you were good at this kind of thing. We ask questions.'

'We ask what questions of whom?'

'Witnesses.'

'But there aren't any.'

She clearly thought I was a complete loss. 'I bet there are; we just don't know about them yet.'

'You've lost me.' Which was true, and I meant lost as in 'completely and perhaps irrevocably mislaid'.

'It's very simple. The Lightollers must have done something to get them murdered, mustn't they? Now maybe the people around them saw something or heard something that will tell us what it was.'

'What do you mean by "the people around them"?' I asked, panic slowly but inexorably rising in what I believe is referred to as my 'craw'.

'Well, the people in the shops on either side for a start . . .'

That seemed reasonable.

'And, I suppose, their son.'

Which didn't.

In the end, I dropped Max off at Dad's house, made her promise faithfully not to attempt another amateur burglary on the Lightollers' now padlocked house, and went on to AMH. Not that there was a lot that I could do there, but I felt that it was my duty to spend a few hours by his side, hoping against hope that he would show some sign of returning consciousness.

Percy Bailey had been relieved of desk duty and was sitting with him. When I came in, he gave me a sad smile and said, 'Smith's supposed to be here, but took sick. I asked if I could do a turn with your dad. He was a good old stick.'

I wasn't too keen on his choice of tense, but I appreciated the thought.

'I understand from the inspector that Smith's a bit of a star on the quiet.'

Percy sucked his teeth; since they were heavily encrusted with nicotine, I suspect he got a bit of high from the act. 'Yes, I suppose he is. The inspector thinks the world of him and, I'll admit, he's pulled a few strokes since he arrived.'

'But?'

More nicotine was extracted from his dental enamel. 'I don't know. He's a little too eager to please.'

'A man has to get on, Percy.'

He nodded in sage agreement. 'Mebbe . . . mebbe,' and left it at that.

'He's young and ambitious.'

He snorted. 'Enthusiastic, I'll give you. A little overenthusiastic, I reckon.'

'What do you mean?'

He made a face. 'I had to have a quiet word not long after he arrived. He wasn't being nice to someone as he brought them into custody.'

'I'm sure he'll learn, Percy.'

He made a face. 'I suppose.'

'Masson said that he'd asked specifically to come and work in the area.'

Percy chortled; there is no other word to describe it. 'Can you believe it? To come and work around here? He turned down a job in the Met. He must be mad.'

With which the conversation died for a while.

Dad's head was securely bound in crêpe bandages and he had a drip running into each forearm, a catheter running out from under the bedclothes. His face seemed just as pale, just as uncaring of life as it had before the operation; someone had combed his beard and I should imagine had regretted ever starting such a gargantuan task, since to my knowledge, Dad had never bothered. It hadn't done much for him, making him look as if he had been spruced up to meet someone, and I could only think that this someone might be God.

I sat next to the bed, opposite Percy who was in the far corner by the door. For a long time a cardiac monitor was the only thing that filled the space between us. I suspect that Percy could have kept going like this until the trumpets blew at the round earth's imagined corners, but eventually, I broke.

'You don't think he's guilty, do you?'

Official caution gripped him. 'Well . . .'

'Oh, come on, Percy. Do you really think he decided to rearrange Doris Lightoller's skull bones with a hammer?'

A deep breath and then: 'No. No, I don't.'

I felt that I had won a small victory, chipped away at a stone in the official wall. 'Have you talked with Inspector Masson about it?'

He shook his head with a sad grin. 'You don't understand.

The inspector isn't interested in what I think about it; he's got your father with means, motive and opportunity, so he's happy.'

I sighed. It was as I had feared. A gap ensued during which the cardiac monitor did its best to serenade us.

I said, 'The inspector said that Lightoller was a bit of a naughty boy himself.'

He nodded warily. 'So they say.'

'Stolen goods?'

Another nod. For a moment, that was it, and then he said, 'And, way back, something else, it was rumoured.'

I pricked up my ears. *Come on, Percy. Don't be shy.*

'Something else?' I tried to pitch my voice somewhere between unconcerned and gossipy.

He looked around, just to make sure that Masson wasn't charging down the ward corridor, waving his truncheon menacingly. 'It was in the early sixties, I think. I remember it because it was on my beat, so I was involved from the start.'

'Remember what?'

'Annie Sage.'

'What about her?'

But Percy, for the moment, was lost in recollection; I suspected that this was sad recollection, but it was difficult to tell because the bag-topped jowls leant a sad air to everything about him. Eventually he sighed and came to. I repeated my question.

'She killed herself. She was a lovely woman, was Annie. Had three children and a husband who was a printer in Fleet Street, so she was never short of a bob or two. She lived in Mayday Road, I recall.'

This amount of detail proved that he would have made a good fist as a troubadour, but I found it slightly aggravating. 'What's all this to do with Lightoller?'

'There were rumours,' he said obliquely.

I jumped to conclusions; the wrong ones, as it turned out. 'They were having an affair?'

While his head moved slowly and deliberately from side to side, there began a sort of generalized shaking about his amply proportioned frame and a deep rumbling made its way

into the room. He was laughing, I realized, and this conclusion was proved correct when he said, 'Gor blimey, no.'

I waited for the tremors to play themselves out before:
'Then what?'

He leaned forward, voice down. 'There had always been
rumours, you see, but no one had any proof and, as I say,
she was such a nice girl, no one could quite believe them.'

I felt giddy, as if on a merry-go-round. 'But what were
the rumours about?'

'That she was having an affair,' he said, apparently
contradicting himself.

I wondered what he was like in the witness box; presumably they added a couple of days on to the estimated
duration of the trial when Percy Bailey was due to appear.
I shook my head, deciding that asking questions did not
seem to elicit much useful information, and said merely,
'I don't understand.'

'Poor Annie was having an affair with one of the neighbours. Chap called Bill who lived round the corner in the
crescent. He was a travelling salesman.'

'Where does Lightoller come in?'

'Bill's mother died, see?' I did not see, but remained taciturn. 'Bill used to live with her, but after the funeral, he
decided to move to a smaller place somewhere in Headcorn
Road, I think. He got Lightoller in to do the house clearance, clear out all of his mother's stuff that he didn't want.'

I suddenly noticed that Percy seemed to be using the
cardiac monitor as a sort of metronome, waiting three beeps
between each sentence. I idly wondered if by tickling my
father's feet, I could get him to hurry up a bit.

'They say . . .' He paused for dramatic effect; three beeps
passed and then: 'That Lightoller found some letters she'd
written to him. They say . . .' Another pause of similar duration before: 'That Lightoller blackmailed her.'

He nodded his head slowly, pleased with the expression
on my face, for what he said had excited me. 'Lightoller was
a blackmailer?'

Apparently I sounded too excited, for Percy began to retract
at once; he speeded up, too, a climactic speech. 'There was
no proof, though. It was only that Annie wrote this note in

which she confessed to the affair and how Lightoller had driven her to suicide. Lightoller admitted that he had found the letters but said that he had only had a Christian chat with her. He denied taking money off her, although her husband, Tony, said that there was a thousand pounds missing from their savings. Whatever the case, it couldn't be found in any of Lightoller's accounts and there was no evidence that he had been spending a lot of late, so the matter was dropped.'

My mind was hurrying through the implications of this news. Blackmail seemed an eminently plausible reason to kill someone; much more likely than a missing watch and the loss of two feet of garden. I asked casually, 'And there was never any other suggestion that he was a blackmailer?'

Percy was definite. 'Nope.'

I did my own counting of the beat, waited for five beeps before: 'Did he do a lot of house clearance work?'

'It was how he kept going.'

'What about his son?'

'What about him?'

'Has he ever been involved in anything criminal?'

Percy delved deep into his stores of memory. 'Not really.'

'What does that mean?'

Percy thought some more. 'When he was young he was a bit of a lad, I recall. Had problems keeping his temper.'

Which fitted in with what Masson had said. 'Nothing criminal?'

More dredging in the same deep places. 'Nothing that he was charged over.'

'But there were suspicions?'

But before he could speak, there came a faint low moan from Dad. It was almost a gurgle, but it was the first noise I had heard him make and I was up at once and leaning over him, hoping to see some signs of animation, my whole attention on him.

TWENTY

Percy watched me and said gently, 'He does that some-times.'

I looked at Dad intensely for thirty, forty, fifty seconds that were counted out by the heart monitor then, when no further sound came and there was no trace of consciousness in his face, I subsided into my chair, feeling even flatter and more depressed than I had before.

Calmly and imperturbably, Percy went on with his tale. 'Young Tom fell in with some "undesirables".' Only Percy and people of Percy's ilk used words like that and then put them in quotation marks.

'In what way "undesirable"?'

'Extortion, mostly.'

'Oh, dear.'

'Yes. Tom got a lowly position as a messenger boy for a gentleman by the name of Frankie Maybery. Frankie wasn't nice, not nice at all. Not long after Tom went to work for him, Frankie died in some sort of altercation with a motor car. Hit and run; no one was ever convicted, but no one was too bothered, if you know what I mean.'

I knew what he meant; I didn't like it, though.

'What happened to Tom?'

'All of Frankie's associates were questioned and quite a few of them were charged, but Tom was relatively new and very young, so he was never really thought to be a major player. That and the help of Alexander Holversum, and he was let go. As far as I understand it, his father took him on as an apprentice.'

'Alexander Holversum?'

'The very same.'

I remembered Holversum's words regarding Tom's father: *I had had the pleasure of working for him on the odd occasion.*

'I'd gathered the inspector doesn't take kindly to him.'

'Absolutely hates him.'

'But why? He's only doing his job.'

'Alexander Holversum keeps the wrong company. Most of his clients are hardened nasty men; it doesn't help your dad's cause to be represented by him.'

'But surely, if he's a defence solicitor, a lot of his clients will be criminals.'

Percy shook his head with a sad smile at my ignorance. 'He's *chummy* with some of them. A little too close, if you get my drift.'

'Oh.'

'I mean, only recently, he's been making a lot of trouble for the inspector.'

'Not Dad's case, surely?'

Percy laughed. 'No, don't worry. It was the Baines and Perry killings. He accused the inspector of exceeding his authority; even got a judicial review. It eventually failed but it didn't half make the inspector mad.'

Not that this struck me as a task beyond the wit of most men. I, for one, seemed able to make Inspector Masson mad with distressing ease. In a strangely compelling way, knowledge of this made me rather admire Alexander Holversum and I decided that he was perhaps the man for me.

The conversation moved on to less intriguing matters, such as Percy's thoughts on the result of England's match against Portugal, and how he reckoned Kevin Keegan was overrated, and had I heard that bloody awful racket that they kept playing on the radio? The one about Galileo, whoever he was.

I looked at my watch and saw that I had been there over an hour and a half. When I stood up, I felt guilty about leaving, though, and tried to tell myself that by going I was not abandoning him.

I thanked Percy for his company and walked away, forcing myself not to look back.

TWENTY-ONE

When I got back to Dad's house, it was well and truly dark and Max was in a state of high excitement. I wasn't even out of the car before she had the front door open and was beckoning to me while crouching down, the hall lights off. In the dim illumination of the street lamp her face sported a look that was three parts thrilled, two parts anxious and finished with a dash of anger. She mouthed something at me, her lips working in a caricature of speech that I could not recognize as words that I had ever known, but it was clear that she wanted me to get inside quickly and that she didn't want me to look over at the Lightollers' house.

I walked as naturally as I could towards her, thinking to myself, She's been possessed by the spirit of Dad. It's the only explanation.

She closed the door gently behind me and before I could speak said in an urgent whisper, 'Someone's been poking around the house at the back.' With which she beckoned me upstairs. Because it was so dark, it was not easy to climb without stumbling.

I said in a deliberately loud voice, 'Are you sure?'

She stopped in her advance up the stairs and swung round, almost losing her footing. 'Shhh!'

'Max, there's no way we can be heard outside.'

A pause. 'Are you sure?'

'Positive.'

She straightened up. 'OK, but don't put on any lights.'

She led me into the back bedroom which had windows on two sides, a large one looking out over the back gardens, a smaller one to its right looking out over the rear of the Lightollers' house.

'Look.'

She was crouched down in front of the smaller one so that her eyes were just above the level of the wooden windowsill; I noticed that it could do with a new coat of paint and there was a faint smell of dry rot as I joined her. While mentally noting to remind Dad to get it seen to, I looked out into the gloom. There was a hint of fog in the air, condensing from the lightest of fine drizzles that had started as I'd reached the house. The back of the Lightollers' house was in almost complete darkness but there was just enough light to make out movement on the small patio. I could see that it was a big shape, but beyond that no detail came to my eye.

Max took to whispering again. 'He turned up about ten minutes before you did. Two policemen had just been looking around, making sure that everything was all right, then, as soon as they'd gone, he appeared; I should think he was keeping an eye on them and waiting for his moment. He must have parked up the road and then come on foot. He went straight around the back and began snooping around, trying the doors and windows.'

'He? You're sure it was a he?'

'I saw him quite clearly under the street lamps.'

'What did he look like?'

The shape was now crouching down on the ground, but doing so in a peculiarly hesitant manner, as Max said after a pause, and in direct contradiction of her previous statement, 'I'm not sure . . .'

I thought it best to say nothing. The shape stood up slowly and, as it approached the French windows, there was suddenly a torch beam illuminating a cone of space before it; the bulb and reflector suddenly appearing in the glass of the doors. Light was cast back upon the figure and, although there were more shadows than elucidation, I thought I recognized something of the figure. Even from this distance and in almost complete blindness, this figure was unmistakably baker-shaped.

I sighed. 'Oh, dear.'

'What is it?' Max was genuinely worried.

'It's Mr Hocking.'

Max was so excited, I feared for her cerebral vasculature. 'Is it?' she demanded in the sort of voice that's considered overacting even on the operatic stage. The figure, meanwhile, was at the French windows, apparently wrestling with the handles; even from a distance it seemed to be hesitant, uncertain.

I said, 'What's he doing here?'

'Isn't it obvious? He's the murderer!' Through the ill-fitting double glazing the sound of wood splintering could be heard. 'He's come back to the scene of his crime.'

'But why?'

The doors were pulled open and the figure disappeared into the darkness of the house. Max said, 'To find the incriminating evidence.'

'Which is?'

She didn't know, but didn't care either. 'Does that matter? We should phone the police.'

I suppose we should have done, but I had access to confidential medical information on Samuel Hocking that Max was not privy to, and it made me doubt that he was the man who had been running around the neighbourhood murdering people. 'I think this has gone on long enough.'

'What has?'

I stood up. 'It's time to confront our intruder.'

She was horrified and, I like to think, awed. 'But, Lance . . .'

'Don't worry. I think I'm safe. You stay up here.'

Like the hero that I felt I ought to be, I left the room, and went down the stairs. After picking up a torch from the kitchen, I went out of the front door and over the brick wall. I made my way down the narrow passageway and only slowed down when I came around the back of the house. The figure was moving around inside the back room, various scrapings, clicks and soft clunks accompanying it; there was clearly a search going on, so in that at least, Max was right. I could tell that the movements were strained and jerky, an impression that they were painful to make made all the more real by the odd groan.

I stepped to the opened doors, and was aware that Max was disobeying orders and was now standing at the corner of the house in the shadows; she had a cricket bat in her hands. I took a deep breath. 'Good evening.' He looked around at once, saw me and jumped. This did his back no good at all, I think, because there was a distinctly painful yelp and I saw him stiffen as if petrified. It was, I am ashamed to admit, a gratifying response. 'I am reliably informed that tampering with a crime scene is a criminal offence, you know.'

He smiled but his cheeks must have been stiff and cold because it was very small and very fleeting. 'I expect you're wondering what I'm doing here, doctor?'

'It had crossed my mind to enquire.' And I thought at the same time, Are you a murderer?

He tried the smile again but with barely any more luck. 'Well, you see—'

I interrupted. 'Why don't you come outside where I can see you a little better?' There was a fine drizzle and I was getting cold to boot, so I didn't see why he shouldn't share a little of the pleasure.

He did so, albeit now moving with the pace and agility of a stuffed gorilla. Max came up to stand beside me. He looked at her but I didn't feel polite and made no introductions. I said, 'So what were you doing, Mr Hocking?'

His face was wet but I guessed that not all of the moisture was due to meteorological factors. He finally found some words; whether they were words of truth was another matter. 'I was getting something. Something of mine.'

'What "thing"?'

A natural question to ask, I thought. Mr Hocking's mouth opened for a moment, or rather his lower jaw dropped and I saw his tongue lying limply in his mouth, before he said, 'An old family heirloom.'

'What heirloom was that?'

He was still pausing a lot, but getting more fluent as he replied, 'A picture ... An oil painting ... Of a landscape.' For a moment it seemed as if Lightoller were a kleptomaniac, what with this and Dad's watch but then Hocking said, 'I wanted him to value it.' This last came out in what was an unmistakably triumphant tone, as if he were pleased with himself for thinking of so clever a story.

Max demanded, 'Why is it at his home? Why isn't it in the shop?'

But Hocking was running smoothly now. 'He said that he wanted to do some research on it; look it up in his books.'

He nodded as he heard the words and thoroughly approved.

I didn't believe him but I had no choice but to accept his story. 'Well, I don't think it's a very good idea to break in to get it, Mr Hocking. The police may not be as trusting as me.'

He relaxed as much as his back would allow. 'No, no, I see that.'

'I'm sure if you go to the police station and explain, they'll be able to help you.'

'Yes, yes.'

I smiled, although I didn't feel particularly happy. 'Good.'

He took a deep breath, clearly a man who was greatly relieved, then laughed. 'I suppose it was rather stupid of me.'

Neither Max nor I said anything. He was just standing there, fidgeting and I suddenly wondered if he was hoping that I would go away and let him carry on. 'So you'll be off then.'

He looked surprised, as if such a concept had never occurred to him. 'Oh! Oh, yes.'

I just stood and watched while he gathered up his burglary tools and put them in a small holdall that was on the ground beside him.

'What about the door?'

'What about it?'

He shrugged. 'Won't the police wonder . . .?'

'I'd be surprised if they didn't.'

He digested this for a while, then, 'Right . . . Goodnight.'

I gave him the benefit of my pearly whites and said, 'And goodnight to you, Mr Hocking. I strongly suggest that you talk to the police about your heirloom.'

Another rather sad nod and then he departed in a stiff, shambling shuffle, trailing clouds of embarrassment.

I went and examined the door. Mr Hocking's attentions had resulted in a large splinter of wood poking out, dislodging the facing plate so that the door latch could be prised away; the door was still held by bolts top and bottom but it wouldn't have taken much more to open it.

'Shouldn't we tell the police?' asked Max beside me.

I had been wondering that. 'I need to think about that,' I said as I jammed the splinter back into place, then examined it closely by the light of the torch. It wouldn't bear close inspection, but fitted quite well and, since the paint-work was fairly cracked and peeling, I was optimistic that the less than penetrating gaze of the local constabulary would not spot evidence of tampering.

TWENTY-TWO

'There's something very odd going on around here,' was Max's perspicacious comment as we digested our conversation with Mr Samuel Hocking, gentle giant, master baker and decidedly unmasterly housebreaker.

'It's not a totally implausible story,' I said, but my heart was not really in it. I kept wondering if Mr Hocking could possibly be more than he seemed.

'Do you believe it, then?'

I sighed. 'No.'

Max was preparing a meal and I was sitting at the kitchen table watching her and drinking a beer; Dad's taste in the art of the hop was not exactly mine – he preferred beers with quaint names like Throgmorton's Kneebuckler and Chumley's Old Disgusting – but I had found something that at least didn't make me feel as if I were swallowing a mixture of kettle descaler and Bovril. It was always a pleasure to watch Max and I found it all rather distracting. She was preparing chilli con carne; I had been brought up to be polite and so didn't tell her that I didn't like spicy food. Nor did I tell her that no one was keeping a watch on the house next door, just in case she went back into *Hong Kong Phooey* mode and made me go and look out of the upstairs windows.

She said with her back to me, 'So what do you think he was doing?'

'He was doing what everyone seems to be doing in this affair; looking for something. The question is, what?'

In the background, Tommy Vance was just beginning his show and the kitchen was filled with the odour of frying onions and Max was opening a can of chopped tomatoes as she suggested, 'Money?'

'Maybe.'

'He was an antiques dealer; they're always rich, aren't they?' Before I could answer, she turned and, wiping onion tears from the side of her nose, asked, 'Is there any red wine?'

'If I know my father, I should imagine there's a couple of gallons of the stuff somewhere.'

I went in search and found it, after some lateral thinking and astute second guessing of my father's thought processes, at the back of the garage in a home-made rack. After returning to the kitchen and opening it for Max, I said, 'I suppose it could be money . . .'

'Perhaps a very rare antique . . .? Perhaps Mr Lightoller found a long-lost Rembrandt in a skip somewhere.'

It sounded unlikely to me, but I couldn't discount it; I couldn't discount *anything*, if I were to be honest with myself. John Lennon's nasal twang was inviting us to imagine some load of tosh about not having a heaven.

Max was quite an expert cook, I was noticing, handling the implements with ease and facility. 'And you said something about Lightoller being a blackmailer.'

'He was suspected of it; nobody every proved anything.'

'So maybe this is about blackmail.'

'Well, the bakery's next to the antiques shop, so it's conceivable that Lightoller got wind of something, or saw something, that Hocking wouldn't want to broadcast.'

Max put in the minced beef she had found in the refrigerator, leaving it to fry with the onions and garlic. 'Perhaps he's been having an affair with one of the customers . . . Passion over the pasties.'

'Kisses over the cakes?'

'Fun beside the fancies!' She burst out laughing which made me laugh too. While she stirred the meat, I returned to the table and the beer.

'I wonder if Hocking's got an alibi for the murders,' I said ruminatively.

'We have to find out.'

'How do we do that?'

To Max, it was simple. 'I'll go into the shop tomorrow and ask a few questions.'

I was slightly uneasy about this. Max poured the tomatoes over the meat and then added seasoning and some chilli powder. Then she covered the pan and came to the table, glass and bottle of wine in hand. 'There,' she said. 'Give that half an hour and I'll put some rice on to cook.'

'Is that a good idea?'

'The rice?'

'No. Poking around in Hocking's shop.'

'What harm can it do?'

'If we're right, he's a murderer, Max. Two people down . . .'

'Even if he starts to think I'm being a bit nosy, what can he do? Drown me in dough? Push me into the oven?'

'Don't joke about it.'

She leaned forward to kiss me lightly on the cheek and whisper breathily into my ear, 'Don't worry, lover. I won't let him get me on my own.'

'It's no joke, Max. People are dying around here.' *Another one may yet die, too.*

Her face fell. In a hurt tone, she protested, 'I realize that.'

And I had to backtrack. 'I'm just worried about you.'

For which I received a bigger, longer kiss and harmony was restored. Cod opera came over the airwaves and I groaned. 'Not again.'

She laughed. 'You're so old, Lance.'

Which rather hurt. 'Just because I have some taste.'

'It's the future of music,' she proclaimed as there came from the radio the voice of someone who had clearly heard too much Wagner.

It was in an attempt to retrieve my credentials as a street-wise, happening guy that I said, 'This lot did "Killer Queen", didn't they?'

'That's right. And "Seven Seas of Rye".'

I nodded sagely. 'Oh, yes.' And I hoped that I said it convincingly. 'Killer Queen' had struck me as unlistenably twee.

Before we ate, I phoned the hospital but there was still no change. I then laid the table as Max dished up the meal. I had found a bottle of Sheepstrangler's Curse to drink while Max was happy with the remains of the red wine, so we settled down for what I expected to be a rather cosy meal.

She waited for about six minutes.

'Mr Hocking obviously thinks that there's something next door of significance.'

I nodded. The chilli con carne was hot, hot, hot and the

consequent pain was occupying most of the space in my brain; already my nose was running and there was an uncomfortable sheen of sweat around my eyes. Max took advantage of this, thus showing how ruthless a woman can be. 'If we could find out what it was . . .'

The chilli would have to have been white hot for me to have missed the dreadful implication of what she had just said. I stopped chewing, and looked at her aghast.

'No.' And with this word I shook my head so vigorously that one or two drops of sweat flew off the end of my nose.

'But it might give us the answer,' she countered. 'If we found what Mr Hocking was looking for, we could go to the police and it would get your father off.'

'*If* we find it.'

'There's that, yes.'

'And *if* Mr Hocking is the one behind all this. We don't know that he is; he might even be telling the truth.'

Max, who seemed to have oral and pharyngeal mucosa that was certified for thirty minutes' fire retardation, carried on ploughing her way through the chilli. She indicated my plate with her fork. 'Eat up.'

But now I had an excuse not to put myself through more agony. I put the fork down and said, 'I don't know how you can suggest such a thing after what happened to you.'

'It wouldn't be dangerous if there were two of us, would it? And anyway, it's hardly likely that someone else will break in; that would make three in one day, which is absurd.'

'No, Max. Absolutely not.'

TWENTY-THREE

E ven a full bottle of Shagnasty's Revenger before we came out could not quell my qualms as we prepared to go into Lightoller's house. We were on the patio where Mr Hocking and I had passed the time of day a few hours before. It had stopped raining but everything was damp, and it was almost as if we were in an underwater cavern; it had grown colder, too. By now it was about two in the morning; one of Masson's patrols had just passed so we reckoned we had about thirty minutes to get inside and lie low. I took the hammer that I had found in Dad's shed and now applied it to the gap between the French doors. Despite the head start, it still took a fair amount of effort to break, but I managed it after a couple of minutes of effort. I stood back and allowed Max to go in first and, in retrospect, I should have warned her then that there wasn't much elbow room. She had barely gone two feet into the room before a decidedly unmuffled crash and squealed cry of 'bugger it' told me that she had found it out for herself.

'Max? Be careful . . .'

She spun around, the inevitable result of which was a second crash followed this time by: 'Sod it!'

'Don't move,' I said, and slipped into the room behind her. She was surrounded by fragments of china. 'What were they?'

'The first one was some sort of china figure.' It probably wasn't valuable, I thought. Max continued, 'And the second was similar.'

I mean the chances that this pair of figurines was worth much were tiny . . .

I took a deep breath and tried not to worry. 'Never mind.'

'Come on then, Lance. We'd better get this over with.'

I don't think I had ever felt so nervous as when I stood in that room with Max and looked around it. I heard the tremor in my voice as I asked, 'What do we do now?'

'We search of course, silly. You'd be no good as a burglar, would you?'

'I never imagined that that would ever be a criticism of me that I should worry about.'

'We could either split up with one of us going upstairs while the other stays down here, or we could stay together and do it room by room.'

The prospect of being alone in there gave me the heebie-jeebies. 'We stay together,' I said at once, adding after a slight pause, 'that way I can protect you if anything happens.'

She gave me a beaming smile of loving gratitude and I felt quite the man. 'What do we look for?'

'Papers, I suppose.' She sounded uncertain. 'Papers and photographs, that kind of thing.'

It all sounded a bit on the vague side. 'Is that all?'

She was already looking around the room, her torch beam picking out the numerous ornaments and the hotchpotch of furniture styles. In a distracted way, she answered, 'And money, don't forget. If there's a safe full of money, that might be what this is all about.'

'I forgot to bring my stethoscope. How am I going to open a safe?'

She missed the sarcasm. She had moved over to a wooden bureau perched upon elegantly turned legs. It wasn't locked and she was soon immersed in ferreting through the various drawers and compartments. Feeling neglected, I made myself busy with peering behind some of the oil paintings that hung from the picture rail. 'Arthur Negus would love this place,' I said by way of conversation but Max said nothing.

We worked our way through every drawer, every possible hiding place, finding nothing except the everyday detritus of normal living. Max was initially excited by the discovery of gas bills, rates demands, a receipt from a local dentist for a check up, a red electricity bill and some shopping receipts, but soon realized that the great majority of the details of a life – any life – are boring to the point of death, and Oliver and Doris Lightoller were no different. These did not bear evidence of an extravagant lifestyle, merely a humdrum one; one not much different from our own. Her enthusiasm was briefly rekindled when she found some handwritten letters which she sat on the sofa and read by the light of her torch, but they proved to be from Doris to a childhood friend in Rhodesia and were filled with news about Oliver's athlete's foot and her prolapsed womb.

'Perhaps it's in code,' she said optimistically.

'Perhaps it's not.'

My beloved gave me a look of such intense irritation that even the darkness could not hide it. She got up. 'Come on. We'd better get on.'

I followed her into the front room where, thankfully, the curtains were half-closed over thick net curtains; even so we had to close the curtains as slowly as we could in order not to signal our presence to the public at large. We could only hope that the regularly visiting police would not notice the change. Max set about her task with a determination that I admired but did not feel inclined to emulate. I followed her with my torch. 'It would help if we knew what we're looking for.'

'We'll know it when we see it.'

But I wasn't as convinced as she was and hung back until she looked over her shoulder as she knelt at a pile of magazines and said, 'Come on.'

She turned back to her work and I did my thing with the pictures on the walls because that seemed to me to be the kind of thing that burglars and spies did. I was looking for pieces of paper stuck behind them, I think, not safes.

Certainly not safes.

So imagine my surprise . . .

'Bloody hell!'

Max looked up. I was standing in front of the chimney piece and had been looking behind an industrial landscape – the kind of thing that conjured up visions of the Poor Laws and Utilitarianism – which I was now taking off the wall to reveal a safe. It was only about a foot long and eight inches high, its metal door painted a kind of dull red and it had a small dial by which to input the combination. It was embedded in the chimney breast above a strikingly unfashionable gas fire.

Max came over at once. 'See,' she said triumphantly. 'I told you.'

'Told me what?'

'I knew we'd find something.'

I found that I couldn't follow in her enthusiasm. 'So? We've found a safe. What does that mean?'

'Whatever's in there is obviously important.'

'Or valuable.'

'Or valuable,' she agreed.

'So how do we get in to find out?'

She pulled at the handle; it didn't budge. 'Can you open it?'

She saw from the look on my face that I couldn't. Having wasted a few seconds with her ear to the red of the metal whilst she twiddled the knob, she stepped away from it with a sigh. 'It's in there, I know it is.'

I didn't ask her what, because I knew that she didn't know; she was just convinced that it held a secret – *the* secret – and that if we could get at it, then all would be revealed. I was thinking that maybe she was right but, equally likely, maybe it held Doris Lightoller's spare pair of dentures and enough books of Green Shield stamps to buy one of those new video recorders I kept hearing so much about. It meant a lot to Max, though, and I said nothing other than, 'We should carry on searching. There might be more to find.'

'Yes,' she said after a pause in which she just stared at the safe as if willing it to roll over, which is what I had a tendency to do when she looked at me with those big, big eyes. We resumed the search and this time, because I wanted her to be happy, I joined in with rather more gusto than previously.

I found the file at the back of a sideboard that looked old and roughly made, perhaps out of ship's timbers or something. It was in the middle of a pile of old seventy-eights, sandwiched between Dame Nelly Melba wrestling with 'Ave Maria' and the Jerusalem Philharmonic doing a job on the 'Brandenburg Concertos'. I thought nothing of it at first, until I opened the flap, whereupon I stood up at once and said in an urgent whisper – we were whispering the whole time – to Max, 'Come over here.'

She put down a brass Russian-style teapot that she had been staring into and complied.

'Wow!'

Wow, indeed. The first item was a report from a private detective agency by the imposing name of A.J. and J.A. Moss, Consulting Detectives. Their office was in Brixton and their headed notepaper claimed that they had associates in New York, Paris, Berlin, Rome and Sydney. The somewhat impressive effect that all this produced was somewhat nullified by their interesting spelling of the Australian city, which was rendered as 'Sidney'. The body of the report detailed the comings and goings of the two shops on either side of Oliver Lightoller's, more precisely the relationship between Samuel James Metcalfe Hocking and Mrs Aurelia Jane Parrish. There was a detailed description of their activities over the period of a month and, for the doubters, a comprehensive set of photographs, many shot with a telephoto lens. They had been taken from over the road, presumably from a first-floor flat, because they peered into a bedroom above Mr Hocking's bakery emporium. In the throes of passion, Mr Hocking had made a poor job of drawing his curtains and what he and Mrs Parrish got up to with a cream cone was clearly seen in all its comestible glory.

'Good Lord,' said Max.

'I think I know how he got a bad back.'

She looked again, as if unable to believe it all, then: 'So that's what Mr Hocking wanted.'

'Looks like it.'

'You realize what this means?'

I nodded but before I could say anything, I caught sight of a shadow moving across the curtains. Someone was walking up the path to the front door.

TWENTY-FOUR

With frantic signing, I got Max to follow my lead and switch off her torch. Then we stood as still as we could, wondering what was going to happen. Max whispered, 'Perhaps it's just a policeman checking the house.'

I thought, What if he checks around the back? I only pulled the doors to; it'll be obvious that someone's broken in.

The shape went to the front door and I suddenly wondered if maybe this wasn't a policeman after all . . .

I said in an urgent whisper, 'Come on,' and with that pulled her out of the front room and into the hallway as quickly and quietly as I could, bending low and trying to avoid passing pieces of bric-a-brac. A vague shadow could be made out through the frosted glass of the front door, backlit by a street lamp, and as we passed it, there came the sound of a key being inserted in the lock. I pushed Max up the stairs and followed as quickly as I could; behind me, I heard the front door open just as we made it to the top, the place where Doris Lightoller had met her manufacturer.

We crouched down side by side on the landing and peered together through the banisters, terrified lest whoever it was should start to come up the stairs. Max was crushed against me, soft and fragrant in a uniquely feminine way; had it been anywhere, anytime else, it would have been wonderful.

But it was here and now, and intensely frightening.

The newcomer, though, did not come up the stairs; the front door opened and closed again very quickly; then we heard whoever it was move away from the bottom of the stairs and I felt Max's body soften in relaxation. For a few moments I wasn't sure where the intruder had gone, but then we heard the sound of hinges squeaking.

Max looked at me, her face illumined by comprehension. She mouthed something at me that at first I didn't catch, then deciphered as: 'The safe.'

No more than two minutes passed before we heard movement back in the hallway; I held my breath hoping that I would very soon hear the front door opening, but for a minute or two there was just silence. In my head, in my ears, the silence screamed; what was happening down there? Would we soon hear the sound of feet upon the stairs?

Well, no, we didn't, but it still wasn't good news. The pattern of sounds from the ground floor told us that our visitor was going into the back room. I looked across at Max and from her expression it was clear that she understood the import of this: the signs of our incompetent break-in would be easily discovered.

We waited again, the sounds now slightly more distant; it was when they stopped completely that we both knew we had been discovered. What would happen now? I could feel my heart accelerating, my mouth becoming dry, gut beginning to churn. The sounds of movement began again, but this time with more purpose; whoever it was, was now looking for us.

Beside me, Max shifted nervously. The newcomer came into the hallway and I began to make plans about what I would do when, inevitably, they came up the stairs: jump out and push them back down again seemed to me the likeliest to succeed.

The noises became slightly but imperceptibly louder with every second that passed. I could feel Max becoming more and more nervous, whilst my own fear was now so huge it was practically blowing steam through my ears. When I heard the first creak of a footfall on the stairs, I only just stopped a squeal from making a run for freedom from my vocal cords.

When I heard the second, I feared for the sanctity of my underpants.

When I heard the third . . .

The front door was rattled and, moreover, rattled quite violently.

There were no more creaks.

The rattle came again and through the banisters I could see the beam of a torch sweep across the wall, making constantly changing quadrilateral shapes. There was a rustle as the figure crouched down.

The torchlight disappeared, leaving perfect calm every-where but inside the two of us. For a dreadful, dread-filled moment, I thought that the figure was going to continue its way on up the stairs towards us, but it didn't. It moved, and moved quickly, but it went back down into the hall, then into the front room; five seconds later and it was at the front door and, opening it quietly and closing it even more quietly, it was gone.

I didn't have time to enjoy my relief, though.

'Come on.' I hauled Max up and dragged her downstairs.

She asked breathlessly, 'What's going on? Who was that?'

'I don't know, but I think that the police are outside.'

At the front door, I paused and listened; it wasn't long before I heard faint noises coming from the back of the house. It was at this point that Max whispered in a voice that was completely confused, not a little alarmed and rather too loud for my liking, 'What are you doing?'

'Shh!'

She was opening her mouth to argue as I opened the front door and pushed her out of the house, then followed, closing the door as quickly but as quietly as I could. Before she could voice her objections, I whispered, 'Keep your head down and run to the road!'

Thankfully, she did as she was told and we sprinted up the driveway and then on to the pavement. I didn't look back but I had the feeling that the front door was opening just as we turned the corner.

TWENTY-FIVE

The ring of the doorbell came forty minutes later. We had lain in bed, still breathing heavily, listening to the muffled sounds of activity outside, hearing it increase slowly as the police arrived. We were both far too awake to even attempt sleep, what with physical exertion and intellectual puzzlement. In the darkness that was broken only by the muted orange shapes of the street lamp on the ceiling and the faint luminance of the alarm clock to my left, we whispered questions to each other; we did not dare put on the light since our alibi was one of an undisturbed night's sleep, and perhaps it was therefore only fitting that the questions produced little in the way of meaningful answers, little in the way of enlightenment.

When I opened the front door it was to find Inspector Masson standing in the porch looking distinctly agitated and angry; behind him was Constable Smith. I suppose, to a certain extent, Masson always looked like that, but now, in the small hours of a dark, damp November evening, the dial was turned up to eleven and he had put a couple of turbochargers in as well. Behind them there were clouds of fog beginning to form. The fog wasn't dense enough and the darkness wasn't dark enough to hide the police activity around the Lightollers' house, with two cars parked in front and five uniforms milling about.

He pushed past me without a word.

I said, 'Evening,' as he came in but wasn't even graced with a return grunt. Rather more loudly, I called to his back, 'Or should that be, "Morning"?'

Smith, following, mumbled something that might have been, 'Hello.'

In the hall Masson turned as I closed the door and said, 'I saw your car in the drive.'

Now, I like to think of myself as a patient man, but I thought that he was being just plain rude. 'Glad to see that your powers of observation haven't failed you.'

'What are you doing here?'

'Looking after my father's house while he's in hospital.' I kept a straight face, even though he stared at me in that uniquely 'Massonic' way.

'Been asleep, have you?'

'Yes,' I lied.

'You don't look sleepy.'

'I don't, when I'm awake.'

Masson frowned. 'You didn't hear the cars arrive?'

I had, but I denied it anyway. He commented, 'You're a heavy sleeper.'

'I like to try to keep to twelve stone.'

Which went down rather badly; I could spot this because icicles formed on the end of my nose as the room chilled.

Masson said sourly, 'Then I assume that you haven't heard anything going on next door during the night?'

'No.'

From the top of the stairs, Max's feet appeared, followed by the rest of her. As she came down, she asked, 'What's going on?'

Masson turned his head to allow her a dose of malevolence. 'Someone broke into Oliver Lightoller's house about forty-five minutes ago.'

Max said at once, 'God! No!' As I looked at her, I appreciated what the RSC had lost when she had chosen life as a vet.

Masson swung round to me, as if to try to catch me out, but I'm confident that I, too, was looking suitably aghast. 'Yes,' he said.

Smith added, 'We're fairly sure that there were two of them.'

Masson put his three pennyworths in, and put it in with an unnecessarily menacing air. 'There are two of you.'

The obvious reply to this was on the point of making its way out of my mouth when Max said, 'I'm really sorry, inspector. We were fast asleep, but we'd have called you at once if we'd known. What did they steal?'

'We're checking now.'

I couldn't resist saying, 'Perhaps it was the real killer, inspector.'

He should have given me a tight smile, but didn't. 'Did you go out at all last night?'

'I went to visit my father.'

'What time did you get back?'

'I suppose about seven.'

'It was seven fifteen,' put in Max.

And I asked, 'Why do you ask?'

'You didn't go out again?'

'We stayed right here,' I assured him, reckoning that 'here' could encompass a fairly large area.

'All night,' added Max and, whether she meant to or not, added with this confirmation a distinctly salacious tint to our alibi. Masson looked less than impressed while Smith just looked embarrassed.

Masson asked with a scowl, 'What time did you go to bed?'

Max answered at once and without a trace of guile, 'About ten thirty, I think; or maybe it was closer to ten forty-five.'

It was obvious he didn't believe her – or perhaps it would be more accurate to say that he didn't want to believe her – but she spoke her lines perfectly and kept a straight face too, her gaze true and unyielding as they looked at each other.

Abruptly he asked, 'Do you two want to get dressed?' Since this clearly was the kind of request that did not expect a debate, we complied while Smith and Masson waited in the back room. When we came back down, and after Max had made some coffee which Masson refused curtly and Smith rather more reluctantly, Masson said without preliminaries, 'We're going over the house inch by inch; in retrospect, perhaps we should have done that before.'

'Perhaps you should,' I said. 'Surely you're now coming round to the conclusion that Dad might just be innocent?'

'I'll admit there might be more to this business than first meets the eye,' he conceded but, before I could celebrate, he went on: 'He's still got a lot of explaining to do, though.'

'Isn't it obvious that somebody is looking for something? Two break-ins within twenty-four hours; admittedly the first one was an opportunist, but this one surely wasn't.'

Masson couldn't help himself. 'The third break-in, actually.' He eyed Max.

The fourth, actually, I thought. If only you knew . . . I asked, 'Have you found anything?'

Masson nodded. 'A hidden wall safe.'

I tried to sound and look surprised. 'Really?'

There was a slight pause, one that was already threatening to become embarrassing, when Max asked, 'What's in it?' She did so with a perfect mix of curiosity and innocence.

'We don't know, and we won't until we get the combination. Luckily Tom Lightoller knows it; he's on his way over now.'

And a light went on in my head.

Max sipped her coffee. 'How did they get in?'

'Nothing very sophisticated. A chisel or screwdriver was used to prise open the French windows at the back.'

Max shivered. 'And to think that Lance and I were only a few yards away.'

Perhaps she over-egged things a bit, because Masson appraised her for a few moments. To distract him, I pointed out: 'If the safe's closed, presumably he didn't manage to open it.'

Masson said, 'Presumably not, although not necessarily. Clearly it wasn't blown open as you two might have heard it, but that doesn't mean to say that it hasn't been opened and then closed again.'

'Oh.'

'Apart from that, we haven't found anything else. Certainly nothing that gives anyone else a motive to kill the Lightollers.'

Out of the corner of my eye, I saw Max opening her mouth. Almost certainly she wasn't going to say something about the report of A.J. and J.A. Moss, Consulting Detectives, but I didn't want to take the chance. 'Maybe when you get the safe open, there'll be something of significance in there.'

'I hope so.' He couldn't resist adding: 'For your father's sake, I hope so.'

When he had gone, we debated whether to go back to bed, but we were too wide awake and Max wanted to look through the dossier. Accordingly, we retreated to Dad's kitchen and from somewhere I managed to find another dose of Shagnasty's Revenger which, although it might not suit the palate of the refined gourmet, hit the spot when I considered all the shenanigans I had just had to endure. I found Max some more wine and for twenty minutes we just sat at the table and looked through the dossier while trying to calm down.

The affair was certainly torrid. During the month that the detective agency had watched them, Mr Hocking and Mrs Aurelia Parrish had met clandestinely – on every occasion in Mr Hocking's bedroom – seven times, their sessions lasting up to an hour and a half. They took advantage of Mr Parrish's visits to the wholesaler which, since he was a successful shopkeeper, were regular and frequent.

Max found some of the photos mesmerizing and, those that she did not find mesmerizing, she found hilarious. Not for the first time, I found her sense of humour and sense of sexuality quite invigorating.

I said, 'It's hardly a family heirloom, but I think it's pretty obvious what Mr Hocking, master baker and inventive consumer of pastry, was after when he tried to break in.'

'Lightoller must have been blackmailing him.'

I nodded. 'Which gives him a very good motive for murder.'

'So he's the one!'

Max's enthusiasm was endearing but, I was very much afraid, premature. 'I suppose he could be—'

'Of course he is!'

'But don't forget the bloke who came in by the front door.'

'Gosh, yes! I'd forgotten him.'

'He had a key.'

'And he went straight to the safe.'

'He was so quick, he must have known.'

She frowned. I think she was getting a bit drunk by now. 'So he did. He knew an awful lot, didn't he?'

'Yes,' I said, thinking. 'He did, didn't he?'

There was companionable silence for a while, each of us communing with our drink. Max said then what I had been thinking. 'Do you think it might have been Tom Lightoller?'

I nodded, wiping some Shagnasty from my lips. 'I think that it's highly likely. Him, or one of his goons.'

'But why?'

Our eyes fell on the dossier that lay innocently on the table between us.

Max whispered, 'He wanted that.'

'He came looking for us.' She was maudlin, her speech slightly slurred, her gaze slightly blurred. Her wine glass as empty as the bottle.

I was getting fairly drunk myself and was desperately tired with it. 'I know.'

'Supposing he'd found us?'

'I'd have fought him off.'

She nodded, thought about it, then looked up at me, her face frowning. 'Would you?'

I thought that her tone was unnecessarily drenched in surprise. 'Of course.'

She continued to stare at me, and I repaid the compliment, until she burst into laughter.

'Why are you laughing?'

But she was so overcome with hilarity that she had no room left for speech and continued to giggle for an irritatingly long time. Several times I asked her again why she had become a chortling imbecile, but these enquiries only served to exacerbate her condition. Eventually, she calmed down and I sat and watched her while she tried to stop gasping for air.

'Better?' I asked, and I like to think my tone was suitably bitter.

'Much,' she said with a smile. 'Come on, Lance, let's go back to bed.'

Before turning in, I phoned AMH. I think that they were surprised to be disturbed by a worried relative ringing at five in the morning but said nothing. Dad's condition was unchanged which, had I been an optimistic sort of person, would have cheered me; being a realist, I had to fight a feeling of dread as I thanked them and wished them a quiet night.

In the event, it was a feeling of dread that was quite misplaced.

When the phone rang, it drilled down into a sleep so deep it was like a tomb, but from somewhere I knew at once that it was the hospital and was picking up the phone before it had completed its second ring. The light through the windows was gloomy but I could see the alarm clock well enough; it was nearly eleven.

'Yes?' My head hurt.

'Dr Elliot?' It was an Australian accent.

'Yes?' No, I decided, my head was hurting *me*. It had decided that it didn't like me and accordingly was taking agonizing revenge.

'It's Atkinson-Morley here.'

I knew that. What I didn't know was whether in ten seconds' time I would be laughing or crying. 'What is it?'

'I thought you ought to know—'

'What?'

He drawled, but then all Australians do, and this just dragged the wait out to an interminable degree, an agony of expectation, fear and worry. 'Your father's . . .'

But what, exactly, was my father? Did this man have a PhD in sadism?

'Showing signs of regaining consciousness.'

TWENTY-SIX

When we got to the hospital, it wasn't quite a case of Dad sitting up in bed, sipping tea and pinching the nurse's bottom; in fact he looked little different to yesterday, save for some more colour in his cheeks and, when you got close, movement of his eyes behind his eyelids. There was definite improvement, though.

The Australian, who was now wearing a white coat on which the name badge proclaimed his name to be Ed Keeping, was writing in his notes. He looked up, his face bearing a look of quiet triumph, although I think that there was a touch of relief underlying it. 'His blood pressure's come down, as has his heart rate. He's responding to pain and has begun to verbalize.'

'What's he said?'

'Oh, nothing intelligible. Just the odd moan.'

Max had sat down and was stroking his hand, peering at him closely. 'So he'll be all right now?'

'He's not out of the woods yet, but it's certainly a hopeful sign.'

In the corner sat a statuesque uniformed woman police officer. She had her notebook out and her pencil poised but I had seen the paper and it was blank. Quite what she had thought my father might mutter in his coma intrigued me; perhaps she imagined that he would say distinctly, 'I did it. I rearranged Doris Lightoller's skull bones with a hammer, and I turned her husband into a shish kebab.'

In the car, I said, 'Half the time, I think that things are becoming clearer, but half the time, they just get even foggier. I thought it was all so obvious. A case of blackmailers receiving their just deserts.'

'Perhaps it is. The problem is, where does Tom Lightoller fit in?' she remarked.

'Whoever came in when we were there, had a key and

knew the combination, remember? Who else but their loving
son? Not only that but I think I recognized the man as he got
away: I'm fairly sure that it was one of Lightoller's employees.'

She considered what I had told her. As we were driving
through Mitcham, the rather scrub side of the common
stretching away on either side of us, she said, 'I think I can
guess.'

'What?'

'I think that Tom Lightoller's carrying on the family business.'

'Antiques or blackmail?'

'Blackmail, silly. He sent his man to get the material that
his parents were using to blackmail people.'

'But we got that, didn't we?'

'Yes . . .Well . . .' She thought about this. 'Perhaps they
were blackmailing other people.'

'But why keep some of the stuff in the safe and some of
it at the back of a cupboard? Why not keep it all in the safe?'

If there is one thing that Max is, it's game. After some
more thought, she said, 'Perhaps they kept the important
stuff in the safe and the less important stuff where you found
it. Perhaps the stuff in the safe incriminates someone famous,
or someone rich and powerful.'

But she didn't sound too convinced by this herself and I
didn't have to say what I thought of it. To change the subject
I murmured, 'In any case, I'm fairly confident that when
Masson gets into that safe he's going to find it empty.'

'So what do we do now?'

We had reached the large Lombard Bank roundabout and
I was going round it to take the last exit, the one that led
back to the Pond. 'We're going to buy some bread, I think.'

'And maybe some groceries?'

I smiled. 'Why not?'

Hocking's was a nice bakery, no doubt about it. Of course,
bakeries have a head start, what with that smell of freshly
baked bread, but this was enhanced by the look of the bread,
the buns, the cakes, the pasties, the sausage rolls, the sand-
wiches and the baps. It was further enhanced by the pleasant
woman behind the counter who smiled at us when we entered
the shop. She was quite tall and greying with a thin face,

but she had kind eyes and gave me the impression that she was delighted to see us, that this was more than just a job for her. I soon discovered, though, that there was a reason for her delight.

'Dr Elliot!' she said.

It was a situation I was used to. I was regularly accosted by people who knew me because at some point I had treated them – usually when it was two thirty in the morning and I was on call and wishing that I had chosen a life as a quantity surveyor – but who had completely failed to remain inside my head. Please do not blame me, for when I am on call I am caring for ten thousand people. I went into automatic mode.

'Hello. How are you?'

'I've been fine of late, thank you. I never thanked you for what you did.'

I smiled broadly. 'There's no need for that. It's my job.'

She turned to Max. 'Your dad was so good to me. I came over all poorly with terrible chest pains and I do believe that if it hadn't been for him, I'd have given up the goat.'

I had the feeling that she did not quite mean what she said but this was overshadowed by the embarrassment that her misreading of our relationship caused. The frown on Max's face told me that she was about to put her right but for a whole host of reasons – not least the fact that we needed this lady (who ever she was, because her name still eluded me) to be on side – I jumped in and said with suitable modesty, 'It's all in a day's work.'

She shook her head. 'Well, all I can say is that I'm glad that you're the one who's doing it. Now, what can I get for you?'

At which point, I realized that I didn't know how I was going to go about establishing Mr Hocking's alibi. I opened my mouth, took in some breath while thinking that I was really only playing for time, then not so much ground – more slammed – to a halt. A moment of silence that seemed like a minute and I was reduced to asking for a couple of custard tarts.

'Good choice,' she said.

Max gave me a pitying look and, as the confections were being put in a white paper bag, said, 'Wasn't it terrible about the murder?'

Our informant froze with the first custard tart midway
between the counter and gaping maw of the bag. 'Oh, I
know! Terrible. Absolutely terrible.'

'Were you here, in the shop?'

'Yes!' She nodded vehemently. 'Yes, I was!'

Exclamations rained down upon us, threatening bodily
injury, but my 'daughter' battled on. 'Did you hear anything?'
Max managed just the right tone, one that suggested excited
nosiness and feminine concern; she had judged her quarry
perfectly because at once a conspiracy was entered into.

'That's what the police wanted to know! I mean I was
here the whole time, serving customers and suchlike, and I
never heard anything. He couldn't have cried out or anything,
because I'd have heard. It gives me the creeps to think what
was going on all that time. I said to my husband that night,
I said, "Supposing the killer had come into the bakery instead
of going into Mr Lightoller's?" Supposing he'd fancied a
pasty?'

It was one of those philosophical questions on which even
the finest of human minds can become stalled. Max almost
gave herself away because she had trouble smothering a
smirk as she asked, 'Did Mr Hocking hear anything?'

'No. Nothing at all. Mind you, he was upstairs in his flat
having his afternoon nap when it happened. He was probably dead to the world.' An unfortunate turn of phrase, I
thought. She continued, 'That's where he is now. He has a
snooze every day at this time.'

For which I was glad, since I didn't particularly want to
meet him just at that moment.

Max asked, 'Has he been shocked by what's happened too?'

Her reward was a nod. 'Terrible. He's a very gentle and
sensitive man, you know. Terribly shy.'

I tried to avoid Max's eye as I thought about the photographs.

During all this, the custard tart had made its slow, unre-
garded way to journey's end in the paper bag where it
waited patiently for company as the events of that afternoon were dissected. I asked, 'Did you know Mr Lightoller
well?'

'Not really. We said, "Hello", and things like that, but
nothing more.'

'What about Mr Hocking? Presumably he knew him a bit better.'

I had hit the right button. Her face went through an almost theatrical change of expressions that had started at polite interest but ended fairly quickly at conspiratorial exhilaration as she leaned over the chocolate eclairs and said, 'Not really.' Then suddenly she said, 'Mind you, there was that time . . .'

But then the shop bell rang simultaneously with the rattle of the door as a very tall but very stooped old man dressed in a black suit with a waistcoat, white shirt and green tie came slowly into the shop. His lower eyelids drooped to expose reddened membranes and his eyes were watering painfully, but despite this he had a bright smile that broadened to expose an irregular array of surviving teeth clinging desperately to his gums. 'Afternoon, Lil,' he said, then stopped to cough; it was a cough that came from deep within him and, from the sound of it, that moved awesome amounts of mucus around his insides.

'Afternoon, Mr Lockyer.' The woman now revealed to be Lil replied in a voice that was considerably louder than usual speech. Despite this, I had the impression that he didn't really hear. He said, 'I've come for my usual.'

'You'll have to wait, Mr Lockyer. I'm just serving these people.'

I said, 'No, serve Mr Lockyer first. We can wait.'

Except that Max then said, 'I can't.'

I turned to her as she was already walking towards the door. 'Where are you going?'

'I've forgotten something. I'll be back in a moment.'

With which she was gone; Mr Lockyer looked at her from under his eyebrows, a large grin on his face, although I am not sure he knew what was going on, and Lil sighed and said in sympathy for me, 'My daughter's just like that. I blame television.'

I opened my mouth, was on the point of correcting her despite my previous intentions, when Mr Lockyer said loudly, 'She's a right cracker, she is.'

'Mr Lockyer!' Lil was horrified and yet perversely delighted, but the old man had already been punished by the gods that be because, once again, he was dredging his own personal phlegm pool. Tutting, Lil was already getting his 'usual', which turned out to be two jumbo sausage rolls. After he had paid his money – which he had ready in a scuffed navy-blue leather purse fastened with a clasp – he left, still coughing and still laughing, although by now it was completely to himself.

'Now,' said Lil. 'Where were we?'

'One custard tart down and you were just on the point of telling me about Mr Hocking and Mr Lightoller.'

'Oh, yes . . .' She picked up the paper bag again and went after another custard tart; I was rather perturbed to note that she used the same tongs for the custard tarts as she had for the sausage rolls. 'Up until recently, they seemed to get on quite well. I mean, they weren't exactly *close,* if you get what I mean, but they passed the time of day, that kind of thing. Used to moan about the rates and about the litter problem and suchlike.'

'And that changed recently?'

She nodded. 'I don't know if they had a row or something, but I saw Mr Hocking cut Mr Lightoller dead last week. Gave him such a look, he did.'

'Really?'

'Yes. If looks could kill . . .' She tailed off, realizing what she had just said. 'Not that . . .'

I hastened to reassure her. 'Oh, no.'

This *faux pas* had forced her to pause but thankfully not before two custard tarts had become conjoined in blessed union inside the paper bag. I changed the subject. 'What about the Parrishes? Did Mr Lightoller get on with them?'

But she was becoming cagey. 'Yes, I suppose.'

'And Mr Hocking?'

I am sure that I asked this in a perfectly innocent voice, but her attitude had changed. 'Yes, of course. Why not?'

And that was all I could get from her. I paid for the custard tarts – now doubtless improved by a hint of sausage roll – and left the shop wondering a lot of things, like what she knew about Mr Hocking's relationship with Mrs Parrish, and how significant it was that Lightoller and Mr Hocking had recently fallen out, and where my daughter had disappeared to.

TWENTY-SEVEN

T he last of these questions was answered almost immediately because Max was standing on the pavement
a little way up the road, beyond Mr Parrish's grocery
shop. She was beckoning frantically to me so I exercised my
legendary powers of deduction and joined her.

'What is it, daughter dear?'

She flushed. 'Don't you start. How dare she? I'm not that
young.'

'I'm not that old, you mean.'

At which, like every female young and old that I've ever
known, she came over all deaf and ignored me. 'I've been
checking out the lie of the land.'

'What does that mean?'

She looked at me with something that the charitable might
describe as 'pitying', the realistic might describe as
'scathing'. 'You're not very good at this, are you?'

'Help me through it, then.'

She led me further up the road past a wool shop, a strangely
empty-looking record shop and a motor factor's until we
came to an alleyway. At the end of this, after dodging some
dustbins, a rusting bicycle and a dead cat, we came to an
intersecting alley that led along the backs of the shops. The
fence that ran down either side of the alley was in varying
stages of disrepair and decrepitude; opposite Lightoller's
shop it had almost completely collapsed.

'See?' asked Max coming to a halt just beyond Lightoller's,
directly at the back of Mr Hocking's bakery.

I saw, although I did not make much of it. The gardens
were short and, being at the back of shops, uncared for to
the point of wilderness. Many of the weeds were dying but
before this fate they had grown to two, three, even four feet
high and dense enough to require something on the scale of
a machete to penetrate. They were damp, too; damp and
cold-looking.

'No, I don't.'

'For a start off, Inspector Masson said that no one had been seen entering the shop from either the front or the rear. This undergrowth is so thick, an elephant could have come knocking completely unseen.'

'True.'

'And then look at the back of the shop. There's a staircase down from the top flat.'

She was right, but it took me a moment or two longer to grasp the implication. 'So Mr Hocking could have got down from the flat without Lil or anyone else seeing him.'

'Exactly.'

'It doesn't look as though he made his way through that lot, though,' I said, indicating the weeds. 'There's no sign of a Hocking-sized hole.'

But she had an immediate answer. 'Judging by the state of the fences, I bet he could get through to his neighbour's garden without too much bother just breaking it down.'

'How did he get into the shop, then? The back door was locked.'

'If the back door was locked, perhaps he knocked and was let in by Lightoller; perhaps he was here to make a payment. In any case, we don't know that the door *was* locked. It doesn't matter. He could have got in and, as I suggested to the inspector, he could have got out again, leaving the door locked and without being seen by anyone.'

'Surely Masson's thought of all this.'

'But he's convinced that your father did it; or at least, he's convinced enough not to be actively pursuing other lines of enquiry. He might have worked out that Samuel Hocking doesn't have a decent alibi, but he almost certainly doesn't know about the blackmail.'

She was right. Masson might well have thought of all this, but it didn't mean anything because he didn't know about Hocking's potential motive. Max said, 'We ought to tell him.'

But something was holding me back from doing that; I didn't know why, but I thought it would be a bad idea. At which point, something occurred to me. 'What about the back of the grocer's? What about their access? I mean, they're not lacking a motive either, are they?'

'You think Mrs Parrish is a murderess?' In those days, we still talked about 'murderesses' and we were still quaint enough to be shocked by the concept.

'Maybe, or even Mr Parrish. Perhaps his wife confessed to him what was going on and he took it out on Lightoller.'

'Wouldn't he be more likely to take it out on Mr Hocking?'

I thought, Well, of course he would, but I'm just casting around for hope here.

The back of the grocery shop proved to have come under the influence of a woman, though. The fence was still intact and relatively well preserved because it had been regularly creosoted. By peering through the knotholes and the cracks around the gate, we could see that it had been, to a certain extent, tended. The weeds had been kept down and the grass, although not ideal for croquet, was relatively short. We were able to see that the fence separating the two properties was intact and robust.

I said, 'Well, it doesn't look as if either of them could have sneaked around the back with too much ease.'

'We ought to talk to them, though. We need to get something to eat tonight, and maybe we'll get some sort of idea of how things lay between them and Mr Lightoller.'

She was right, but I was none too hopeful. I was also wondering what Mrs Parrish would say when she saw me.

TWENTY-EIGHT

M r Malcolm Parrish had not been around when I had raised the alarm about Oliver Lightoller's death. He was a portly man, with a cheerful face that was craggy and seemingly a tough job for his razor, given the number of minor cuts spread out on it. He had no neck to speak of and jet-black hair that doubtless looked just like the packet said it would; possibly to inject yet more illusion of youth into his appearance. His establishment was one of those shops that seemed to stock everything, that was so crowded that wherever the eye looked there was something different to see. It called itself a grocery store, but that term was stretched to include stationery, small items of hardware, greetings cards, toys, equipment for dressmaking, a large selection of second-hand books and an array of magazines, some softly pornographic. It smelled of furniture polish laced with a soupçon of something that at first I could not place, appreciating only after Mr Parrish had reached up to a top shelf to fetch a large tin of baked beans for Max, that it was his body odour.

Max said, 'Do you have any bacon?'

He indicated a small cold cabinet. 'Only streaky.'

'I'll have one packet, please.'

He complied with her wishes. Max asked, 'Eggs?' and eggs were duly inspected and then supplied, half a dozen white, each with a little lion stamped on it. Mrs Parrish entered the room and, while we both struggled to suppress the image of what Mr Hocking had done to her with a chocolate eclair, she began making room on the shelves to our right for some more tins of vegetables. Max was just choosing which type of sausage to have – Walls best with or without skin – when Mrs Parrish straightened and caught sight of me. Her face betrayed instant recognition and before she could speak, I began with, 'Hello again.'

'Hello.'

Mr Parrish looked on with an interesting expression. Mrs Parrish had dropped her gaze from me and found something that she liked about her shoes. She was still attached to a cigarette and from closer quarters, I could see was a good fifteen years younger than her husband; she had made an effort with make-up, too, but it was a doomed attempt because it was failing to make up for the lines of tiredness and anno domini that the life of an English shopkeeper's wife had given her.

'Do you two know each other?'

His tone had changed quite noticeably; gone was the affable shopkeeper, eager to please and therefore perhaps make a few more bob; now there was an injection of curiosity, and none too passive curiosity either. Mr Parrish was a jealous man.

I said, 'We met when I raised the alarm about Oliver Lightoller's death. You weren't here, I think.'

'Oh?' This in a tone that came across as paranoid, an impression compounded by the way he looked me up and down as he spoke.

Max chipped in with, 'Wasn't it awful?'

Mrs Parrish agreed at once. 'It was dreadful.'

'And then his wife, too . . .'

Mr Parrish, it then transpired, was not a man of great tact. 'I read in the local rag that your father's under suspicion. Is that right?'

'My father's seriously ill in hospital,' I pointed out. 'No one knows what happened.'

He made a face that said quite clearly that he wasn't fool enough to fall for *that* one, which I ignored and said, 'You missed all the excitement, Mr Parrish.'

'I'll live.'

'At the cash and carry, were you?'

He patently thought was none of my business but replied anyway, 'We'd run out of frozen chips. What with the weekend coming up, I wanted to get in a good stock.'

I smiled. 'Of course.'

'I would have been here, only I had a puncture on the way back. Bloody nuisance it was.'

Max asked, 'How much do I owe you?'

He totted the total up on a cheap paper pad with a pencil that was well chewed at one end and, at the other, trimmed to a square point with a pen knife. 'Two pounds thirty-three.'

As Max proffered the money, she said, 'We were just in the bakery. Mr Hocking's very upset.'

This lie produced a gratifying reaction. Mr Parrish's face darkened, while that of his spouse blanched. These equal and opposite reactions almost cancelled each other out, so that the overall colour balance remained undisturbed. Then, Mrs Parrish left the shop muttering something about having to get on, while Mr Parrish crashed down the keys on his till with what I thought was a quite unnecessary amount of violence and said tersely, 'We're all upset.'

As if completely unaware of the atmosphere, Max enquired, 'Did you know Mr Lightoller well?'

The money safely deposited, he slammed the cash drawer shut and said, 'Not particularly.'

'But surely, you were neighbours, after all.'

He handed over the receipt and gathered up the handles of the plastic bag that contained our purchases. 'That's all we were.'

There was a tone of finality in these words that prevented either of us from probing further. We left the shop, none the wiser but considerably more intrigued.

In the car on the way home, Max went through what we had learned.

'Neither Mr Hocking nor Mr Parrish had an alibi for the time that the first murder took place, and both of them had a potential motive.'

'From the way that Hocking's name went down with the Parrishes, I would say that there's some sort of history there.'

'Surely, though, it was Mr Hocking, not Parrish, who was being blackmailed.'

'We don't know that. Perhaps Lightoller judged Mrs Parrish to be the weaker party. She's got more to lose, after all. He blackmails her; she tells Hocking; Hocking goes round and does him in.'

'But it's still Hocking doing the murdering, not Mr Parrish.'

'OK, then. Lightoller blackmails Mrs Parrish who then

breaks down and confesses all to her husband. He decides the best way to deal with matters is to bump Lightoller off, then, at a later date, go after Hocking. Perhaps he's just biding his time.'

'Or maybe he was hoping to frame Mr Hocking for the murder . . .'

I shook my head. 'He didn't do a very good job, then, did he? It's my father who's in the frame for it.'

'But that's because he barged in as Doris Lightoller was being killed. That meant that he had to change plans. He *was* planning to implicate Hocking, but now he's got to think of something else.'

She had missed something obvious. 'Why did he kill Doris? She wasn't obviously involved.'

'They were both in it together, maybe Tom, too. Anyway, we know why he went to the house – to find the evidence – so perhaps Doris Lightoller was just in the way.'

'I still think that Hocking has the strongest motive. It was Hocking who turned up at the house, trying to break in.'

There was a pause. We were nearly back at Dad's house when Max asked, 'So what's going on between the Parrishes?'

I shrugged. 'Probably nothing more than paranoia. Parrish strikes me as the pathologically jealous type. I bet over the years he's suspected everyone from the coalman to the delivery driver of having an affair with his wife.'

'For a moment, I thought he was suspecting you.'

'For a moment, so did I.'

I parked in the drive in front of Dad's house and, as I got out, I could hear the phone ringing inside. I sprinted for the door and just got it open in time to pick up the receiver. It was AMH. Dad was conscious.

TWENTY-NINE

H e wasn't sitting up and cheeking the nurses, but he was most definitely alive and awake and wonderful to see. He was lying slightly more upright than he had been, still hooked up to a cardiac monitor and two drips, but with more colour in his cheeks and without that sunken expression that so nearly caricatures death. Percy was standing outside the room when we arrived, looking pleased with himself.

'He came round about an hour ago. He seems quite his old self, though a bit croaky.'

We went in. He turned his bandage-bedecked head to look at us, although he didn't try to raise it off the pillow. 'Ah, Lance. About time.' His voice was dry and husky.

'Hello, Dad.'

Max said, 'Hello, Dr Elliot. I'm so glad to see you getting better.'

He regarded her for a moment and then said formally, 'Thank you, Miss Christy. I'm touched by your concern.'

I suppressed an urge to chastise him. We sat on two chairs by his bedside as Percy slipped into the room, presumably to make sure that he didn't miss Dad's confession to a double murder. I asked, 'Does it hurt?'

He gave me the benefit of what can only be described as a baleful look. 'What do you think? That gentleman with the peculiar accent and irritatingly cheerful demeanour tells me that he cracked open my skull and scooped out several pints of blood. From the way that he described it, he used a foot pump and a ladle, so, yes, it does smart rather.'

Max asked, 'Can you remember what happened?'

I was aware that Percy sat up a little straighter in his chair. Dad thought about things. 'I'm told I was found at the bottom of the stairs in the Lightollers' house.'

'That's right.'

'I think I remember hearing a commotion coming from

next door. I was outside servicing the motor mower before putting it away for the winter, and I heard Doris screaming and shouting. I hurried to the front and banged on the front door, called out a few times, but Doris was making such a row I don't think she heard me.' He paused and frowned. 'I think I nipped around the back, but that's where it starts to go hazy . . .'

I said carefully, 'Has anyone talked to you about Doris?'

He was concentrating hard, lost in a past that he could not quite claim as his own, and had to come back to what I had said. 'Doris? No. Is she all right?'

I was about to tell him when Percy coughed. 'I'm not sure you should be discussing that, not until the inspector gets here.'

'If Masson wants to talk to Dad first,' I suggested, 'perhaps he should pull his finger out of wherever it is and get here.'

'He's a bit stretched,' admitted Percy. 'Constable Smith's phoned in sick again.'

Dad asked somewhat plaintively, 'What's going on?'

I looked at Percy with my eyebrows raised and he responded with a faint shrug while the look on his face suggested that he was washing his hands of the affair. To Dad I said, 'Doris Lightoller's dead.'

His eyes widened and his mouth opened slightly. 'Oh, no,' he whispered. Then: 'How?'

I tried not to hesitate, but failed. 'She was attacked with a hammer.'

His eyes closed. I knew Dad, knew that he might not have liked either of the Lightollers but the last thing in the world he would have wanted was to see them dead. 'Dear God.'

There was an awkward silence; I could feel the presence of Percy behind me taking all this in, an audience of one following the action with an opened mouth and tongue that peeped shyly out of the dark. Inevitably, Dad asked, 'Who did it?'

I glanced up at Max who was on the other side of the bed. Her grimace said it all: *rather you than me*. Percy's cough wandered into the room from his position in the corner. Dad frowned at me and I saw the beginnings of comprehension peeping like rosy-fingered dawn over the horizon. 'They think I did?' he asked quietly.

I nodded. 'Your fingerprints were on the hammer. They think you attacked her and then somehow fell down the stairs.'

Being my father, he took this in a completely unexpected fashion. What he should have done was protested his innocence with passion and gusto, shouted incredulity from the chimney tops, expressed loudly his scorn for the notion. Instead, all he did was say, 'I wonder if I did?'

Max squeaked in alarm as I said through teeth that were threatening to buckle under the strain so tightly were my jaws clamped together, 'No, Dad, you didn't.'

Percy had sat up; several decades of less than exhilarating police work behind the counter at Norbury police station might have turned his detective abilities from razor sharp to something with all the cutting ability of a lead pipe, but even he could tell something worth listening to when it wandered past his lugholes.

'I hope not,' Dad continued, his tone suggesting that, in his own mind at least, he was merely having an absorbing academic discussion. 'But I can't be sure at the moment, can I? I can't remember doing it, but then I can't remember *not* doing it.'

'Of course you didn't do it, Dad. You're not a violent man.'

He thought about this. 'I don't think I am . . .'

'You're not, Dr Elliot,' put in Max.

He turned to look at her. 'Not normally, at least.'

'Not ever,' she said firmly. 'You're one of the kindest, most caring, most gentle people I've ever met.'

He looked at her intently. Perhaps he was checking for insincerity, for the merest suggestion that she was being patronizing and, accordingly, I found that I was holding my breath. Then he smiled just a little and reached out his hand to pat hers, the drip line swaying as he did so. 'Thank you, my dear. It's very kind of you to say so.'

I decided to concentrate on the positives in what Dad had told us. 'You said that you heard Doris making a commotion. Did you hear anyone else?'

He thought about this. 'I don't think so.'

'And when you went into the house, there was nothing to suggest the presence of someone else?'

'Not that I recall.'

I gave up. Dad's refusal to give himself any means of escape – to offer any doubt, no matter how small, that someone else was in the house when Doris Lightoller had died – was to me ample evidence that he was innocent in every sense of the word, but I suspected it would mean nothing to the more cynical ears that resided beneath a policeman's helmet.

Percy was noting things down in his notebook and I had a strong suspicion that it wasn't his shopping list. In desperation, I looked around the room for a subject to change to, my eyes lighting on a crumpled copy of the *Croydon Advertiser*. 'Catching up on everything you've missed?' I asked, picking it up and brandishing it.

Dad nodded. 'I like to keep abreast. One of the nurses gave it to me. Nice girl; about your age, Lance. Not married, either.'

Ignoring him and hoping that Max was not taking offence, I peered at the date on the front page. 'It's last week's.'

'Is it?' he asked, then shrugged. 'I did wonder.' He sounded vague, almost musical and for a second I thought that he was having some sort of turn; I looked across at Max who was watching Dad too, but then the door opened.

Ed Keeping came in, Dad's medical notes under his arm and looking, as ever, as if he was either on his way to, or on the way back from, a beach, although there wasn't one for sixty miles. 'Hi, guys. How's tricks?'

My father eyed him. 'If, by that strange idiom, you are asking after my health, Mr Keeping, I can tell you that I am fine.' He seemed to be back to normal.

'Call me Ed.'

Dad looked less than impressed. 'I'd rather not.'

Ed Keeping was looking at the nursing chart which he put back down as he said with a smile, 'As you like.'

I asked, 'Would you like us to leave?'

'Nah. I won't be more than a couple of minutes.'

To Max, Dad said loudly, 'I can't help feeling that there is a worrying degree of informality entering into the doctor-patient relationship. It's not a good idea; not a good idea at all. It interferes with the necessary degree of clinical objectiveness that the doctor must have to give of his best.'

We moved back as Keeping began a brief clinical examination, first feeling Dad's pulse, then checking his eyes and
his chest. When he had done this, he said through a large
and amused smile, 'You're doing just great, Dr Elliot.'

'That's nice to know.'

Keeping was writing in the notes. 'The drips can come
down tonight. Are you eating and drinking?'

'I'm trying, although to judge from the quality of the muck
on the plate, the canteen staff don't want me to.'

'Do you have a headache?'

'Only when I eat.'

Of me Keeping asked, 'Have you noticed any change in
his personality?'

When I shook my head, Keeping asked with a sly glance
at Dad, 'You mean he was always like this?' Before Dad
could vocalise his outrage, he continued quickly, 'Another
five minutes, no longer. He's getting tired.'

'I am not.'

Keeping looked at him and then turned to me with a
perfectly straight face. 'It often happens after a serious head
injury.'

Dad demanded, 'What does?'

He was ignored, though. 'It's nothing to worry about.' And
with that he winked at me.

Dad wasn't going to be left out. 'What isn't?'

I nodded. 'I understand.'

Keeping walked out, leaving my father demanding loudly
of anyone and everyone, 'What on earth is that man talking
about?'

THIRTY

Darkness fell as we drove back to Dad's house. We let ourselves in and I was looking forward to a nice fry-up courtesy of Max, hopefully followed by . . . well, who knows?

It wasn't to be, though.

I know that in crime thrillers and suchlike, the hero is at once instinctively aware of something being amiss when he enters a room or a house, that he has at his fingertips an unerring sixth sense of danger, but it didn't happen with me. Max went in first, and I followed, I switched on the hall light, and we took off our coats. We went through into the kitchen, switched on the light in there, and only then for the first time saw that we had visitors.

Tom Lightoller sat at the kitchen table, one of his goons – the big one with a brow big enough to stand under should it rain – behind him. The cheeky devil had helped himself to a cup of coffee which he was now ostentatiously sipping; Igor, or whatever his name was, had to content himself with chewing something that I could quite easily imagine was a small furry rodent. They looked to me as if, as undertakers, they offered the complete service, including providing the cadaver.

Max squeaked, I said something that might have been, 'What the hell?' and Tom Lightoller said politely, 'Good evening.'

Igor scowled; perhaps he had bitten into the gall bladder.

Tom Lightoller put the coffee cup down and continued, 'You weren't about, so we made ourselves at home.'

'What the bloody hell is going on here?'

'I want to speak to you.'

'You can't just barge in like this.'

'I did, though, didn't I?' He said this not arrogantly, merely in the spirit of getting things right.

'I'm going to phone the police,' I said but before I could

actually do anything towards this end, Igor moved out from
behind the shadow of his diminutive boss and stepped towards
me. That was all he did – he didn't have a gun, a knife, a
flame-thrower or even brass knuckledusters – but it was
enough. He made his point.

'Sit down,' advised Tom.

Max and I looked at each other, then sat down. Tom
enquired solicitously, 'You sure you don't want any of your
coffee?'

It was a nice offer and, I'm sure, well meant. I spoke for
both of us. 'No, thanks.'

He looked distressed for a second but, from the expression on his face, he was remarkably resilient, an impression
that was strengthened when he said with a shrug, 'OK.'

He took a sip of his – of my – coffee. 'You should get
Nescafé Fine Blend. It's ten times better than this stuff.'

You probably can't imagine the shame I felt that I had let
my guest down but I bore it all with fortitude and muttered,
'Thanks for the tip.'

Despite the pain that he professed to feel, he managed to
finish the coffee and put the mug down. 'Now,' he said. 'To
business.'

'If you wouldn't mind.'

'Your old man killed my old man.'

'No, he didn't.'

'And then he killed my mum.'

'No, he didn't.'

'The old man, I could take or leave, but my mum, she
was a bit special. I loved her.' He had become ruminative.

'Dad didn't kill anyone.' Nobody could say that I wasn't
persistent.

'Of course, Masson thinks it was over some watch or
something, but I know different.'

I tried upping the volume a tad. 'Tom, Dad didn't kill
anyone.'

It had no discernible effect. He had previously been looking
at his fingers clasped on the table in front of him but now
he looked up at me. 'You know different, too.'

'Do I?'

He suddenly banged the table hard with his fist and the

coffee mug jumped, thought momentarily about falling over in surprise, then thought again. It made us both jump and it made Max squeak and clutch my arm. 'Yes,' he said. 'You do.'

I didn't argue and into the silence of my agreement he continued, 'My old man had something . . . of value.' I began to see what he was getting at but I didn't say anything; beside me Max stirred, presumably because she, too, was seeing some light. He continued, 'I want it. It's mine. The way I look at it, it's my inheritance.'

I cleared my throat. 'Well . . .'

This proved to be a mistake because it provoked him to turn on me and say crisply, 'Don't argue, else my companion here will pull out your tongue and lick your arse with it.'

Max couldn't help herself. 'Charming!'

There was a moment of something that I can only describe as incipient menace as Tom appraised her, then he bowed his head slightly and said, 'Sorry.'

I think he meant it, too. I didn't feel that I ought to comment and it was left to Tom to pick up the conversation. 'Somehow, your father found out about it and he went looking for it. He looked in the shop and then he looked in the house, but he didn't find it.'

This was fantasy, of course, but in the interests of keeping my tongue inside its usual orifice I tried to make the argument against his hypothesis using facial expressions alone. It didn't have the same oratorical force and he carried on obliviously, 'I'm told your girlfriend was caught snooping around my parents' house.'

Max flushed. 'It wasn't like that . . .'

'That's not what I heard.'

'You heard wrong,' insisted Max.

I added, 'She was attacked by a real thief, too.'

'Oh, yes.' I'm not sure whether I had hoped to evoke some sympathy in his breast; in any case, I failed.

'Some would say she deserved what she got.'

Max squeaked. 'Well!'

'You or your family and friends always seem to be in the vicinity when these things happen,' he pointed out.

'A coincidence.'

Tom's eyes narrowed as he pushed on. 'There's a safe in my parents' house. If ever the old man had anything valuable, that's where he'd put it.'

'Really?'

'I expected it to be there, yet, hey presto, when my man looked in it, it was as bare as Mother Hubbard's cupboard.'

Max joined in with: 'How odd!'

'And he had the distinct feeling that someone was in the house with him when he was there.'

'Imagine!' I ventured.

He looked at me sharply. 'It wasn't you then?'

We both looked as innocent as possible, eyes wide and mouths straight. 'We were asleep,' I assured him.

'In bed,' added Max, rather unhelpfully, although neither Tom nor Igor noticed the slight incongruity.

There was silence for a short while. 'Are you sure?'

'Totally,' I said.

'Completely,' added Max.

He pursed his lips and frowned and had me fooled completely into thinking that he was on the point of accepting this when he banged the table again, only this time with even more force, so that the coffee mug fell over and played dead. It must have hurt him – I once broke a bone in my hand doing something similar – but he was made of stern stuff and didn't flinch. Max jumped, too.

'No,' he decided. 'I don't believe you. I don't know how you did it, but I think you managed to steal my inheritance from the safe.'

'Max and I aren't safe crackers. How could we have got into a locked safe?'

'I don't know,' he admitted. Our joy at this was short-lived. 'But I do know that it wasn't there when my man looked.'

'Tom, this is nothing to do with us.'

He waited, might have been in a different room. Nervous silence descended; at least it was nervous on our part; Tom looked completely impassive whilst Igor just looked ugly. After a short while, I tried again. 'Think about it, Tom. Do you really think that we were the ones who got into the safe and stole your "inheritance"? I'm a GP and Max is a vet.'

This time he did shrug. 'Your old man was after it – killed

to get it – and you sent your girl in to get it when he came unstuck.'

I was surprised, shocked even, to hear how his mind worked. He had struck me as a cold fish and Masson's description of his activities whilst at school only reinforced that impression; now, though, he was talking as if he felt no remorse at all for his parents' deaths, as if he had seen everything as a business and he now interpreted the actions of my father and the two of us in the same light. There was no room for affection in his world view.

'Tom . . .'

The fist came down again; the coffee mug which hadn't got up since the last time, rolled a bit as he shouted, 'YES, YOU DID!'

It might have been the third time he'd done it, but I still jumped a little and Max did likewise. Into the silence – albeit a silence that was spoiled by the ringing in my ears – he continued, 'And if you're not going to do this the easy way, then you're going to do it the hard way.'

With which he gestured to Igor. Igor uttered a soft grunt – it was difficult to tell but it might have been uttered in a lugubriously excited tone – and moved into action. He came around Tom in a distinctly threatening way, so I stood up, ready to repel all boarders. 'What are you doing?' I demanded.

'Get out of the way,' advised Tom.

Igor moved forward and I resisted.

At least I tried to resist.

Igor pushed and I moved backwards; I pushed back and I still moved backwards. When I was out of the way, Igor turned to Max, so I took a swing at him.

Now, I'm not a fighter – never had boxing training, done no martial arts, always considered pugilism to be recidivism repackaged as entertainment – but I thought for a moment that I'd made a reasonable job of it. My fist connected with the left side of Igor's face, and I'm fairly sure that I immediately felt a bit guilty about spoiling his good looks, but then it all went distinctly fruit-shaped.

He paused, turned to show me a deep and angry scowl, then grasped my throat.

Yes, I said 'throat'.

I gurgled at first but then that soon stopped because there was nothing getting either in or out of my chest. The room went that sort of lurid blood colour that you see in horror films and the ringing in my ears came back big time, as if it had been orchestrated and was now being played by the Royal Philharmonic. I vaguely heard Max screaming but then everything went dark.

THIRTY-ONE

When the world came back to me, I was sitting on the floor and my back was against the wall; Max was bending over me as she held my hand and rubbed the back of it, saying my name. My throat felt as if someone had hit it with a sledgehammer and my head was pounding so much I was surprised that the blood wasn't squirting out of my ears. Behind her, Tom was at the table and leafing through something while Igor had taken up station behind him again.

He didn't look happy.

As Max helped me up, he lifted his eyes from it and asked, 'What's going on?'

I said, 'You gave it to him.' My voice was an interesting mix of croak and squeak.

'And you're alive, Lance. Spot the connection.'

I saw her point but before I could acknowledge this, Tom interrupted rather rudely. 'Are you two taking the mickey?'

Max replied, 'It's the file you wanted.'

He opened his mouth but I'm not sure that he was going to say 'Thank you'.

The doorbell rang.

He shut his mouth, and looked concerned; Igor frowned but that, I feel, was the utmost limit of his thinking on the subject. I said at once, 'I'd better get that,' and, since we were between Igor and the front door, I rushed out into the hall, taking Max with me. Tom cried out but, strangely, I didn't feel it wise to listen too closely.

When I opened the door and found Smith standing there, I have never been so delighted. In fact, I was so pleased – and the look on my face was so ecstatic – that he looked first alarmed, then nervous, as if he feared an outbreak of dementia in the Elliot household. Max, too, let out a loud sigh and smiled broadly, hardly adding to the impression of normality. I said loudly for the benefit of Laurel and Hardy in the kitchen, 'Constable Smith! Come in!' My voice was still polyphonic and shouting caused no little pain.

He was ushered in, murmuring, 'Sorry to bother you, doctor.'

'It's no bother. No bother at all.' I kept it nice and loud. 'Are you all right?'

'Fine, fine. Come into the kitchen.'

I led the way into a kitchen shorn of undertakers; the back door was open and the file was gone. No one had cleaned the coffee cup. He didn't say anything, but I watched him look around the room, at the opened back door, and I could see that he was aware that he might just have interrupted something.

Max said, 'I'd better close the door; it's getting rather cold in here.' Even I heard the tremored relief in her voice.

'It is a bit, isn't it?' he agreed. There was a hint of something in his voice that might just have been amusement, as if he'd guessed that we hadn't been alone.

I hesitated, unsure of what I was about to say when he peered closely at my throat and remarked, 'Has someone tried to strangle you, Dr Elliot?'

I sat down with a loud sigh. 'We've just had a visit from a small psychopath and his pet gorilla.'

He raised a copper eyebrow. 'Tell me more.'

Max made coffee and chipped in with her own observations as I related what had happened. At the end of it, both of his eyebrows had made the journey northwards and he was silent for a moment. When he spoke, it was in a wondering tone. 'It seems we've been missing a trick.' But before we could congratulate ourselves on being ahead of the local plod once again, he went on: 'But you have just confessed to at least two criminal acts in your account.' There was a smile twitching about the corners of his mouth, as if he found our shenanigans privately amusing.

'Done with the best of intentions,' I protested.

Max had put down the coffee in front of him and he was now shovelling sugar into it as if afraid that at any moment the sugar bowl was going to vanish for ever after. 'We all know where that particular path leads.'

'If we hadn't done that, you wouldn't know about Lightoller's blackmail schemes.'

He took a sip of what could only be coffee-flavoured syrup. 'Yes, we would,' he countered flatly. 'We'd have found it this morning when we did the thorough search.' Amazingly, he seemed to like the taste.

'Not necessarily . . .'

'Yes, we would.' There was no arguing with him. 'And, what's more, it would be tucked up safe and sound in the evidence cupboard at the station, instead of in the possession of Tom Lightoller.'

Max had joined us at the table. 'He's horrible, constable. He nearly killed Lance.'

He did at least show some sympathy for me, which was more than Masson would have managed. 'I can see that.'

'Well, then . . .'

He shrugged. 'It doesn't really matter. Even if you had thought to do the sensible thing and hand it over to me immediately, it would have been useless in court.'

'Why?'

'Because of how you obtained it. You can't go around stealing things and then presenting them as proof of innocence. It's a fundamental tenet of how justice operates.'

'That's stupid.' This from Max.

He smiled sadly at her. 'Be that as it may, that's the law.'

'Then the law's stupid.'

He declined to comment. 'I'll have to tell the inspector what's been going on.'

I grimaced. 'I was afraid you'd say that. What will he do?'

'At the worst, he could have you both arrested and charged on several serious counts because of what you've told me.'

Max, still relatively unused to the ways and temper of the good inspector, said at once, 'He wouldn't!'

He shook his head from side to side in consideration. 'No,' he agreed eventually, 'he probably wouldn't. He'll give you both a bollocking you'll never forget, though.'

I had expected no less. Trying to look on the bright side, I pointed out: 'Still, it gives Samuel Hocking, and maybe the Parrishes, a good motive for wanting to do away with the Lightollers.'

'I suppose,' he agreed grudgingly. That smile again; he clearly thought we were just being stupid.

Max added, 'And Mr Hocking has no alibi and easy access.'

And then I remembered. 'Except that Mr Hocking's done his back in, so I can't see him running swords through people or battering them to death.'

'Oh, gosh, no,' said Max sadly.

'And your father also has no alibi and easy access,' he pointed out.

'Oh, for God's sake!'

He held up his hand. 'I'll admit, it's certainly food for thought, if all you say is true. The problem is, we haven't seen this stuff, have we? You're desperate to prove your father's innocence, so maybe you've made all this up.'

Max became incredulous. 'How can you think that? We haven't done anything of the sort. We're telling you the truth, honestly we are.'

'I'm sure.'

'Look at my throat,' I said. 'Do you think I did this to myself? Or perhaps you think that Max did it.'

'There is that,' he conceded.

'All you have to do is go and talk to Tom Lightoller.'

He laughed. 'You think he'll corroborate your story, do you? My, how trusting you are, doctor. What a pleasant world you must live in.'

'But you've got the testimony of two of us . . .'

'And, if he's the kind of man you say he is, I can guarantee that he'll have the testimony of at least six people to say that he was dishing out soup to the homeless, or knitting tea cosies with the Women's Institute.'

Max was about to do that exploding thing again, so I said quickly, 'So what are you going to do?'

He took a long time to think about that one, during which time he finished his coffee. 'I'm not sure. It's up to the inspector, and he's very stretched at the moment, what with tidying up the killings in Greyhound Lane.'

'You mustn't let him lose sight of the Lightoller case,' I said forcefully. 'I think we've shown that there might be more to this than was at first apparent.'

More of that smile. I was starting to get irritated by it; he seemed to think he was dealing with morons. 'Don't worry, doctor. We won't.

'I'll report to him at once what you've told me. I'm sure we'll pay Tom Lightoller a visit; if nothing else, it'll show him that we know what he's been up to. And then, tomorrow, at ten o'clock, the inspector is going to have a little chat with your father, now that his doctor tells us that he's well enough. At that meeting, I don't doubt that he will be formally cautioned. You might care to have a lawyer there for him.'

Max beat me to it with the horrified surprise. 'He can't!'

Smith shook his head. 'I wouldn't advise telling the inspector what he can and can't do.'

'After all we said? After the evidence of the blackmail?'

'I'll admit that if you haven't been telling me a pack of lies then it's a potential motive for those being blackmailed. You've demonstrated that Hocking does not have a reliable alibi for the first murder, but what about the second?'

'We didn't have the chance to find out.'

He snorted. 'Which means we'll have to.'

I thought, That's what you're paid for. I said nothing, though.

He continued, 'And, in any case, Samuel Hocking wasn't found at the bottom of the stairs with Doris Lightoller battered to death at the top.'

'That's not fair,' I protested.

'From our point of view, it is.'

Max tried. 'But you aren't just going to ignore what we've told you, are you?'

He paused. 'I told you. I expect we'll have a chat with Tom Lightoller, make it plain that I know what he's been up to. We'll also warn him about threatening innocent – or, at least, more or less innocent – citizens.'

'And you'll talk to Hocking and the Parrishes?'

'We've talked to them already, but we'll have another chat, I expect.'

'Good.'

As I showed him out, curiosity at last broke me down and I asked, 'How did you get that beautiful shiner?'

'It was when I was off duty. I broke up a brawl outside the Norbury Hotel, during which I got in the way of a swinging fist. Why?'

'Just wondered.'

I closed the door behind him.

Because I'm stupid, I didn't realize what was wrong with all this until we were in bed and drifting off to sleep. When I did, I was at once very much awake.

'Max?'

'Mmm?'

'We're being dim.'

I heard her fighting to come back into consciousness. 'What do you mean?'

'Tom Lightoller wasn't after the blackmail stuff. I'm not sure he even knew about it.'

There was a pause as her cerebral functions kicked into motion again. 'What do you mean?'

'Don't you remember what he said as he looked at it? "Are you taking the mickey?" They're not the words of a man who's just been given his heart's desire, his "inherit-ance".'

She thought about it. 'No, I suppose not.'

'So, if he wasn't after the blackmail evidence, what was he after?'

Another pause before, 'Does it matter? If the Lightollers were murdered because they were blackmailing someone, it's not relevant, is it?'

But I wasn't so sure. I began to suspect that we were very far from getting to the bottom of the Lightollers' deaths.

THIRTY-TWO

There is a certain cosmic inevitability about the fact that it was my father who set us on the right track, although, of course, he did so unwittingly. We had slept as late as we dared, breakfasted quickly and then gone to AMH to visit him, arriving at a quarter to ten. His uniformed companion of that morning was a large Afro-Caribbean policewoman who looked on sternly throughout our visit and never uttered a word; I'm not even sure she changed either expression or posture, a show of stoic implacability that I could only admire.

Dad was getting better and better, now sitting up in bed and moving his head quite freely; his colour was better and the drips were down. There was evidence in his beard that he had breakfasted well. Another welcome advance was that he seemed to be treating Max with more warmth, so that he talked directly to her and had great fun ridiculing me – sure signs that she was being invited mentally into the Elliot fold.

Dad was aware that Masson was coming to undertake a formal interview, but seemed strangely inured to the prospect. He showed no anxiety, no emotion at all when I broached the subject, saying only, 'Well, of course he has to talk to me. I was found at the bottom of the stairs at the same time as poor Doris was killed.'

Despite Masson's warnings, I had turned once again to Alexander Holversum (since I didn't know any other solicitors) and he arrived at just before ten. Every possible facet of him, whether material or spiritual, was twinkling: eyes, teeth, feet, smile and personality.

'Dr Elliot!' he said as he entered the room and there was for a moment some uncertainty as to which Dr Elliot was being addressed; perhaps it was both, I reasoned. It soon became clear, though, that his pronouncement was addressed to my father as he said, 'I am told that you have been seriously injured.'

'Very much so,' confirmed Dad. 'Very much so indeed.'

'But you are better?'

Dad couldn't resist playing the injured soldier. 'A little,' he admitted, adding then, 'a very little.' This last was graced with a sigh, as if he were just being brave about it all.

Holversum turned to me. 'And you, doctor. Are you well?'

'Fine,' I replied, feeling that I was lacking the cachet of a serious head injury and consequent major surgery.

'My dear!' was Holversum's next shot, this time addressed to Max. 'What a pleasure to see you.'

Max didn't exactly blush, but there was something about Holversum that made her smile. 'Thank you very much.'

Masson entered the room and, I have to tell you, the temperature in the room seemed to drop. When he caught sight of me, he scowled and beams of dislike shone over me; the reappearance of Holversum made sure that any chance of a break in the clouds disappeared instantaneously. 'Mr Holversum,' he said. Just like that. Nothing else.

Holversum clearly had his winter long johns on because he didn't notice how frigid the atmosphere was. He smiled and bowed his head as he said, 'Inspector.'

What then followed was neither fascinating nor productive. Masson kept asking my father the same questions – Why did he go into Doris Lightoller's house? How did he get in? Where was Doris when he went in? If there was someone else there, who was it? If he didn't know who it was, what did he look like? Why couldn't he say? – and all the while, Mr Holversum did what Mr Holversum did best, which was to thwart Masson, constantly advising his client to say nothing and to say it loudly. Not that Dad had much to say. He still had amnesia for the critical period just after entering the house, not that Masson professed much belief in this.

'You're not the only person to have caught amnesia in that house,' he observed with his customary sarcasm, looking with great meaning at Max who dropped her eyes with an apologetic grimace.

'Really, inspector?' said Holversum. 'I do hope you're not implying that my client is feigning his illness. He has quite clearly suffered an extremely grave injury and is the innocent victim of a serious assault. He is anything but a criminal.'

'So you say, Mr Holversum. So you say.'

'I do, inspector. I do.'

They looked at each other, Masson with an angry glare, Alexander Holversum with a sweet smile that I am sure was calculated to infuriate rather than appease.

It ended after perhaps thirty minutes with Masson informing Dad that he was technically in custody, under arrest on suspicion of murdering Doris Lightoller, and that he was not to leave hospital under any circumstances. Since Dad wasn't going anywhere for several days, this seemed to be a touch unnecessary. As Masson was leaving the room, he turned to me and said savagely, 'I want a word with you, doctor.'

Outside, he didn't quite pin me to the wall with my feet off the ground – he was about six inches too short to do that – but he did invade my personal space and, were I a lawyer, I am fairly sure that I could have had him for assault as he poked my sternum with a finger apparently made out of oak. 'Smith's been telling me what a prat you are.'

'A bit harsh, inspector.'

'Yes?' he enquired. 'You think so?' It was a rhetorical question. 'I don't, Dr Elliot. I think you have potentially fatally hampered an investigation into a double murder; I think that, if I weren't such a nice, accommodating sort of person, I'd have you charged with perverting the course of justice, breaking and entering, interfering with a crime scene . . .' He ran out of books to throw at me, and had therefore to finish up rather lamely with: 'And half a dozen other crimes.' He was full of self-pity. 'My life is hard enough without all this. Four deaths in three weeks, for goodness' sake. That's not fair, so it's totally out of order that I should also have to put up with amateur sleuths wandering about like Lord Peter Wimsey's bloody butler after a lobotomy.'

'But at least, now you have to admit that it might not be as straightforward as you thought.'

With which, he backed off a bit, perhaps exhausted; it was a relief because his breath was ever so slightly pungent. 'Do I?' he demanded. 'Do I?' There was a pause in which

I thought that maybe he had tossed another rhetorical one into the ring and a stand-off ensued. He broke first. 'I've been to see Tom Lightoller – he seemed to think I was a lunatic, putting to him some cock-and-bull story about threatening and assaulting you; knew nothing about any photographs and private investigation reports. He spent last night at the Masons' dinner, and he's given me a list of names as long as my Aunt Fanny's washing line to corroborate that.'

'Look, inspector. You may not like me, but you do know that I'm not a liar, or a criminal, or stupid. Inexperienced and naive, maybe, but not dishonest. What Max and I told Smith is the truth. Lightoller was a blackmailer and we found the evidence. His son took it from us—'

I was about to go on to say that I wasn't sure that it actually mattered, that maybe there was another motive altogether, but Masson was still fairly steamed up. 'All I know about you, Dr Elliot, is that you are a complete and utter pain in my behind. In future, just stay out of my way, OK?'

With which, and before I could give him another theory to chew on, he was off down the corridor.

Alexander Holversum hung around for five minutes after Masson departed, solemnly informing Dad not to say anything in front of whichever uniform happened to be in the room, and optimistically telling us that they didn't have anywhere near a strong enough case against Dad, something which neither Max nor I considered to be remotely close to the truth.

With Holversum gone, Max and I stayed on but our conversation was somewhat constrained by the spectre who sat in the corner and looked as though she would rather be doing anything else than be with us, and in truth I wanted to tell her that the feeling was mutual. Despite this I told Dad what we had discovered regarding Oliver Lightoller's blackmailing activities and Samuel Hocking's bedroom activities.

'But there's something else, Dad. I know there is. Tom Lightoller's been after something, but it wasn't the private detective's report.'

'I told you Lightoller was a crook. You wouldn't listen, but I knew.'

'Yes, Dad.'

'He never listens to me,' he told Max. 'Always been the same.'

'Has he?' she replied curiously, and rather unfaithfully, I thought.

An enthusiastic nod from my progenitor. At least, I comforted myself as the expected embarrassing story was told, he was showing distinct signs of returning to normality. 'Oh, yes,' he said, 'I remember when he was fourteen – old enough, you'd think, to know better – he insisted on picking at the scab on his knee when he fell off his bike. I kept telling him not to, but he always knew better. Of course, it went septic and he had to spend four days in hospital on intravenous antibiotics.'

'Really?' Max eyed me with mock surprise, as if she would never have believed me capable of such stupidity.

'And that wasn't the only time, far from it.'

I enquired coldly, 'Is this how we're going to spend the time? Embarrass Lance?'

'But Max wants to hear what kind of a person you are. Don't you, dear?'

At which Max nodded enthusiastically and, in disgust, I picked up the *Croydon Advertiser* and cut myself off from the conversation. It was the same old copy I had looked at before, but I would have read the telephone directory with intense concentration just to blot out Dad's humiliating stories.

Now, the *Croydon Advertiser* is, as you may have guessed, the local paper for Croydon and its environs. I didn't take it regularly and had not bothered with it for some weeks. I would imagine it was much like many local papers: week after week full of screaming but ultimately uninspiring head-lines about drunkenness, the theft of bicycles and the exploits of the local football club (Crystal Palace – known, inappro-priately, as 'The Eagles'). Its staff probably prayed every day for some real news and, every so often, they were rewarded. The story of Ricky Baines and Eddie Perry, of course, had been pure unadulterated manna.

Much of what Jessie Trout had told me had been accu-rate, but it proved to have been a somewhat patchy account. Thus, the main thrust – that Ricky Baines and Eddie Perry had robbed a jewellery shop in Covent Garden, during the course of which a prostitute by the name of Eleanor Johnson had been run over, that they had been fairly quickly arrested but that the booty had never been found – was substantially true. It was in the details, though, that I found interest.

It was not jewellery that had been stolen, but unmounted diamonds; only small ones, but then they didn't have to be big to be valuable: two hundred and fifty thousand pounds worth, to be precise. It had all happened twenty-two years ago, since which time Ricky Baines had been inside Wormwood Scrubs and Eddie Perry in Dartmoor. They had been released within weeks of each other, with Ricky Baines taking up residence more or less immediately in a rented property in Greyhound Lane, although how he had afforded to do so was the subject of much speculation. It seemed that Eddie Perry had done a bit of speculation himself and concluded that Ricky was spending money that belonged at least in part to him. He had come looking for Ricky and the diamonds and, what is more, found him.

The boys in blue of the Croydon Constabulary, led by Inspector Masson, had come running as soon as the reports of two shots fired in Greyhound Lane had been received, and they had found Ricky Baines and Eddie Perry in the back room on the ground floor. They faced one another, each with a single bullet wound: Eddie's in the chest, Ricky's in the throat. The house was a tip and the speculation was that Eddie had broken in and been turning the place upside down in his eagerness to get hold of the diamonds, then been disturbed by Ricky. Professor Crawford had concluded that Eddie's wound would not necessarily have been immediately fatal – it had nicked the superior vena cava but missed the heart and the aorta – whereas Ricky's would have been; Ricky had shot first, thought that his man was down and had been fatally mistaken.

Not everyone accepted that explanation, though. A passing motorist claimed to have seen someone sprinting down the road just after the incident, although no one else had seen this phantom and all enquiries regarding it had proved subsequently fruitless. The house and grounds had been thoroughly searched but no jewels found. Inspector Masson was quoted prominently as saying that the case was now officially classified as 'solved'.

What caught my eye was in the last paragraph.

> Eddie Perry did not leave any next of kin. Ricky Baines is survived by his estranged wife. When asked to comment on events, she said, 'I'm not sorry he's dead. He was a bad man and a terrible husband. I feel as though I've been living through a bad dream, and now it's over. I'm going to get the house cleared and then sell it. I just want to start over fresh.

I put the paper down and stared into space as Max burst into delighted giggles over some story about an unfortunate encounter between me and a farmyard cesspit. I thought I could guess who had done the house clearance.

THIRTY-THREE

'It's not blackmail, it's diamonds!' I said to Max as soon as we were out of the hospital and in the car park.

'What?' We were hurrying – I was hurrying – and she was having trouble keeping up.

'Someone's looking for the diamonds, not the file on Hocking's affair with the grocer's wife.'

'How do you know?'

'I just know.'

We had reached the car and I was unlocking her side. As I went around the back she said to me, 'Is that why you were in such a rush to get out of there?'

It was true that I had been impatient to leave but I had thought that I had hidden it well. I had withstood Dad's inexhaustible supply of oh-so-funny stories regarding little Lance and his juvenile idiocy for over half an hour before saying as tactfully as I could, 'I think it's time we got going, Dad.'

He had looked disappointed but in a way only he could manage; it was disappointment cooked in a sauce of disapproval. 'Oh. Are you?'

'Well . . . You know.' His face told me quite plainly that he didn't, but I was experienced enough when dealing with him just to plough straight on. 'Come on, Max.'

With which – and a promise that we would be back that evening – I had hustled her out.

'There are things we need to do.'

I got in and she did likewise. 'Like what?'

'Go to the library.'

'Lance, it's Sunday.'

'Is it?' I'd forgotten.

'What do you want to go for?'

'I want to read the last few weeks' copies of the *Croydon Advertiser*. In particular their coverage of the Greyhound Lane killings.'

'Oh, I've got back copies of that, if you want.'
'You have?'
She nodded. 'For Twinkle.'
'What for?'
'Bedding, of course, silly.'

Max took the *Daily Mail* and the *Mail on Sunday* as well
as the *Croydon Advertiser,* old copies of which she kept in
a pile by the back door of her house; the rabbit hutch was
outside, also by the back door. Sod's law was in full operation and of all the back copies of the *Croydon Advertiser*
that were available to us, the one that I wanted was under
Twinkle's paws and had suffered grievously.

'I need to clean him out, anyway. The neighbours' children are very good about feeding him, but I can't ask them
to do the dirty jobs.'

Thus Twinkle, clearly feeling somewhat aggrieved at being
turfed out of his cosy cubbyhole, was put into his run and
sat in a hunched posture, wrinkling his nose and managing
to look like one angry bunny. I let Max handle him, which
she did with great aplomb and much cooing and stroking;
Twinkle took it all with great disdain and I wondered if the
basic source of his dyspeptic attitude to life in general was
being saddled with such a bloody awful name.

I stood back, too, when it came to removing said pet's
bedding. An aroma of sweet, dusty hay and ammonia flowed
out of the hutch and into our nostrils as Max put the old
bedding into an old plastic shopping bag to expose the
Croydon Advertiser on the floor.

It was damp and variably stained in a huge range of shades
of brown. I took the paper from her and, holding it by my
fingertips, took it into the house.

'Put some fresh paper on the table before you lay that
thing on it,' advised Max. 'I eat at that table.'

Since this was the edition on the Friday after the shoot-
ings, the story took up the whole front page and most of the
following four. There were brief biographies of the dead
men, eyewitness reports (including that of Jessie Trout),
diagrams of the house, background stories on the rising level
of gun crime in the borough of Croydon, and a thundering

leading article demanding increased police presence on the streets.

I started reading with great enthusiasm, sure that the information I was seeking would be easy to find, but soon became disillusioned; it was undoubtedly informative – if somewhat repetitive – but I found little that was new and certainly not what I was after: the name of Ricky Baines' wife.

Max came back inside, washing and peeling off her rubber gloves in the sink. 'Any luck?'

'Not really.'

She came over and sat next to me, reading through the various articles. With the logic that only women know, it was only after a while that she asked, 'What are we looking for?'

I explained and she returned to her reading. She was a quick reader and after only ten minutes was at the bottom of page three and waiting for me to catch up. When I eventually did, she turned the page over and almost immediately said, 'There.'

She pointed to a small photograph of a late middle-aged woman with blonde hair and sharp features. Nadia Baines was quoted as knowing nothing about her husband, that she had been separated from him for six years and, as far as she was concerned, he could 'rot in hell'.

'Charming,' remarked Max.

'I'm not sure we should judge her too harshly. I suspect that the late Mr Baines was not a kind and attentive partner.'

At the end of the piece, though, there was a surprise.

It did not, as I had hoped, give any indication of where she lived, but it did mention where she worked. At the Wimpy Bar, St George Street, Croydon.

I looked again at her photograph. It was the pinch-faced woman behind the counter.

THIRTY-FOUR

I was not looking forward to interviewing Mrs Baines. I suspected that she would not take kindly to anyone taking an interest in her affairs and that dislike would have been honed to a pitch by the fact that we would not be the first. The police and press had got there before us and I knew from my own experience how aggravating these two groups could be when they were doing their jobs. We had driven straight into the centre of Croydon and were now parked just down the street from the Wimpy Bar. As it was Sunday, Croydon took on a different aspect, but one that, to me, was even more forbidding and unwelcoming.

At least during the week and on Saturdays, commuters and shoppers added a dimension of humanity to the grey concrete world that post-war planners had envisaged and built for the delight of the teeming masses. It was as though the powers that be had decided to forgo architectural evolution and plump for revolution. Thus, what had at first seemed like the coming thing – the *Jetsons* and *Flash Gordon* with a hint of *Brave New World*, perhaps – had too quickly become yesterday's bad idea.

The Wimpy Bar was open and the familiar tableau in place: a group of youths looking seriously disaffected, some sort of tramp looking wild-eyed and seriously insane, a gentleman of Mediterranean aspect with the kind of cigarette addiction that suggested his colouring was actually a mix of sun exposure and nicotine staining, and Nadia Baines. Previously unaware of her identity, I had seen her perhaps thirty times before, and on none of those occasions had I been lucky enough to witness her smile. We soon saw that today was to be no exception.

As it was approaching lunchtime, Max and I decided that it would be a wise move to buy something and thereby engineer an introduction; it struck me as an approach fraught with difficulty, but we could think of none other. Accordingly, we entered the smoky atmosphere of the Wimpy and bathed ourselves in the familiar ambience of hostility, grease and grubbiness. The wild-eyed man did his thing, adding for good measure, a bit of wordless talking as if he were going through some sort of incantation; the youth section pretended to ignore us while in actuality talking about us; Mrs Baines and her colleague busied themselves doing nothing.

'Two cheeseburgers, please,' I announced. I was aiming for commanding and insouciant; managed only loud and timorous.

Nadia asked, 'Chips?' I could not detect any real interest in this enquiry.

I looked at Max; we had not discussed this option beforehand. She shook her head and I turned back to our quarry. 'No, thanks.'

'Something to drink?'

Max said, 'Coffee, please.'

I duly reported, 'Two coffees.'

She looked around to her colleague and said tiredly, 'Two cheese.' I felt that communication without verbs might, under certain circumstances, become confusing, but she showed remarkable versatility by then asking of me, 'Eat in or eat out?' Her command, then, of auxiliary verbs was intact.

'We'll eat in here.'

She raised her eyebrows and pursed her lips, possibly surprised at our judgement; was that a shrug I saw?

'That'll be one pound, thirty-eight pence.'

'And one pound thirty-eight pence well spent,' I said as I handed over two pound notes. It sounded, I think because I was uncommonly nervous, a trifle sarcastic. It at least had the advantage of catching her attention, albeit hostile.

She paused, pound notes in hand, till drawer open. 'You what?'

I found that I had no plans for further verbal engagement and therefore stood there, mouth slightly open, staring into her belligerent gaze. Beside me, Max rode to the rescue. 'Mrs Baines?'

Her eyes jerked quickly to the left, narrowing as they did so. 'Who's asking?'

Max's smile was as sweet as it could possibly have been,

but I feared it would have no effect on the incarnation of sourness at which it was aimed. 'You are Mrs Baines, aren't you?'

I glanced around and realized that I shouldn't have. The knowledge that everyone was staring at us did not improve the constitutional crisis my innards were experiencing; even the wild-eyed man was caught up in the action, although he was twitching regularly like a silent metronome. The chef was doing wonders with his spatula, periodically flipping the burgers, then pressing down on them, making them sizzle loudly on the hot plate. The eyes of Nadia Baines were by now slit-like. I suspect she was going to give us some advice regarding where we could go and how we could get there but Max seemed to have less problem with stage fright than I did and forestalled her.

'We're not press and we're not the police.'

The pound notes descended into the cash drawer, held there by a clip that Mrs Baines snapped down with a loud crack. As she slammed the drawer shut, she said, 'I can see that.' There was a distinct tone of derision.

'Can we talk?'

She handed the change back to me. 'I've got nothing to say.'

I decided to join in. 'I'm a doctor, Mrs Baines. I know that you've recently been bereaved, but it's quite important that I ask you a few questions about your husband's death.'

She added a frown to her face. 'What's it got to do with a doctor? Ricky was shot.'

'It's a long story. Can we sit down?'

It took her a long time to decide and I think it would have been against us, except that Max said, 'My father used to beat my mother, Mrs Baines. I know how you feel . . .'

I looked at Max, once again staggered by the size of her audacity, the breadth of her conviction, the depth of her deceit. She was looking at Nadia Baines, eyes as wide as marbles, the merest trace of moisture brimming the lower lids.

The burgers arrived on plastic plates. As she handed them over, Nadia Baines said tersely, 'Five minutes, no more.'

She called over her shoulder, 'I'm taking a break, Manny.'

She did not wait for assent and, indeed, would have waited a long time, because Manny, having scraped the hot plate more or less clean, had retreated behind the *News of the World* with the only movement coming from a curling tendril of smoke that rose from behind it.

We sat around a table just by the till, Nadia opting to do her bit for air pollution with a Players No. 10 while we tucked into our cheeseburgers liberally garnished with tomato ketchup.

'So what's all this about?'

I had been wondering what to say and had decided that honesty was probably best; even if Max's grasp of this rare and precious commodity was somewhat lax, I felt that one of us should remain on the straight and narrow path to salvation. 'My father's under suspicion of murder.'

She was surprised. 'Is he?'

I nodded. 'The police think he killed Oliver and Doris Lightoller.' I watched for a reaction and got one, of sorts.

'The Lightollers? Your old man's the bloke they found in the house, is he? The one in hospital?'

'That's right.'

'I read about that.' She considered things and then asked, 'Why did he do it?'

'He didn't.'

Something that I can only describe as a smirk appeared. 'Yeah, right.'

'He didn't,' I insisted, wondering why everyone automatically thought Dad was guilty. She shrugged; I could say what I wanted, it wouldn't have changed her opinion. I asked, 'Have you ever contacted Oliver Lightoller?'

She handled the cigarette as I would think she imagined elegant and refined people did – film stars and society people – holding it at the tips of her fingers, her lips pursed as she blew out the blue-grey smoke. 'No.'

She said this simply, definitively, without doubt. I asked for clarification. 'No? You're sure?'

'Yes. Why?' It was obvious from the way that she said this that she wasn't lying.

'You didn't ask him to clear your husband's house?'

'No.'

Bugger. I sighed. I had lost my appetite, at which point I realized that I had been staking a lot of hope on getting the right answers in this interview. The door opened and a mother with two small children came in, both talking loudly, clearly excited at the treat ahead. The woman was about thirty, dressed in a thick, pink overcoat; it was starting to rain outside and she had on a clear plastic rain hat that was dotted with drops.

Nadia Baines stood up having stubbed out her cigarette in the cast metal ashtray. 'I've got to get back to work.'

I would have let her go and was on the point of thanking her for her time when Max asked, 'Who did clear the house?'

She stopped and looked back down. 'I don't know.'

Which was surprising. 'Why not?' asked Max.

'Because I didn't arrange it.'

Before we could respond, she went to serve the woman and her children. Max and I exchanged looks; what did that mean? While we were waiting, Max ate the last of her burger with the small, precise bites and contained chewing movements that I was starting to know and love. I just sat there and wondered how she could be so calm, impatient as I was to find out more.

The woman took a tray replete with glasses of Coke, a cup of something and plates of burger and chips to a table near the door. We went back to the counter.

'Excuse me, Mrs Baines, but who did arrange the house clearance?'

She was fed up with the conversation and said tiredly, 'My solicitor.'

OK. Fair enough.

'Can you give us his name so that we can contact him? We really need to know who did the house clearance.'

She shrugged. 'If you like. His name's Holversum. Alexander Holversum.'

THIRTY-FIVE

'**W**hat?'
It was a somewhat hackneyed reaction but a real one. I had thought that we would be given an anonymous name that we would contact to find out what we needed to know, nothing more. 'Holversum?'

She said, 'Yes.' There was the merest of pauses before she added for emphasis, 'Holversum,' and said it in the kind of voice my teachers used when I was being particularly stupid at school.

I looked at Max and she looked at me and I saw in her eyes my own question mirrored. What was the significance of this? Max turned to her. 'Has he always been your solicitor?'

'Ricky's, not mine. He'd represented Ricky for years and years.'

The door opened and two more youths came in and were greeted enthusiastically by those already present. Nadia looked across at them, then back to us. 'If you've finished . . .?'

We could think of no more questions but I wasn't sure if we were irrevocably done. With my brain still trying to work out what this meant – if it meant anything at all – we left the Wimpy Bar and made our way home.

'Mr Holversum?'
'That is I.'
'It's Lance Elliot. Sorry to bother you on a Sunday . . .'
'Think nothing of it, dear boy. What can I do for you?'
'I don't know if I told you this, but I saw something in Mr Lightoller's shop which has me somewhat puzzled.'
'Really? What would that be?'
'A brooch. It belonged to my mother but was stolen from my house about six months ago.'
'Good grief! Are you sure?'
'Absolutely.'

'But I don't understand; how can I help with that?'

We were nearing the nub of things and, I had to admit, I was also feeling that my purported reason for ringing him was somewhat tenuous. I looked across at Max who was looking on with interest. We were in Dad's sitting room, cups of tea in front of us on a low table. I felt slightly sick, the burger lurking in my stomach, a bolus of indigestion.

'It occurs to me that Mr Lightoller did house clearances.'

'He did.'

'So he might have acquired the brooch that way.'

'Yes, I suppose he may.' He sounded puzzled.

'You don't happen to know which houses he might recently have cleared, do you?'

'Me?'

'Yes, well . . .'

'Why should I know such a thing? I hardly knew the man.'

On the face of it, this was a good question. I had reached the tipping point and either now plunged in, or pulled back and lost the initiative. 'I understand that you arranged the clearance of Ricky Baines' house; I don't suppose you used Mr Lightoller, did you?'

There was a long pause at this. I heard him draw in breath before he said, 'Yes, as a matter of fact I did.' *Bingo!* I looked across at Max and nodded with my eyebrows raised. Meanwhile, Holversum was asking, 'But what can that possibly have to do with your mother's brooch?'

I had prepared my explanation, knowing that it would sound pathetic but hoping, thereby, that it would sound authentic. 'Mr Baines was a jewel thief. I just thought . . .'

Holversum's laugh came down the phone complete with a full load of condescension. 'I don't think Ricky Baines had anything to do with the theft of your brooch; he was still enjoying the hospitality of Her Majesty six months ago.'

'Oh, yes.' I waited for a heart's beat, then went on: 'How stupid of me.'

'Oliver Lightoller did many house clearances,' he went on, forgetting that he 'hardly knew the man'. 'He might have picked up the brooch in probably fifty houses.'

'Of course.'

'Is there anything more I can do for you?'

I wasn't entirely planning to say what next came out of my mouth. 'Did you know the Lightollers well?'

His answer came in a slightly different tone, a more defensive one, perhaps a more hostile one. 'I believe that I have already explained my relationship with Oliver Lightoller. I did some legal work for him, nothing more. I did not know his wife at all.'

'Oh, yes. You said.'

'And now, I really must get on. If you have no other questions, doctor?'

I did, but none that I could reasonably ask and, accordingly, I rang off.

Max asked, 'It was Lightoller who did the clearance?'

'Yes.'

'So it's possible that he found the diamonds amongst the possessions.'

I pointed out, 'The police apparently went through the house, practically ripped it apart, and they didn't find them.'

'But they're so small they could have been hidden in anything. I mean, it's not as if we're talking about gold bars or wads of pound notes.'

She had a point and because of that, it seemed hopeless trying to prove anything. Max was right and I felt then that there was nothing more we could do. We had speculation and we had coincidence, but that was all we had. And anyway, what did it matter? Even if we were right, if Lightoller had found the diamonds amongst the possessions in Baines' house, and somebody was doing a lot of killing to find them, it didn't indicate *who*, and certainly didn't point at Holversum, even if he was a little shy about how well he had known the dead antiques dealer.

But Masson clearly had his suspicions about Holversum. He had implied that he was rather too well acquainted with the criminal fraternity, yet did that mean he was himself a criminal? Might Masson's prejudices merely be those of a man who was continually being bested? Certainly, from what I had seen, Holversum's behaviour was guaranteed to outrage and vex someone like Masson, but that didn't in any way mean that he was a murderer. If anything, it seemed somewhat odd that Holversum, were he after the diamonds, should have allowed Lightoller to clear the house. If Lightoller had found them, how had Holversum found out? Why would Lightoller have told him? Wouldn't he have been better advised to keep quiet?

I finished my tea, and looked at my watch. It was half past two and the long stretches of a dull November afternoon lay ahead. Nothing but *The Big Match* and *Kung-Fu* to look forward to on the television. Since the radio offered only delights such as *Down Your Way* or the *Mitchell Minstrel Show*, I turned to Dad's bookshelves for entertainment. Not that I was overly optimistic. My father's fictional entertainment was drawn heavily from John Buchan, Robert Louis Stevenson and Trollope, redoubtable authors all but impossible to characterize as 'light' reading; his non-fiction choices, to describe them charitably, were eclectic, and to describe them realistically, were bizarre. In the end, I plumped for an ancient tome on the English Civil War which I found on the top shelf in the back room. The shelf was so high that I had to stretch even though I was on tiptoe; it was wedged in, too, just to make things really difficult. Because of this, I had to tilt it towards me by pulling on the spine and I almost succeeded, but then the binding tore with a soft rasp.

I was truly mortified; Dad prized his books and he had instilled in me a sense of the importance of them, the reverence with which they should be treated. No book, no matter how old, how peculiar, should be abused. I would not enjoy telling him what I had done, because I knew that he would excoriate me for such vandalism. But perhaps I needn't tell him, I thought; all I had to do was push it back and go and look for something else. It was highly unlikely that he would spot it for years, if ever.

I reached back up, fighting a small pang of guilt and beating it.

As my finger made contact with the spine of the book, I saw for the first time that something had been revealed as the spine had come away from the binding. Old and yellowed, it looked like a folded slip of paper. Intrigued, I changed my mind; I would quite like to take a peek at it, see what it was. Accordingly, I strained every muscle and just managed by so doing to get forefinger and thumb around the book.

Eventually it came free from its cramped home and I had it in my grasp.

In the event, it was inexplicable. In faded ink and a cursive hand that was neat and clearly decades old, it was a billet-doux, asking for a meeting. To Cecily from Bertram, it asked the lady to attend at the War Memorial at seven in the evening on the Tuesday next. It spoke of love and affection, and was somehow Edwardian in its tone and sentiment. I looked at it and thought how strange it was that it had been there for so long and remained undiscovered. Why was it there? Had Cecily hidden it in a hurry as her father had come into the room? Had she been supposedly studying the English Civil War but instead dreaming of this tryst? Perhaps her parents did not approve of this Bertram, had forbidden her from having contact with him.

For a moment, I became inexplicably sentimental, hoping that Cecily had managed to keep her appointment with Bertram, that the relationship had prospered . . .

And then the true significance of the note burst upon me.

THIRTY-SIX

'The inspector's not here.' Smith said warily, as if feeling unprotected.

'Where is he?'

Smith's tone suggested that he didn't take kindly to being the subject of interrogation. 'Out,' was the response.

'It's quite important that I speak to him. Will he be back soon?'

'I'm not too sure. If you like, I'll pass the message on when I see him.' He sounded to me as if it wasn't going to be top of the priority list, though.

'If you could. As I said, it's important that I speak to him.'

'Can I help?'

I hesitated. Maybe he could. 'You remember the petty thief who stole that book from the Lightoller's house?'

'Victor Robbins.'

'That's him. He just stole a book; is that right?'

'Yes. Hang on a minute . . .' There was some faint rustling for a moment or two. 'Here we are. *Diamonds Are Forever* by Ian Fleming. It's an early edition, but not that valuable. At most a tenner.'

I wasn't listening because the fireworks of triumph were exploding in my head. I managed to ask, 'What condition was it in?'

More rustling. 'Fairly tatty. The spine was ripped apart.'

More fireworks. 'Listen, constable, I need to talk to you. I think I know who killed the Lightollers.'

I said to my audience, 'It's Holversum. It has to be.' Max glanced across at Smith to judge his reaction. She had already heard my theory but I don't think she had bought a large number of shares in it, something that made me all the more nervous in front of what was always going to be a difficult audience.

We sat in a cramped office in Norbury police station that

had been made to accommodate two desks, but only by placing them so close together that they practically kissed at one corner. Masson's desk, naturally, was larger and he had more leg room; Smith looked, in comparison, like a large schoolboy squashed behind his. From the expression on his face, I guessed that at least one of his legs had gone to sleep. The chairs on which Max and I sat were similarly intimate, so that she was almost, but not quite, keeping my left knee pleasantly warm.

Smith looked perplexed. 'Has to be what?'

'The killer.'

For a moment, he looked startled, as if I'd accused Masson, then that smile again; he really did think I was an idiot. 'Holversum?'

Max was giving me looks that melded sympathy with 'I told you so', and Smith was shaking his head slowly again, which I've always thought is not a good sign. 'That's right.'

'Alexander Holversum?' he asked for clarification as if the case were riddled with them.

'If you'd only hear me out—'

'Are you sure about that, doctor? Your track record isn't good. Samuel Hocking and both the Parrishes all have alibis for the time that Doris Lightoller was being killed.'

'I'll admit that our theories regarding Samuel Hocking were probably a bit off the mark . . .'

'Completely and utterly wrong, you mean. At the time of Doris Lightoller's death, Hocking was visiting his mother in Kennington. She's in a home and four of the staff have corroborated his alibi. The Parrishes were at a rehearsal for the Norbury Amateur Dramatics Society production of *Snow White and the Seven Dwarves*.'

'It's not about blackmail.'

Smith didn't seem to be listening. 'Samuel Hocking also denies he was ever blackmailed.'

Max came to my defence. 'They're all lying about that!'

Smith said only, 'Very probably. That doesn't change the fact that, as a story, it is completely and utterly unsupported by any evidence.'

'But you're not listening, constable. I told you, this whole business had nothing to do with the blackmail. It's all connected with Ricky Baines' diamonds.'

For the first time during the conversation, I gained the advantage. Smith was surprised into silence by what I had said, allowing me to plough my furrow a little further. 'Holversum was an old associate of Ricky Baines, wasn't he? He'd represented him on many occasions in the past, he represented him when he was sent to prison for the jewellery shop robbery.'

'Holversum? Alexander Holversum?' Smith sounded worryingly incredulous.

'Yes. You said yourself that he was a bit dodgy.'

'Dodgy, yes, but not a double murderer.'

It wasn't going well. 'The petty thief, Robbins; Masson said that it was Holversum who was representing him.'

Smith sighed; I got the impression that he felt sorry for me. 'That's what Holversum does. He defends the real criminals. As soon as he turns up in the station, you might just as well put on a striped jersey, black beret and mask, because only the criminal uses him. Not many honest people come to him, so the ones who do – like your father – tend to get looked at askance.'

'You said that all Robbins stole was a book. *Diamonds Are Forever.*'

'That's right.'

I was looking at him, unable to believe that he had missed the significance. 'See?'

'See what?'

'*Diamonds Are Forever.*'

But he was either genuinely obtuse or making a good impression of it. 'What about it?'

'Diamonds.'

He smiled condescendingly. 'Oh, yes. Of course. Silly me.'

Before I could go for his throat, Max said, 'It's a funny thing to steal isn't it? An old book?'

'He didn't have time to find anything more. You interrupted him and he just grabbed what he hoped was valuable and scarpered.'

'Is that what he says?'

Smith smiled. 'Robbins is saying nothing because he's taking Alexander Holversum's advice.'

'And you're certain that it was Lightoller's book?'

'We have our reasons for believing so.'

'What are they?'

'There was a recent receipt made out to Oliver Lightoller tucked in the back.'

'That's not proof of ownership, or that Robbins stole it from Lightoller,' I pointed out.

'And also we've found it listed in Lightoller's records.'

'Do his records say where he got it?'

For the first time, Smith was uncertain. 'No, I don't think so. They just include the date that he acquired it.'

'Which was when?'

Smith had to consult a file that was at the bottom of a foot-high pile on the floor by his chair; as if that weren't already inaccessible enough, a portable typewriter was precariously balanced on the top of everything. Eventually, and slightly red of face, he came back up for air and said, 'October 29th.' His injured eye, now healing well, was accentuated by the blush of blood to his skin.

'And when did Ricky Baines have his house cleared?'

But this was beyond his knowledge. 'Why?'

'Because I'll bet a pound to a penny that it was on October 29th. Lightoller did Ricky Baines' house clearance and that's where he got that book.'

I could see that, despite himself, Smith was starting to become just a little intrigued; not convinced – very far from that – but certainly no longer just condescending. He asked thoughtfully, 'And if it was?'

'You said that the spine was ripped.'

'So?'

'That's where the diamonds were hidden. In the spine of the book.'

Two ginger eyebrows met for a confab in the middle of Smith's face. 'Let me get this clear. You think that Ricky Baines hid the stolen diamonds in the spine of this book and that Lightoller found them?'

'More or less.'

'Meanwhile, Alexander Holversum knew where they were, and killed the Lightollers to get his hands on the book.'

'Exactly. He killed Lightoller, then searched the shop.

When he couldn't find it there, he went after Doris. He was interrupted by Dad before he could properly search the house, so sent Robbins back to find the book, which he did.'

Smith thought some more. I glanced at Max, who was in turn looking at Smith with a look of deep worry on her face. After a while, Smith asked, 'Could you clarify a few things about this theory?'

'If I can.'

'Where are the diamonds now?'

I admit, that he had me on that one. 'I don't know.'

He nodded, as if he understood my problem. 'Well, we can assume that Holversum doesn't have them, I think.'

'Can we?'

'I think so, because if he did, Robbins wouldn't still have had the book, would he? Unless Holversum took the diamonds from it and then gave it back to him, which is unlikely.'

I saw what he meant. 'No, I suppose not.'

'So,' he went on, 'the fact that Robbins still had the book suggests strongly that he hadn't made contact with Holversum by the time we picked him up. This, in turn, suggests that the book was probably in that condition when he stole it . . . unless you're hypothesizing that Robbins took the diamonds.'

I began to sense danger in his words. 'No . . .'

'So whether or not Robbins has a connection with Holversum, neither of them has the diamonds.'

It took me a moment to catch up, but I had reluctantly to agree with him. 'I suppose not.'

He then asked simply and directly, 'So where are the diamonds?'

I had anticipated the question but it had done me no good; I didn't know. I tried to put a good gloss on it, though. 'I'm not entirely sure.'

To his credit, he didn't crow or even smile. All he said was, 'Neither am I,' and he said it sadly.

Max decided that it was time to play the part of the cavalry. 'How do we know Robbins didn't take the diamonds?'

This produced silence. How *did* we know?

Smith said eventually, 'Because if the diamonds were in

that book and Robbins took them, he'd have disposed of the book pretty sharpish. He'd have claimed to Holversum that he never found it.'

We digested this for a moment before Max tried again. 'In which case, Lightoller found them. He and Holversum were in league to share the money, but Lightoller found the diamonds, wouldn't hand them over and got killed for his trouble.'

'Theories are very nice, but as far as I can make out, you have no proof of any of this – no proof that it's Holversum and not even any proof that it's about diamonds. And why Holversum? Why not Tom Lightoller? It was only a day or two ago that you were telling me that he was after "his inheritance". If anyone employed Robbins, it's more likely to be him, I'd have thought.'

'So you admit that Robbins might have been employed by someone to snatch the diamonds?'

'I said, "if anyone employed Robbins"; once again, there's no proof of any of this, is there?'

'But Holversum's name keeps cropping up . . .'

He had the perfect riposte.

'So does the name of Elliot.'

THIRTY-SEVEN

'I can't blame him,' I said gloomily as we drove back. 'All we've got is speculation to support our theories, we have no proof.'

'No, I suppose not.' Max said this from deep in thought. Then: 'The question is, how are we going to find it?'

My eyes were on the road and it was only with the greatest of efforts that they remained so as she said this. The striking thing was that her tone was so matter-of-fact; it had not occurred to her that there was any other course of action.

'Now, wait a moment—'

'Lance, of course we have to prove it. For your father's sake, if nothing else.'

It sounded dangerous and I said as much, but Max had no truck with this. 'Pooh! I never realized what a rabbit you are, Lance.'

'Two people have already been murdered.'

'That was because someone thought that they had the diamonds. No one any longer thinks we have them.'

'Even so, Max. I think we've done all we can.'

She didn't reply.

Because I'm stupid, I thought nothing of it.

The next morning we were both going back to work. Max seemed subdued over breakfast and, when I asked her what was wrong, she said only, 'Nothing.' She said it distantly, though; I assumed that she was sickening for something, although she denied this. I dropped her off at her house at eight o'clock where we kissed and I promised to ring her that evening, after I had been to see Dad. Uncharacteristically, during all this time she barely said a word and I admit to being sorely puzzled as I drove on to the surgery.

Were my colleagues pleased to see me back? I suppose so, although it took much searching and not a little imagination to find the signs. After some fairly perfunctory questions on my father's condition, Brian told me in exhaustive detail how hard life had been, how the winter flu epidemic was really beginning to take off, how he thought he might be coming down with it himself, etc. etc. while Jack just asked sarcastically if I was well rested. Only our staff exhibited what I considered to be an appropriate attitude towards a man whose father is recovering from a life-threatening illness. Jane seemed to think that maybe I had found the whole thing extremely stressful and showed some empathy for me, while our two receptionists, Sheila and Jean, kept tutting whenever they saw me and then looking at each other in that way that only women of a certain age can achieve. It was all pretty much as I expected: just another working day.

When I got to see Dad, he was sitting in a chair and looking very much his old self. He moaned at me for an hour and I kept telling myself that it was a lot better to have him moaning and alive than silent and not. Percy Bailey was back on duty in the corner, looking as if a few hours of Dad's unique blend of surreal non sequiturs liberally sprinkled with scathing dissatisfaction with the universe had worked their magic on him, and that he ought to be a front-runner for the Queen's Gallantry medal. As I left, I said to him in a whisper, 'Hard going?'

He grimaced and said in a low tone, 'Bloody hard these chairs.'

I knew what he meant, though.

I got home at about eight, the night becoming enveloped in fog and dankness. As always happened, sounds became dulled, as suffused as the yellow-brown street lights, the whole world a thing of creepiness. In the hallway, I debated whether to ring Max or have something to eat first; as it happened, the decision was taken from my hands because the phone rang and I discovered Max on the end of the line. We went through the usual formalities and once again I detected that all was not well with my soulmate; this time, however, I discovered what it was because she told me.

Her confession came in the lull in the duologue which followed her asking how Dad was and me telling her.

'Lance?'

'That's me.'

'I think I might have done something a little unwise.' Her voice betrayed a degree of hysteria that found me feeling a trifle worried.

'Unwise?'

'Yes . . .'

I knew that Max could understate for England, so I was becoming dreadfully afraid at this point. 'In what way, Max?'

There was a pause. 'I had this idea.'

Max had ideas like plague rats had fleas; it meant trouble, and usually it was trouble for me. In this respect she could have been using the same plans as my father; I found myself wondering if this was actually telling me something very significant about my psyche.

'What have you done, Max?'

'We didn't have any proof of who it was, did we?'

'Who what was?'

'Who the murderer was; who was after the diamonds . . .'

Oh, no . . .

'So I got the idea that we could do what they do in the movies.'

I tried to keep the tremor out of my voice as I enquired, 'And what do they do in the movies?'

'They smoke the baddy out.'

Baddy. In the use of that word, Max told me an awful lot of how she saw the world. 'You decided to 'smoke' the killer out?' I asked, just on the off chance that I was panicking unnecessarily.

I wasn't.

'I hope you don't mind.'

'How have you tried to smoke him out, Max?'

'I rang Mr Holversum and I told him that we had gone back into the Lightollers' house and found the stolen diamonds.'

I couldn't speak for a moment; it was an odd feeling but one I was used to given the fact that I had been brought up by my father. Max kindly left me alone for a few moments until I once more had the sacred gift of speech. 'What did he say?'

'He went quiet for a while, then asked why I was telling him.'

'To which, of course, you replied . . .?'

'I said that we thought it was something he might like to know . . .'

That didn't sound too bad, I thought. Then she went on: 'And that unless he contacted us within the next twenty-four hours, we would go to the police and share with them what we knew.'

At which my legs – until then doing their best but feeling distinctly under the weather and very definitely on the wobbly side – buckled completely and I sat down heavily on the stool by the telephone table. She began to say something. 'And there's one more thing—'

I, though, was in the middle of exploding. 'You do realize what you've done, don't you?'

A longish gap followed before Max said somewhat plaintively, 'It seemed like a good idea.'

'Max, if Holversum's killed two people because of those diamonds, he's not going to stop at killing a couple more, is he?'

'He might not be the killer,' she pointed out. Her voice was slightly strangled as if she were holding back a sneeze or something.

'He might be, and his idea of coming to some arrangement might involve one or both of us getting very dead.'

'No, I'm sure . . .'

'Are you?' I asked. 'Are you absolutely sure, Max?'

To which she said, 'No,' and then burst into tears. I felt immediately awful and tried to stop her but it was to no avail. She howled down the phone at me and every second made me feel more and more like a pig. I ended up assuring her that she had done exactly the right thing and that I had been totally unreasonable in getting in a stew about it.

And all the time I was wondering what she had done. Maybe we were wrong and the stolen diamonds had nothing to do with the affair, and maybe Holversum wasn't a killer – Tom Lightoller, was a distinct possibility, too – and neither Max nor I was in the firing line, but what if we weren't? What if Max had just told a man who was willing to kill to get his hands on the diamonds that I had them and that she knew I had them?

'I'm coming over to get you, Max. Don't answer the door to anyone else but me.'

The fog had grown a lot thicker; whereas before it had been patchy, now it was intensely thick and claustrophobic. It reached into the house as soon as I opened the door five minutes later; immediately I was wondering what was hiding in it, who was watching me, who was thinking of killing me. I had tried to phone Masson but had been told that he had been in conference at Croydon police station all day and couldn't be disturbed.

A journey that should have taken less than ten minutes took twenty but at least in the car I felt reasonably safe, once I had checked underneath it for bombs and the ignition had started the car and not triggered a detonator. Max was waiting for me and we were back at my house in another twenty minutes. Her face was tear-stained, her eyes large, possibly with fear, possibly with remorse. She kept looking around us in the fog. There were a few people walking along the pavements, one or two with a dog on a lead, others with no obvious purpose, but who they were was impossible to say.

Back safely inside, the atmosphere lightened and I began to think that I had been unnecessarily spooked by the fog and my fears. I said to Max, 'I'm sure nothing's going to happen, but it's just as well to take precautions.'

She nodded. She still wasn't talking much. I asked, 'Have you eaten?'

A shake of her head.

'Well, the menu's changed, but I expect I can make an omelette.'

'Fine,' she said.

In the kitchen she stood and watched me beating eggs in a glass bowl. I said conversationally, 'I expect even now Holversum's sitting at home wondering what you were talking about.'

'Lance . . .?'

'It wasn't a bad idea, in its way. It could have been a quick way to get at the truth, but Holversum's probably got nothing to do with it. I mean, thinking about it, Tom Lightoller's a far likelier bet. I wouldn't put it past him to murder his parents for money.'

'Lance . . .?' This was said more loudly.

I stopped beating. 'What is it?'

Her eyes were even larger as she looked at me.

Then . . .

'I rang Tom Lightoller, too.'

At which point a baseball bat came through the glass in the back door of the kitchen.

THIRTY-EIGHT

n the next thirty seconds, an awful lot happened. I dropped the bowl and four half-whisked eggs, Max first squeaked, then screamed, and Igor, then Igor's friend (whom I had last seen helping with Doris Lightoller's body) and lastly Tom were in the room. Aforementioned small psychopath looked down at the egg and broken glass mess at my feet and tutted. 'Oh, dear. You've made a mess.'

The fact that he had done serious damage to my back door and was now standing in quite a bit of broken glass of his own direct making seemed to have passed him by. Igor's friend laughed at his boss's witticism but perhaps it passed Igor by because he had to concentrate on breathing regularly and standing upright. My heart was beating so fast and so loudly that I swear I could feel a slight pain as it thudded against my chest wall; Max had scurried to my side and was hiding partly behind me. I thought briefly about outrage, then remembered the last time I had made a nuisance of myself with Igor in the room and abandoned that thought.

It was with a slightly tremulous voice that I said, 'Hello, Tom.'

He nodded, looked around. 'Nice kitchen. Nicer than your old man's.'

'It was,' I said.

At that he looked back at the door and said, 'Sorry about that.'

Max shivered and I'm sure that it wasn't just because of the cold dampness that was seeping into the room. I put my arm around her and squeezed gently. 'What can we do for you, Tom?'

He frowned. I realized then that Tom had two frowns; one was the slightly quizzical version he used when he suspected that someone was 'taking the mickey'; the other was the one that he used when he *knew* that someone was 'taking the mickey'. It was the latter one he used now.

'You what?'

'What can we do for you?' I repeated. Max squeezed my arm again, although I'm not sure why.

'Are you taking the mickey?'

'No.' I wasn't; I was sure of that.

He opened his mouth, deepened his frown a little, looked first to his left at Igor, then to his right at Igor's little helper, then back to me. 'DO FOR ME?'

It made both of us jump and in the course of which Max tightened her grip on my arm so much that tears came to my eyes. I sighed. 'Point taken.'

And immediately he was happy again; he took in some breath, flexed his neck a little and then said in something that might have been relief, 'Good man.' Another sigh, then: 'Shall we go and sit somewhere a little more comfortable?'

I took them into the living room where we sat in a rather incongruous party: Tom, Max and I on the comfy chairs, with Tom's chums on the two dining chairs that I couldn't fit around the table in the dining room. It was a motley crew, all right, and it could only have been more surreal if we had offered to serve up tea and chocolate fancies to them while discussing the hymns for next Sunday's sermon.

'I'm glad you saw sense,' said Tom. He sat back in his seat, perfectly relaxed, perfectly at ease, although all three of them had made dirty wet footprints on the carpet which Max had seen and might even have told them about had I not strenuously shaken my head whilst making wild-eyed expressions at her.

'You see, Tom . . .'

'I thought you were taking the mickey when you gave me that crap about the baker's love life.'

I smiled. 'Merely a misunderstanding.'

He nodded. 'I see that now. Mind you, you were a bit near the knuckle sending the inspector round to have a chat.'

'Terribly sorry.'

He pondered for a moment. 'I see what you was up to now, though. In fact, I like your style. Like it a lot.'

This had me a trifle perplexed. 'Do you?'

'Oh, yes. When I got to think about it, I realized you were

playing a clever game. Very subtle, I thought. We all did, didn't we?'

This last was addressed to the rest of the team, who nodded, albeit without obvious sign of comprehension. He then turned back to us. 'And then your girlie's call. I like that, too.'

I had the feeling he was talking across me, at an oblique angle, so that the meaning of his sentences only appeared to head in my direction while missing me completely. I hazarded my response: 'I thought you would.'

He liked the fact that I agreed with him, seemed to want everyone to. 'Nice touch.'

'One does one's best.' I shot a glance at Max who was looking at the two of us as if we were both mad and, who knows, perhaps we both were.

One final nod before he smacked his hands together and said, 'And now, to business.'

'Yes,' I said nervously. 'To business.'

'You have something I want, I think.'

'Yes, well, I wanted to speak to you about that . . .' I began.

But then Max joined in. 'There's been a bit of a misunderstanding.'

For a second he was perplexed, then angry, then he broke into a wide grin. 'Oh, that!' he said. 'You've no need to worry about that.'

Once again I had the feeling that Tom and I were out of phase somewhere. I would have probed a little more deeply had he not continued: 'I fully understand. Business is business. The ends justify the means. You can't make an omelette without cracking eggs.'

It could have been a reference to our aborted supper, but I don't think Tom's mind worked along such lines. Whatever this gibberish meant, we had no need to worry, since he had embarked on something of a soliloquy. 'In my line, you tend not to be squeamish, else you don't last long. You never saw an undertaker who didn't want to touch a bit of cold flesh and, once you lose that inhibition, well, things take on a different perspective.'

Were all undertakers like this? Was it a side effect of the business of embalming – a process that I knew involved inserting pointed pipes into various body cavities and flushing out as much blood as possible – that you became certifiably bonkers? My covert look at Max told me that she, too, was considering the same imponderables.

'I've done a really nice job on Mum and Dad,' he said at this juncture and I thought at once, A confession!

He was lost in thought for a moment and I wondered what horrors he was recalling. It was clear that he was a 100 per cent, unalloyed, true-blue and gold-certified psychopath. Surely, only a beast such as this could so cold-bloodedly consider the murder of his parents.

'Nothing but the best, of course,' he said.

Which was odd, even for a madman. Max asked tentatively, 'What do you mean?'

'English oak coffins, silk linings, real brass fittings. I'm quite looking forward to the cremation tomorrow.'

'You're talking about the funeral?' I asked.

He was surprised. 'Of course. It's tomorrow at two p.m.' He paused. 'What else would I be talking about?'

'Not the murders?'

This was met with frown number one. 'No. You did those.'

'No, we didn't,' I said firmly.

Max followed up with: 'We thought you did.'

'Me?'

Max, who hadn't worked out the signals vis-à-vis frowning and therefore did not notice that we were in danger of moving on to number two, nodded. 'Yes, you.'

There was the proverbial calm and then: 'ME?'

Max jumped, but only a little. The rest of us were clearly more inured and didn't even do any eyelid batting. I tried to explain, 'You're after the diamonds. We thought that you had killed your parents to get them.'

His expression was comical: open-mouthed and wide-eyed, he had stopped breathing, and behind him, although Igor was staring straight ahead as per normal, his colleague was shaking his head slowly.

I said as gently as I could, 'I see you didn't.'

'You thought I had done Mum and Dad in?' He couldn't believe it, as his tone – one of stupefied wonder – told us.

'Sorry,' I said, just in case he was taking umbrage.

'But you did it,' he pointed out.

'No, we didn't.'

'But you've got the diamonds.'

'No, we haven't.'

Bit by bit I was dismantling his belief system. He indicated Max. 'But she said you did.'

'I said that to smoke you out,' Max explained.

'What the bloody hell does that mean?'

Max had the grace to look embarrassed. 'Well, we thought that whoever killed your parents had done so for the diamonds. You were after the diamonds, so we thought that you were the murderer.'

'You think I killed my parents?' I fully expected that we were in for a dose of frown number two followed by a bit of bellowing, but I then realized that he was completely taken aback by the concept of being the killer of his mother and father. He was, it seemed, a loving child.

'It seemed likely,' I admitted.

For several moments we were cast into silence, as Max and I looked at Tom, and he sat glumly staring into the television that was switched off. The eruption, when it came, was slow in starting but worth waiting for. He began by shaking his head in a way that might at first have been sorrowful but rapidly became clearly incandescent. He then passed quickly from frown number one, on through two and was well on his way to an unprecedented number three before he found voice and a Vesuvian eruption followed.

'NO! YOU ARE TAKING THE MICKEY!'

There seemed no point to me in entering into a debate but Max gave it a go. 'No, Tom, we're not—'

'YES, YOU ARE!' He was getting hoarse and I think that was why he toned it down a bit from then on. He was now breathing quite heavily, in fact almost panting, and becoming more and more agitated. 'I'm being stupid, Arnie.' He addressed this to the little chap who, clearly knowing on which side his bread was buttered, was nodding enthusiastically. 'I'm losing my touch, I am. I almost fell for their scam. This was designed to put me off, make me think that they're a couple of innocent idiots.'

Under other circumstances I would have taken exception to his use of this rather pejorative term, but I bit down hard on my tongue. Tom stood up. 'It's like I thought all along. Your old man was after the diamonds and he killed Mum and Dad to get them. You've dreamed this up just to throw me off the scent.' He was pacing now, and becoming ever angrier. 'Yes . . . yes, I see it now. You and him are nearly clean away, aren't you? I'm the only one who suspects you, so if you can persuade me, then no one's going to think to look in your direction.' He was nodding at his own brilliance. 'What do you say, Arnie?'

'I think you're right, Mr Lightoller.'

He turned back to us. 'Good. So do I. Now, where are they?'

'We haven't got them,' I said tiredly.

He snapped his fingers. 'Arnie. Malcolm.'

I remember thinking, *Malcolm?*, then everything went blurry again. My field of view was immediately severely restricted by the rather unpleasant sight of Malcolm's trousers as he came to stand in front of me and then that familiar feeling of being throttled came upon me as his hand clamped its rather sweaty fingers around my neck and, at the same time, he lifted me with that arm alone to a standing position. I dimly heard Max do her familiar squeak as Arnie went for her and through watering eyes I saw him standing behind her, his left arm around her neck while his right hand was forcing her into a half nelson.

Tom said brightly, 'Now. You know the routine. Where are the diamonds? Where is my inheritance?'

Max said in a voice that was encouragingly combative although agonized, 'We don't know. We honestly don't know . . . ow!'

When I heard that I tried a bit of struggling but Malcolm put a stop to that by grabbing my manly vegetables and squeezing so that I did a bit of squeaking of my own. Throughout this, his expression did not change.

Tom shook his head. 'No, I don't believe you. One last chance. Where are the diamonds?'

I tried to speak but could only manage a feral noise. There was a pounding in my head that was growing louder and more booming, and in my eyes there was a throbbing that was so painful I thought something was sure to burst. Max had given up on being combative and had settled for straight agonized. 'We honestly don't know!'

'Wrong answer.' He sighed. 'The wrong answer.' Then, brightly: 'Now. Who shall it be first?'

'Please believe us,' begged Max. 'We don't know. We never found them.'

Tom came over to Malcolm and me, and stood beside his pet gorilla, dwarfed in stature but not authority by him. He had a wide grin on his face exposing perfect teeth replete with two gold crowns. 'You?' he asked.

Then he swivelled round to face Max; her face was bright pink becoming worryingly blue at the lips. 'No!' he announced loudly, then pointed at Max. 'You!'

As he strode over to where she was sitting, he said to Arnie, 'Make her squeal.'

THIRTY-NINE

And Max squealed. I struggled but all Malcolm did was to tighten the grasp of both his hands and I soon stopped. Then Max squealed again . . .

The door burst open and in came Constable Smith, followed by three burly forms in the dark-blue sackcloth that passes for high-end tailoring in the constabulary. A lot of confusion followed, much of which passed me by, since my attention was wholly taken up by the relief as first my throat and then my private parts were released. I fell back into my chair but already my thoughts were on Max. Malcolm was just standing there, the arrival of a contingent of plod apparently causing central nervous system overload, so he did nothing when I struggled to my feet and headed for her. Arnie, meanwhile, demonstrated that he had a few more functioning neural pathways by releasing Max and backing away from the approaching wave of blue, looking around for an exit route. Tom was alternating between frowns number one and number two, his mouth quivering, eyes wide as he stood in the middle of the room and presumably tried to think of explanations.

Smith went for Tom, two of his friends went for Malcolm and the fourth went for Arnie. Max had slumped back in her chair, still conscious but in a lot of pain. I hugged her as hard as I could while around me a fair amount of tussling, struggling, blasphemy and breaking of my property went on. Only Tom didn't struggle and, after Constable Smith had whispered into his ear, he said in a loud voice, 'OK, lads. Enough's enough.'

After that, it all went a bit quiet. Malcolm, Arnie and Tom were led away by Smith and the three uniforms while I sat with Max in the mess that was the living room, each with a glass of brandy. I had checked her arm and it was still intact, and her throat seemed to have suffered no serious harm; various parts of my body to which I was rather attached

ached appallingly but only time would tell if they had suffered serious permanent damage. Max was shaking quite badly but I didn't say anything because I was shaking more.

Eventually Smith returned and sat opposite us as we hunched together on the sofa. His black eye had almost gone as he sat there, relaxed and happy. 'Tom and his friends have been escorted back to the station. We can relax a bit.'

I looked around at the mess in the room, thinking that I had a lot of clearing up to do. He caught me looking around and said complacently, 'We got here just in time.'

Max asked plaintively, 'How did you know?'

He smiled broadly. 'Holversum.'

Which surprised me. 'Holversum?'

'He phoned the station this evening and told us about a peculiar phone call he'd received from you. He had been pondering what to do about it, and then decided that contacting us would be the best thing to do.'

Max and I looked at each other. We hadn't discussed it, but clearly both of us had assumed that now Tom Lightoller had shown himself innocent of the murders, it must be Holversum who was the guilty party. Smith was prattling on, though. 'The inspector and I discussed it, and he decided that I should come over and see you, try to find out what it was you were up to.'

I heard the words, wondered why my head was whispering a question to me. That was surely a lie. Why would he lie? 'With three hefty colleagues?' I said. 'That was prescient.'

He laughed. 'Oh, no. I came on my own, but when I got here, I saw Tom Lightoller's van outside and wondered what was going on. I thought it wise to do a bit of reconnoitring first, and that way discovered the damage done to the back door. I stayed back but saw Tom and his heavies hustling you out of the kitchen. I called for backup straight away.'

'Thank God you did,' I said fervently.

'You can say that again. I think he was about to do you a bit of damage, miss.'

She laughed nervously. 'Just a bit.'

He nodded earnestly. 'Still, all over now.'

'Absolutely,' I agreed. I had thought about offering him some brandy but decided against it given that well-known dictum concerning 'drink and duty'. I had seen *The Sweeney* – quite enjoyed it, too – but still couldn't come to believe that this was how the police really behaved. Smith surprised me, though.

'I couldn't have one of those, could I?'

'Brandy?' I asked. 'Yes, of course. Ice?' He declined and I went to the kitchen to get another glass and when I returned Smith was leaning forward talking earnestly to Max, trying to reassure her that Tom Lightoller would be charged with breaking and entering, assault, illegal detention, and whatever else they could think up. I filled the glass, then handed it to him.

'Many thanks,' he said, taking the glass and then some of the brandy; in fact, taking quite a lot of it. A sigh. 'That's better.'

I said conversationally, 'You look stressed.'

He had been looking at the carpet but at my question paid attention to me. 'You're right there.' He was shaking his head, and had already finished the brandy. 'It's been bloody busy over the past few weeks, what with the deaths of Baines and Perry, then the murder of the Lightollers.'

Things were going around in my head; not normal things, but fantastical objects, dreamlike concepts. 'You'd only just arrived when it all kicked off, hadn't you?'

His attitude changed; just slightly, but noticeably. 'That's right.'

I took a sip myself. 'And the work's not over yet.'

He shook his head sadly. 'No.'

'If it wasn't Tom Lightoller and it wasn't Alexander Holversum, then who killed Doris and Oliver?'

Smith was lost in reverie but came back to answer my question. 'It was your father, wasn't it?'

But he asked it in what was almost a teasing manner, and he had trouble suppressing a smile as he did so.

'No, it wasn't,' I replied calmly.

He considered. 'I must admit that it's always struck me as a poor motive for a double murder,' he said. 'An argument about blocked access, a few inches shaved off the boundary, a stolen watch.'

'Have you told Masson of your doubts?'

He shook his head sadly. 'The inspector's a very good policeman, but he's a bit prone to irritability.'

'Tell me about it.' I felt suddenly elated; at last someone was listening to us. 'He's closed his mind completely to any other possibility.'

'And any other motive,' he agreed.

'Exactly.'

This was going swimmingly. The stress of the evening's events was dissipating as the brandy did what brandy does and Smith's confessions worked a bit of their own magic. Max had at last relaxed against me and might even have been dozing off. I offered Smith another glass of brandy which he accepted readily.

Having satisfied his desires, I sat back down and he took another sip. 'Very nice.'

I concurred; I would have been very upset if he hadn't liked it, in fact. I had bought the stuff on a holiday in southern France about three years ago and it had cost me a bomb. 'Constable, I don't want to put you in a difficult position, but is there anything you can do to influence the inspector?'

He pursed his lips, drew in a whistling breath. 'That's difficult, very difficult.'

'I know, but if anyone has any influence with him, it must be you.'

He smiled sadly. 'There are two pretty big obstacles in the way of success.'

Max asked, 'What?'

He took another large sip of the brandy and, as he did so, I watched a worryingly large amount of money disappear into his buccal cavity. 'Well, firstly, I've learned that the inspector is a stubborn man. A very stubborn man indeed.'

It was a sentiment with which I could heartily recur. 'And the other?'

'That's an even bigger obstacle.'

Max and I looked at each other; he sounded so sad. 'What is it?'

'I don't want to.'

I didn't know what to say but, bless her, Max did. 'But you must! If you think that Lance's father is innocent, it's your duty to make sure that he isn't wrongfully convicted.'

He nodded enthusiastically. 'Absolutely, absolutely,' he agreed. 'And in normal circumstances, I'd be right there in his office tomorrow morning telling him just where he's going wrong . . .'

'But?'

'But these are not normal circumstances.' With which he uttered a deep sigh.

Max asked incredulously, 'Why not?'

I sighed; Max had missed the subtle but quite distinct transformation in Smith. His hand was in the pocket of his raincoat; if it had been Masson, I would have been fairly convinced he was feeling for cigarettes, but Smith didn't smoke. 'I think that the good constable is trying to intimate that it suits him to have my father as the one and only suspect.'

'Why?'

To Smith, I said, 'There's no proof. I haven't a shred of anything approaching evidence to implicate you.'

Max gasped and Smith took a gun from his pocket. 'But you've been putting things together in your head, haven't you?'

'What things?'

'My arrival in the neighbourhood just before the Greyhound Lane killings for one.'

'That's nothing but a coincidence.'

He shook his head. 'It just needs a single question to start people digging. Maybe they'd find something out, then something else, then, before you know it . . .'

Max asked in a high-pitched voice, 'You're the killer?'

That smile again. 'Terribly sorry.'

FORTY

I t wasn't a very big gun, and maybe it wouldn't have made very big holes in me, but I wasn't an expert and thought it safer to take a cautious stance on the issue. Max had resumed her act with the big staring eyes and she was using them to stare intensely at the barrel of said gun. Smith was again crouched slightly forward, his elbows on his knees, the handle of the gun in both hands.

I thought it wise to initiate some conversation. 'Why did you kill them?'

'It's a long story.'

'I think we've got time.'

His smile this time was less than encouraging as he said, 'Don't bet on it.'

'Start, at least.'

'The detective duo have been expending a lot of energy trying to find that out, haven't they? I was quite amused by the blackmail theory; very ingenious and quite fortuitous for me. It couldn't last, of course, but it provided me with a bit more time.'

'But why the Lightollers?'

He frowned. 'Because they wouldn't tell me where the diamonds were.'

'So it is the diamonds,' I said.

'It always was.'

'Why are you after them?'

'They're my inheritance.'

I couldn't stop myself from bursting out, 'Not another one.'

He reacted at once. 'No, the only one. They're mine by right. Tom Lightoller's got no claim on them.' His voice had taken on a different voice, one of obsession.

'How do you justify that?' I asked as calmly as I could; I had the feeling that the wrong question, or perhaps the right question in the wrong tone, would result in his index finger getting twitchy.

'As compensation for the death of my mother. No child should be deprived of his mother so young.'

'And you were?'

He looked briefly angry, as if I were being stupid. 'Yes.'

Looking at the gun barrel and aware that it probably wouldn't be good for my health to annoy him too much, I asked, 'How did you lose her?'

'Haven't you worked that out, yet?' he sneered.

Max had, it turned out. 'She was killed in the original robbery,' she said slowly, working things out. 'She was Eleanor Johnson.'

He nodded. 'Well done.'

I blurted out, 'She was the . . .?' and then stopped myself. Thankfully, he was back in his past.

'She was beautiful, although I can't remember directly. I've only got a few pictures, you see. I was brought up by my aunt and uncle and they didn't want to talk much about her. I had to do a lot of digging to find anything out about her.'

Max asked gently, 'How old were you when she died?'

'Nine months.'

She looked sincerely sad as she said, 'I'm so sorry for you.'

He wasn't listening, though. 'She was a *prostitute*. She was *scum*. That's what Uncle Greg taught me; not just by what he said, but equally clearly by what he didn't say, by his actions and facial expressions. And not just him; there was Auntie Jennifer and even their children, Andrea and Jonny. I was supposed to forget her, be grateful for what was done to her, as if I had been saved from some sort of hell. They kept on and on. Preaching at me, dragging me to church and Sunday school every sodding week. Droning on about prostitutes, how they were evil and went to hell.

'But their brainwashing didn't work. The more they did to blacken her, the more I wanted to know about her, and when I eventually found a photo of her, I knew why they were doing what they were doing.

'She was beautiful, see? Drop-dead gorgeous, isn't that what they say? How I laughed – laughed and cried, too –

when that phrase occurred to me. It could have been invented for her.' He became ruminative. 'She didn't deserve what happened to her and certainly didn't deserve what they said about her.'

The gun barrel had been dropping slightly but quite perceptibly for a few minutes now. I debated the wisdom of being heroic but only for a moment. Smith continued, 'They were ugly compared with my mother, and that was why they hated her; it was sheer envy, nothing more.'

'How come your name's Smith?' Max asked.

'My adopted name. Smith! What a banal, tedious, excuse for a label. Not a name, not a thing that resonates; just a way of identifying someone, of making sure that you are immediately regarded as run-of-the-mill, average, a small part of a large crowd. There is nothing louder in proclaiming nothingness than to be called Smith.'

'You killed Baines and Perry.'

Once again, anger flared. 'Of course, I did. Who else?'

'Because they killed your mother.'

He smiled. 'Not hard, is it?'

I admit that it was out of a fascinated curiosity that I asked him, 'How did you make it look as if they'd killed each other?'

'Sheer good luck,' he replied happily. 'I'd kept tabs on them for years, not that that was difficult, given the fact that they were banged up in prison. In the meantime, I'd drifted into the police force, had even found that I quite liked it. I made sure I knew when Baines and Perry were going to be released, and manoeuvred a posting here, where I knew Baines had a property. He duly did what I hoped and moved back to his house. I watched him as best I could, and struck lucky one evening. He left the house under cover of dark and travelled all the way to a lock-up near Streatham Common. I didn't get close enough to see what he got out of it, but I could guess.'

'The diamonds?'

'I thought about smacking him then and there but I wanted both of them; only then could I enjoy them.'

'Your inheritance?'

He nodded. 'I'd lost my mother; nothing was going to

replace that, but I was damned if I was going to let her murderers make money out of her death.'

'So you waited until Perry was released and had turned up at Baines' house?'

'I had to go sick for a while to make sure that I didn't miss it. When it came, though, there was no subterfuge about it. He just waltzed up the path and knocked on the door. I couldn't believe it.'

'Convenient.'

He agreed enthusiastically. 'Superbly so. I had spent a long, long time stuck in my car, so it was a relief to get out and stretch my legs, even though the rain was torrential.'

'What happened then?'

'I sneaked around into the rear garden. They were in the back room, enjoying their reunion, sitting opposite each other with a can of beer in hand; good mates they must have been; delighted to see each other. I watched them, mesmerized, for I don't know how long; it could have been hours. My feet grew numb, I was shivering, but it didn't matter; nothing mattered then. I just stared at them, a rising anger within me. They were laughing and I wondered at what; they talked and I wondered what about. My mother? Was she the butt of their joking? I didn't know what would have been worse – if they were talking about her or just choosing to forget her, as if she were nothing.

'And then Perry went out of the room. I woke up then, realized that if I was going to act, it had to be then. I walked to the back door, and was delighted to find it unlocked. I slipped off my shoes and crept to the door of the back room, where I had the pleasure of surprising Baines. He didn't know who I was but he knew that I had a gun and, when I told him to be quiet, he did as he was told.

'I stood behind the door, gun pointing at his chest, waiting for Perry to return, which he did fairly quickly. Baines proved to be stupid, though; it could have been relatively painless, had he cooperated, but he chose to be clever. I saw his eyes flick to me as Perry came into the room, saw a slight movement of the head. I shot him at once, of course, but in the throat; my aim was spoiled by Perry who barged into the door. That was when I got the black eye; I dropped the gun at the same time.

'Perry fought well. He had his own gun out and for a moment I thought everything was going to go wrong; he was ferocious and strong but I had one advantage. I hated him; I wanted him dead with a passion that he couldn't hope to match. My only problem was to keep him alive long enough to find the diamonds.'

The gun barrel was definitely drooping quite appreciably and, when I glanced at Max, I saw that she had seen it too. Suddenly I was afraid that she would do something stupid. I asked of Smith, 'Perry was killed with Baines' gun, wasn't he?'

He shook his head. 'No. Perry was killed with his own gun. It was just found in Baines' possession.'

'How come?' This from Max.

'We grappled for a minute or two. I managed to grab hold of the gun and keep it pointing away from me. When it went off, I was nearly deafened. I wasn't sure until that moment which way it was pointing, and was relieved to discover that it wasn't at me. He fell away from me, a bleeding mess of a hole in his chest and, although, not dead, clearly dying.

'My main hope was that Baines had already told him where he'd put the diamonds – I knew they were in the house somewhere – but either he wouldn't say or perhaps he didn't know. Anyway, he died in fairly short order and I had a problem. I knew that the shots would have been heard and that I didn't have long. I wiped Perry's gun and then put it in Baines' hand; then I wiped my gun and gave it to Perry. I did a bit of ransacking and then disappeared.'

'You were seen,' I remarked.

'I was, wasn't I? But the trail led to nothing and, in any case, Masson was already in the process of making up his mind that there was no one else involved.'

'But you didn't have the diamonds.'

He snorted. 'No, I didn't and, more annoyingly, I didn't have the chance to look for them. Masson had us searching the house for three days and every minute I was in agony that someone would find them, but no one did. Baines had done a good job.'

He seemed to be hypnotized by his own story and the gun was being held only loosely. I shifted my weight and Max, good girl that she was, distracted Smith's attention by asking, 'Didn't you go back and look on your own?'

'Every night, but I couldn't do too much for fear of someone noticing that things had been disturbed.'

'And eventually the house was cleared by Oliver Lightoller.'

'Yes. I was so near and yet so far.'

'But you had killed the two men who murdered your mother. Wasn't that enough?'

It was a good question but an unfortunate one because it angered him and the gun barrel jerked back up. 'Don't be stupid. There can never be enough revenge for the killing of your mother.'

Max said nervously, 'I didn't mean . . .'

'I wanted the diamonds. Having them wouldn't have been enough alone, but it would have been a further, small piece of justice.'

I sought to calm him. 'So Oliver Lightoller had everything from the house; is that the only reason you killed him?'

He laughed. 'I knew his reputation. He was as bent as a safety pin; he'd been fencing stuff for years and we'd never proved anything, but that was only because he was bloody clever. I figured he was smart enough to know a good deal when he saw one, so I went to him and suggested that if he should find an unexpected bonus in the stuff from Baines' house, he would do well to discuss the matter with me.'

'But he didn't?'

'Unfortunately for him, no. He thought he could get things past me, but I found out that he'd discovered the diamonds.'

'How?'

'He had one of them valued. Unfortunately, he had it valued by a man who might, or might not, have felt up a little boy in a swimming pool and who owes me for giving him the benefit of the doubt on that occasion.'

'So you went to see him?'

'He told me that he had only found a single diamond, that Baines had split the diamonds and he was still looking for the others.' A sigh. 'Silly man.'

'You didn't believe him?'

'I'd spent a long time studying Baines and I knew that

he was just a stupid thief. If he'd had a stash of diamonds, he wasn't going to split them up; he'd have forgotten where he'd hidden them.' He shook his head. 'Wherever they were, they were in one place.'

'Which made you cross?' I suggested.

'I gave him a chance and he decided that he didn't want to take it. Fair enough, don't you think?'

Max, bless her, was looking for logic in his words. 'But wasn't killing him a bit unwise?'

He could only agree. 'He made me cross,' he admitted. 'In retrospect, running him through wasn't my best move.' He spoke sadly, full of regret; it was one of those moments where I wasn't sure whether the best course of action was to concur or demur. He brightened up though and then went on: 'But, having done so, I had to make the best of things. I searched the shop as thoroughly as I could, keeping away from the front window and putting up the closed sign to deter intruders; it was just before lunchtime, so I didn't expect it to excite too much attention. Unfortunately, I couldn't find the diamonds and, once again, time wasn't on my side. I had to open up the shop again, slip out the back and wait. All I could do was hope that nobody connected Lightoller with the deaths in Greyhound Road.'

'Which they didn't, initially.'

He nodded. 'I couldn't waste time, though. As soon as Masson let me off the leash, I went to see Doris, to see what she could tell me.'

'And what could she tell you?'

'At first, not a lot. I had to use the hammer to get her to cooperate.' Max shivered and I have to admit that the calm way he said this made me feel a bit queasy as well. Smith added, 'But eventually she opened up a bit. She told me that hubby had hidden them in a book, and that it was some-where in the house, but she swore that she didn't know precisely where. I was about to persuade her to change her mind about that, but it was at that point that your old man came snooping around and I had to make myself scarce. I'd been interrogating Doris at the top the stairs – that was where I came upon her as she came out of a bedroom – so when he started coming up, the only place I could hide was upstairs.

When he started up, I knew that my only chance was to push him back down again; I charged out, head down, and pushed.'

This man is mad, I thought.

'He cried out as he fell, I remember. Not loud, but almost plaintive. I peeped over the handrail but he was out cold. Once again, I had little time to act. I picked up the hammer, went down the stairs and wrapped his fingers around the handle, then dropped it beside him. I didn't know then whether he was dead or alive, but I didn't have the time to find out. I had to find that book.'

Max asked in a slightly strained voice, 'What about the safe? Did you know that was there?'

'Not at first, but I came across it when I searched. I was rather annoyed that Doris hadn't told me about it in the first place. In fact, I went back upstairs and told her off.'

I think that both Max and I could tell what he meant by that; from her expression, she felt as sick as I did. Smith felt no such nausea as he said, 'She gave me the combination, though, but imagine my disappointment when it was empty.'

'Yes,' I said softly. 'I can imagine it.'

'I was going to tell her off again, but she was no longer very communicative, so I went through as much of the ground floor as I could, but then I heard a key going into the front door and I decided that I would be advised to make my escape.'

His use of terms – 'annoyed', 'told her off' – when describing murders, some of them atrocities, suggested that he was completely unhinged. Max was staring at him, her mouth slightly open; I doubt she had ever had the chance to study a stark staring loony at such close range before and, clearly, she didn't want to miss a moment. The gun barrel was dropping again.

'I take it that it was you who employed Robbins to break back in and look.'

'Yes. Another one who owes me. A little matter of forged MOT certificates that I hushed up for him; he does odd jobs for me now and again.'

'And he found the book.'

'Yes, but the diamonds were gone. The spine was ripped open and the only thing inside the book was a receipt of some sort.' He frowned. 'I was starting to think that there were supernatural forces working against me.'

'Are you sure that Victor didn't take the diamonds himself?'

He smiled. 'You know, I thought about that. I questioned him fairly closely and assured him that I would take a similar approach to his little boy should he lie, but he was fairly convincing that that was how he found the book, and I believe him.'

With every sentence, his mental state became plainer; every syllable painted a further detail in the picture of his criminal insanity. The gun barrel kept going up and down as if it were bouncing on elastic; his grip on the handle was quite loose but there was no chance that either of us was going to get to him before it tightened on the trigger.

'So, again, I had to wait. I had really begun to think that it was all over, that I would never find them, but then Mr Holversum so kindly came to tell me about a peculiar phone call he'd received this morning.'

'But that was a lie,' insisted Max. 'I just made the calls to—'

'To open an auction,' he interrupted. 'Yes, that's what I thought. Very clever.'

'No, we told Tom—'

'You told Tom that you had the diamonds, and then you denied it again. I know.'

'There you are then.'

He was shaking his head. 'He doesn't believe you, though, does he? He was about to find out the truth when I came in.'

'He wouldn't have found them, no matter what he did,' I said. I kept my voice as calm as I could but made sure that it was also urgent and forceful. 'We really don't have them.'

'I don't believe you.' There was no arguing with that decision. 'You're the logical ones to have them. You took up residence in your father's house; you –' he indicated Max – 'broke into the Lightollers. The diamonds had already gone from the book by then. No one had any other chance.'

Max looked at me, her face full of horror, but I was looking at the gun barrel; it was horizontal and perky again, pointing purposefully away from a fist that gripped the handle and the trigger tightly. We had missed our chance.

'Now,' he said calmly and he was smiling again, 'I want you to give them to me, or I will kill you.'

FORTY-ONE

Out of the corner of my eye, I saw Max looking in
my direction but all I could think about was the
hole of that gun barrel looking in front of me. It
was obvious that he was serious and that he was just mad
enough to shoot us both if we didn't do as he wanted very
quickly. Which, considering that we didn't have the diamonds,
was a problem.

But there was something . . .

'Come on,' Smith urged. 'Don't dally. I have to get back
to the station.'

Max still thought he was contactable by the kind of logic
that the rest of us lived by. 'But you don't understand,
constable. This was just a trick we played to try to entice
the murderer to make himself known.'

I would ordinarily have taken issue with her choice of
personal pronoun, but this was not a time of ordinariness
and, anyway, I was thinking . . .

Smith sighed and was not taken in. 'And you succeeded,
Miss Christy. Your scheme was wonderful in its simplicity
and for that I applaud you. Now, though, it is time to hand
over what I want.'

'But we haven't got them!'

'Yes, you have. You must have. Nobody else has.'

Max looked again to me, her face showing understandable stress but things were happening in my cranium and I
was undergoing a completely novel experience.

I was solving a mystery.

Smith stood up and walked around the room; he did not
take his eyes from us, did not dissuade the barrel from its
fascination with us. When he was standing behind us and
we were craning around to look at him, he said, 'Who's
first?'

Which is one of those questions to which there can never
be an answer.

But I was close to an answer to another question.

He put the barrel to Max's forehead. She pulled away but the barrel followed her. When she squealed and twisted round to grab my arm and bury her head in my shoulder, all he did was to lean forward on the back of the sofa and dig it into the back of her head. 'I think you,' he breathed. There was an unmistakable pitch of excitement in the sound of his words.

Max cried out and squeezed my arm so tight that I almost lost the thread of my thoughts and, to gain time, I said loudly and urgently, 'OK! OK!'

I was craning my head to look at him, hugging Max to me. He didn't withdraw the gun. 'OK, what?'

I still hadn't worked it through completely, but I couldn't let that stop me. I had to say something to stop him firing that gun. 'I'll take you to the diamonds.'

The only movement he made was on his face as his expression changed to one of suspicion. 'Take me to them? What does that mean?'

'They're not here.' I managed to say that with total sincerity.

'Where are they, then?'

I took a deep breath. I didn't know and I would have to lie.

'On my father's allotment.'

FORTY-TWO

At which he grinned. 'No,' he said. There was a degree of certainty in that syllable that no one of sound mind could ever produce. 'No, you're having me on.'

The gun dug into Max's neck; I could feel her shaking as she in turn pressed ever harder into me. 'No, not this time. Believe me, Smith. I'm telling the truth. The diamonds aren't here; they never were, because Dad found them when he called at the shop just after you killed Lightoller. He lied when he said that he hadn't found Lightoller.'

He considered me, looked at me and I saw him wondering, judging, calculating. 'Masson told me that your old man was crackers but honest. He couldn't ever get his head around the possibility that he might have killed Oliver Lightoller, let alone Doris. Are you saying he's a thief?'

'But Dad didn't like the Lightollers, remember? He might not have had the temperament to kill them and he might not ordinarily be a thief, but he was mad at Lightoller because of the watch. He only found the diamonds because he was looking for his watch.'

'Where did he find them?'

'In the watch cabinet.'

I held my breath and tried not to show that I was doing it; if he had happened to look in the watch cabinet, then Max and I were dead.

'What about the book, then? Why did Doris Lightoller say that they were in the book?'

It was a good question.

A bloody good question, actually . . .

Suddenly Max emerged from my arm and said, 'Probably because they were, once. I expect he hadn't told his wife that he'd decided to take them out of the book; it was a stupid place to hide them, don't you think? *Diamonds Are Forever*? Do me a favour. You said that Baines was stupid, and that proves it.'

I saw it work on Smith. He couldn't resist a spot of staring, but it was qualitatively different; it held now a faint dawning of realization that she might have a point.

He hesitated a long time but then stood up. 'Take me to them.'

My father, who likes to believe that he is of a philosophical bent of mind, has talked often of his belief that allotments are the spiritual centre of the universe, that they are a perfect microcosm. 'All of life – not just human life – is here, Lance,' he used to say and I, for one, thought he was talking rubbish but never said so. He also used to go on about the Circle of Life long before Disney ever got in on the act. 'Everything comes back to this place, you know,' he would add. 'And then there is rebirth.'

Since my father is allowed out without a straitjacket only because he is clever enough to fool the psychiatrists, I had always thought these words to be mere ravings but I have to admit to a certain sense of coming home as I drove to the allotments, Smith in the back of the car with the gun still pressed into Max's side, aware that the climax of this whole episode was once again going to be enacted on my father's allotment.

I just hoped that the silly old fool hadn't listened to me for once and disposed of the grenade.

All through the trip I kept catching Max's eye in the rear-view mirror; understandably, she had a puzzled and worried expression, since she didn't know about Dad's little souvenir; the trouble was, I *did* know about it, and I still wasn't feeling particularly chipper. Even if it was in the shed, I wasn't sure how I could use it on Smith without a fair amount of collateral damage to both myself and Max. It had been a plan borne of desperation, to get us out of the house, to prolong our lives for a while, nothing more.

As we drove on to the allotment site, Smith looked around us; it was very dark and very cold, with the fog as thick as ever. 'How did the diamonds get here?' he asked.

I had been wondering about that myself.

'Because this is where Dad hid them as soon as he found them.'

It must have sounded unlikely to him; I couldn't blame him because it certainly sounded so to me.

'Why didn't he hide them in his house?' he continued.

'Because my father's rather eccentric.'

He thought about this. 'Masson told me he was cracked,' he admitted.

There was silence for a moment, and then he asked, 'So how do you know where they are?'

'His memory's coming back. The last time we were visiting, he waited until Percy Bailey had gone to the toilet and told us where they were.'

He made a noise that sounded very suspicious, but said nothing more. I drove as slowly as I could along the lane, trying to formulate some plan all the while, then stopped at Dad's plot. Maybe it was my imagination, but maybe I really was walking as if through molasses; who could tell?

He made me get out first, then got out himself, pulling Max after him roughly. We stood there, in the dark until I switched on the torch that he had made me bring. He said, 'This gun is going to remain in contact with your girlfriend come what may, so just be sensible, Dr Elliot.'

We moved along the path, through the long damp grass; it wasn't long before my shoes had let in enough freezing moisture to make me worry about trench foot. I crossed over the allotment, past Dad's bean trench, heading for the shed with Smith and Max following. I called over my shoulder, 'They're in the shed.'

'Get them, then.'

Dad, of course, had not locked it (he would not consider the presence of an ancient explosive device to be sufficient reason for such responsible measures) and I opened the door. I pointed the torch here and there, trying to locate first the tin with the grenade. I saw a lot of large spiders suspended worryingly close to my head but I had other things to worry about. If I couldn't find the tin of Crawford's biscuits, I would have to adopt plan B. The trouble was that I hadn't yet got around to formulating plan B.

For a minute or two I shone the torch around, looking for the telltale red of the tin without success. I tried not to panic, tried to think. Perhaps, I decided, he had hidden it away, just in case.

My eye fell upon some brown paper bags lined up on a shelf that tilted at an angle of at least twenty degrees. The first two were filled with substances that would not have looked out of place in a witch's toilet, but the third was a different shape – perhaps biscuit tin-shaped.

I had found the grenade.

FORTY-THREE

'What's taking the time?' Smith's voice, as it came into the shed, sounded angry, jumpy.

I called out, 'I can't find them.'

'You've got two minutes, Dr Elliot. Two minutes and then I'm going to fire this gun.'

In fact, what I couldn't find was a screwdriver, but I managed to locate one in the old rusty toolbox that Dad kept by his Thermos stove. From my pocket I took Mum's brooch and began to prize off the fake diamonds, one by one. I didn't have the foggiest idea how many diamonds Smith was expecting to get, and could only hope that it was about the same number. They were fairly obviously fake, but he would be looking at them only for a moment or two, I hoped.

When I had the last gem out of its setting, I kissed the remaining emeralds, apologized silently to Mum, then slipped the butchered brooch back into my pocket. I put the diamonds into one of several old Golden Flake tobacco tins that Dad kept about the shed, took a deep breath and then muttered a short prayer.

I loosened the belt on my trousers, then picked up the grenade and without thinking too much about anything, pulled out the pin, holding the lever tight against its side; I didn't know too much about Mills bombs, but I was fairly sure that as long as I did that, I would be safe. I then tucked it under my belt and tightened it again. It was uncomfortable but it held in place, the lever pressing into my stomach.

My head was full of uncertainties, but there was one that drowned out all the rest: was this grenade fitted with a four-second fuse or seven-second fuse?

There were cases when the sods kicked it back and blew one of us up. I remembered my father's reminiscences from a few days ago.

I opened the shed door.

Smith smiled. 'About time, Dr Elliot. I was starting to

think you were trying to tunnel your way out of there.' He still had Max's arm in a tight grip, the gun pressing into the side of her chest.

I walked forward, came to stand just beside the gaping chasm of Dad's bean trench. It looked like a mass grave awaiting filling; perhaps it would prove to be so. 'Here they are.' I held up the tin and rattled it and felt the grenade shift slightly. I hurriedly put my arm down.

'Throw it over here.'

'Let Max go first.'

He was standing about ten yards away and in darkness but I heard the grin in his voice. 'When I know that those are the real diamonds, I will.'

I hesitated, not least because there was a danger that the act of tossing the tin over to him would dislodge the Mills bomb with unfortunate consequences for my trousers and their contents.

'Come on, doctor.'

So, with a somewhat stilted action, I threw the tin over to him; it landed in the mud about two feet in front of him. He looked down at it and at that moment I surreptitiously pulled the grenade from my belt, still squeezing the lever. He glanced across at Max and I could see he was wondering what to do; I was hoping that he was going to have to let go of Max to get the tin but, unfortunately, they train policemen well these days. He said to Max, 'Bend down and pick it up.'

She flicked a nervous glance at me, then complied.

'Open it.'

She did so and I held my breath. There was barely any light for him to see by, since I had been the only one with a torch and I had deliberately left it in the shed. He peered into the tin; he did this for what seemed a very long time indeed . . .

So long that I began to think that he knew, in which case I couldn't see how Max was going to come out of this alive.

He looked up; I have never been so relieved as I was then, because I saw a smile on his face. 'You've been very wise, Dr Elliot. Very wise indeed.'

'Let Max go, then.'

He looked at her and for a moment I thought that he was just going to kill her there and then, but all he did was to lean down and kiss her lightly on the cheek, then release her arm. 'Give me the diamonds, miss.'

The plan was that she would give him the diamonds, she would run to me, I would release the lever on the Mills bomb and throw it, and the two of us would leg it as quickly as we could.

For obvious reasons, however, I hadn't consulted Max.

Which is perhaps why a look of determined aggression came across her face and she deftly threw the tin into the air.

At once, the tin was lost in darkness and weather and Smith watched his inheritance sailing away with a stunned, almost idiotic expression. Max took her chance and bolted . . .

Smith was quick, though. He grabbed and almost got her arm as she sprinted towards me. Only almost, though . . .

She collided with me with such an impact that I almost dropped the grenade. Smith's attention was torn between us and the diamonds; uncertainty flickered across his face for a second.

I released the lever on the grenade.

Smith smiled, a decision made.

One . . .

He raised the gun and pointed it at us. He said sadly, 'I can find the diamonds at my leisure.'

My father's words came back to me. *You've got either four or seven seconds then before it explodes, so you don't want to throw it too early.*

But which was it?

Two . . .

Max said desperately, 'Someone will hear the shots.'

He was puzzled. 'So?'

Three . . .

I threw the grenade.

Four . . .

He looked at the grenade as it headed towards him but didn't recognize what it was – why should he? – and he began to dodge it, moving to the right so that it would pass harmlessly by. He almost certainly thought that it was a pebble or something, so dodging it would be easy and then he could get on with shooting us.

Five . . .

I fell to my left, pulling Max with me. As we disappeared into the maw of the bean trench, I saw it had fallen to the ground in the darkness behind him, and he was concentrating once again on us. He began striding towards us purposefully, the gun following us, as we fell into the ditch.

He was smiling again.

Six . . .

I thought that I had blown it. It had been a seven-second fuse and been thrown too hard. Every step he took meant that he was walking away from it, towards safety.

And then the Mills bomb did what Mills bombs do and there was a huge explosion about ten yards behind him.

It was an explosion the like of which I had never known before; as we fell into what seemed to be a bottomless pit, I remember thinking that Mills bombs were certainly more powerful than I had imagined them to be, after which we hit the bottom.

Actually, a bottomless pit would have been far nicer than the rotting vegetables, fruit, tea leaves, worms, beetles and slugs that we ended up in.

FORTY-FOUR

Dad's bandages were off and he now wore, in lieu of a full head of hair, a rather fetching, and somehow appropriate, purple woolly hat. He was fully mobile and was due to go home in the next few days, and he no longer had a police escort, but he was not happy.

'Bloody vandalism,' he said.

It had been three days since that night on the allotments and my ears were still ringing with the noise of the grenade exploding. His words had to fight to get through to my brain. 'What is?'

He looked at me sourly. 'The way my souvenir was destroyed.'

I didn't follow for a moment, then, when I did, I looked across at Max for support. She only smiled sympathetically. To Dad, I said, 'Are you serious?'

He was outraged. 'Never more so.'

'You're moaning because I used the grenade to save our lives?'

He shrugged but still looked disgruntled. 'Valuable, that was.'

'More valuable than my life? More valuable than Max's?'

He had the grace to soften at Max's name. 'Of course not,' he said and smiled at her.

Even after years of this treatment, I found it hard to keep quiet.

Silence followed, into which Max asked timidly, 'Can you remember what happened at the Lightollers' house now, Dr Elliot?'

'Oh, yes. It's all come back now.'

'Did you see who pushed you down the stairs?'

'Not at all. It all happened too quickly.'

I joined in sulkily. 'That was why Smith didn't want to be around you when you'd come through the operation; he was afraid you might just be able to identify him.'

Max asked, 'What about the watch? I don't understand where that came in.'

Dad was at once enraged. 'Oh, the watch! Do you know, that mountebank Lightoller only had the sheer, untrammelled gall to have it out on display in his sitting room! I saw it when I came in to see what was going on. It was in a display cabinet. I opened the cabinet, grabbed it and then made my way further into the house; I remember thinking that I would have a bit of fun with that watch.'

'So you had it in your hand when you fell down the stairs?'

'I suppose so. I don't really remember.' He scratched his head and said to Max, 'I do hope you're fully recovered from your ordeal, Max.'

He had never called her by her first name before. I was fuming inside because he always made me fume inside, but I thanked him for that. She replied with a demur smile, 'Yes, thank you, Dr Elliot.'

He nodded and smiled and I knew that she had passed a very high hurdle. Of me he enquired, 'So where are they?'

'Where are what?'

'The diamonds.'

I shrugged.

'You don't know?' His voice suggested not just incredulity, more despair, almost disappointment that once again I had failed to live up to his expectations.

'No,' I sighed, trying to find some affection in my irritation; this man was, at heart, made of the right stuff, after all. 'If they ever were in that book, where Lightoller put them after that is anyone's guess.'

The expression on his face suggested that he took this defeat personally. I swear that he even muttered, 'After all I've been through . . .'

Silence descended again until he overcame this personal slight and, perking up, he said brightly, 'Ada's been to see me.'

'Ada Clarke, the stool pigeon?'

He frowned. 'That's not very nice, Lance. Ada is a good Christian woman who found herself placed in a very difficult position. It was my fault and I don't blame her in the least.'

I murmured, 'You'd better hope she's not *that* Christian . . .'
But he didn't hear me.

After a few seconds during which he seemed to be working
himself up to something, he finally broke down and asked
me with a hint of suppressed excitement, 'Tell me, Lance,
did it make a big bang?'

'What?'

'The Mills bomb. Did it make a big bang?'

Max looked rather unwell at this. In fact, Constable Smith
had been fairly comprehensively blown apart; it was not a
sight I was going to forget for a long time. As if that weren't
bad enough, because a man had died, there was going to
have to be a police investigation into what had happened.
Masson had assured me that I would be exonerated, but even
so, I could not but feel a little anxious. I said non-committally,
'Fairly.'

He said, 'Really?' in a tone I found a trifle odd.

'Don't you know?'

With that asperity I knew so well, he said, 'I wouldn't
know, would I? I wasn't there.'

'But what about all your experience of them during the
war?'

He looked for a moment nonplussed, then slowly smiled.
'To be honest, I never got around to using one,' he admitted.
This ought to have been in a sheepish expression, but there
was an unmistakable air of sangfroid.

'No?'

He shook his head. 'No.' I was about to pounce with a bit
of triumph when he added, 'I never got the chance. To be
honest, I always had the tommy gun.'